I0635748

Across the Great Divide

Book 3

THE FOUNDING

By Michael L Ross

Copyright © 2022, 2023 Michael L. Ross

Published by HistoricalNovelsRUS

TM

All rights reserved.

ISBN 13 978-1-7359931-3-3

Dedicated

to my wife Marti, and the people of Lubbock and Nicode-

mus who quested for freedom

Prologue

Evansville, Indiana, August 1865

Luther heard shouting and smelled smoke. His fingers nervously touched the butt of his revolver in its holster. He looked at Ned, his father-in-law, eyes wide with fear and speculation. They had come to Evansville, a four-day drive from Madison, Indiana, to drop off an order of tools for a local business, made in their blacksmith shop.

"What's going on over there?" Luther peered down the street, seeing a gathering mob.

"I don't know," said Ned. "But I think we'd best load up and get out. White folks with torches can't mean nothin' good for us."

Down the street, the shouts grew louder, and the mob began moving in their direction. Luther could hear men yelling things like, "Dirty blacks! Lynch'em!" As they moved closer, he saw they were carrying one black man and driving another, bound, in front of them with kicks, fists, and clubs. Having escaped slavery some years earlier and finding freedom, Luther had no desire to suffer under the cruelty of whites who hated him simply because he was black. His fists clenched in anger and helplessness.

"You're right. I don't know what's going on, but we can't do anything. There's too many of them."

Luther, spurred by fear, loaded the rest of the raw iron they had bought into the wagon. By the time he finished, the mob was close enough to make out faces, and someone started throwing rocks at them.

"Hey, there are two more coons! Let's get'em, boys!"

Ned mounted the wagon box to drive, and Luther jumped on, drawing his revolver. He dodged a rock and sent a warning shot over the heads of the crowd, causing them to draw back. Ned slapped the reins, and the horses took off at a fast trot, moving them away from danger. The crowd seemed ill-disposed to charge Luther's bullets, but looking back, he saw them put ropes around the necks of the two Negroes in their control. He didn't want to see what happened next and turned away.

Luther and Ned drove away in silence, looking back to

make sure they weren't followed. In his mind, Luther re-lived his mother's torture at the hands of slave catchers and his own whipping when caught off his Kentucky plantation, Ashland, by a patrol. Fear and anger warred in him. He'd settled with some of his demons and thought now that the war was over, and he was here in the North, he could find peace.

"What you think those men did?" asked Ned.

"Don't have to do anything. I don't know. Maybe there was a reason, maybe not. I just know I'm glad my child gonna be born free!" said Luther.

Ned smiled. His daughter Ruth, Luther's wife, had just discovered she was pregnant before they left on the trip. Both men were excited at the prospect.

"That grandchild gonna make a great family tradition, blacksmithing," said Ned.

"Huh. What if Ruth has a girl? Or what if she has a boy who wants to farm, on his own land?"

Ned smiled and shook his head. "Guess we'll see."

Passing through Boonville, they stopped to water the horses. Luther saw a poster on a barn proclaiming free farmland.

Ned saw him looking and shook his head. "I doubt it applies to us," he said. "Ain't nobody gonna give a black man somethin' for free."

"Maybe, maybe not. Worth looking into."

They got back on the wagon and began driving again.

"Luther, don't chase the impossible. Look, we got a good business in Madison. There's steady trade at the blacksmith shop. We're on the river, so it's easy to make things to sell. Who are you gonna sell to on the frontier? What I hear, you be lucky to keep your scalp."

"You know we don't get paid what a white blacksmith would get for the same work. And think—to own your land, answer to nobody. I did enough farming in Kentucky. And if thousands are coming west, then think how many horses and wagons that is—and they'll all need a blacksmith. Won't be so many to choose from. We can charge a fair price."

"You mean you *watched* farming in Kentucky. You worked up in the big house. Ain't the same thing."

"You put seeds in the ground. Rain comes. They grow. You take out the weeds and harvest. How hard can it be?"

"And if the rain doesn't come? Or if the bugs eat it? My daughter gonna have a baby—who gonna help her out there? Where does the child go to school? With Miss Albinia's school, a black child can learn."

Luther grimaced. "Maybe you're right."

***

A few days later, they arrived back in Madison. Luther got up early, eager to beat the heat of the day and finish an order. He was pounding at the forge, thinking about what Ned had said. Luther and Ruth had moved into town after their marriage, from Albinia's farm in the country. Luther's mother, Jemima, and sister, Olivia, stayed on the farm in the cabin Albinia had built for Will but came into town every day to help Albinia with the colored school she had started. It was a good life, he reflected, but still not one of complete independence and freedom.

Luther hefted a sack of coal and was adding some to keep the fire going when a portly white man in a bedraggled suit entered the shop. Luther wiped his hands and the sweat from his brow with a towel and came to see what the stranger wanted. He assumed he was a prospective customer, so he was careful not to look him in the eye or offer a handshake.

"Yes, sir? What can I help you with today?"

The man smiled, but his eyes did not. Handing Luther a paper, he said, "What you can do is get out of Indiana. We don't want your kind here. I'm the sheriff and part of the Superintendent Board for the Colored just formed here in Madison. Maybe you can't read that, but it says that you came into this state illegally, in violation of the Indiana constitution. You're an escaped slave from Kentucky. War or no war, slavery is still legal in Kentucky, and unless you have freedom papers or permission from the state of Indiana to be here, you need to git! Someone recognized your wagon—you were at the riots in Evansville. The sheriff there sent me a wire. You're a troublemaker. You fired a gun at white men. You slaves are just a bunch of escaped monkeys, trying to overrun us. You have twenty-four hours to get out of the state, or I'll be back with chains and ship you to your owner in Kentucky."

"You can't do that!"

"Oh no? Just watch me!" Quick as a snake, he grabbed a pitchfork and jabbed the handle end into Luther's midsection. Luther gasped for air. "Twenty-four hours," the man said, turning and laughing on the way out.

Ned came in, passing the man, and rushed over when he saw Luther holding his stomach.

"What's wrong? What was that all about?"

Luther handed Ned the paper, which he read line by line. "We can fight this—things are changing."

"Not that much, and you know it. Indiana doesn't recognize that I'm married. It says I don't have a right to be here. Looks like I don't have much choice. Ruth, she could stay, but not me."

Ned shook his head. "We need to pray. We need to show this to Pastor Peter and Albinia."

Luther sighed. "Fine, you do that. Meanwhile, I got to pack."

***

Madison, Indiana, August 1865

"Luther, you have to let us help you," said Albinia. "You can't just go off to nowhere with a pregnant wife. And what about your mother and sister? Jemima will have a tough time traveling at her age. And Olivia has gotten settled in here."

Katy, Ruth's mother, came in carrying a wooden crate. "The Lord made us wayfaring strangers, it seems. But we're family. We go together."

Luther sighed. "I know you mean well, Miss Albinia. I owe you everything after you helped us to freedom. But I don't want trouble. That guy and more like him will be coming back. Do you think they'll spare Mama because she's wore out? Or Olivia because she's a girl? You know they won't. And Ruth and me, we're not gonna be separated again. I have been reading like you and Ruth taught me. Out west, there's land. There's a territory where almost no one is, and them that's there, no one cares what color you are, long as you ain't red."

"And what *about* Indians? How will you work? What do you know about farming? How will you get land?"

"I don't know yet. But God, He told Abraham to go,

14

and he didn't know how he'd manage or where he was going. I figger He'll take care of us. I'll head for Colorado. I hear there's a gold rush. Bound to be folks coming along with wagons. They'll have horses to shoe, wagon tires that need repair, and tools they want to buy. I'm a good blacksmith now. We'll manage somehow."

Ruth entered the barn, carrying a box. "We will," she said. "I'm not losing Luther again. And my little one isn't going to grow up where black people are hated. We've started over before. We can do it again."

Jemima and Olivia came in, carrying bags of clothing. Jemima said, "I'm going with my boy. And the Lawd God Hisself go before us. Men here, they want to come and kill us. I don't mind for me, but I want all the children I got left to live free. I want to see that grandchild come."

Olivia said, "Ruth gonna need help when the time comes. Mama and I, we can do it. And we know about fieldwork." She held up her hands for Albinia to see. "These aren't soft woman hands, meaning no offense. I worked in the fields as a girl. I can do it again. For myself, this time."

Luther saw the fight go out of Albinia. She raised her hands, let them fall, and shrugged. "All right. Since you're determined," she said. "At least let me help you get started.

You'll need a wagon, mules, and supplies. I know Julia will help too."

"I can pay for that," Luther said. "I've been working."

"But Luther . . ."

"No buts, Miss Albinia. I'm a free man—or I will be. I can pay my own way. You just help some more children to read. Someday black people gonna have rights. You teach them so they'll know the rights God gave them. All men are created equal. We'll keep going west until we find a place where they believe it. Got to be freedom somewhere in this country. Maybe in Colorado Territory."

Chapter 1

Wyoming and Colorado, August 1868

Will Crump traveled southeast, following the old
Pony Express route through Wyoming, then dropping
south at Rock Spring through Colorado Territory. His
companions now were Lightning, his bull mastiff,
Dusty, his horse, and an Appaloosa packhorse he'd
named Sadie that he'd bought at Fort Bridger. She
would need all her strength and stamina for the mountains they would climb. As they went farther south, the
leaves spun like whirlwinds, a show of green, yellow,
and scarlet. The wind blew down from snow-covered

peaks, bidding them come and dance to the tune of the oncoming autumn.

Will's other companions were loneliness and longing. Losing Dove was an open wound sending shooting pains throughout his whole body. After leaving Washakie's camp, he'd felt as if he were alone and forsaken until he'd gotten his father's letter at Fort Bridger. Learning of his mother's death added to his sorrow. The invitation to join his father in Colorado and the promise of connection and family made him ache from wanting to see his father. They had parted in Indiana on fair terms after their conflict over the war. The letter brought back all the times his father had been there for him, even trying to get his freedom during the Camp Douglas days. He practiced what to say to his father, talking to his dog as they wound through the mountain passes.

"Lightning, Pa was right in so many ways that I never admitted. He was right about the war and how girls don't always stick with you. I wish I could have a marriage like he and Ma had."

His time with Dove flashed through his mind and heart—they had come so close and risked everything to be together, only to have death snatch it away. His dream of a quiet life with her, hunting and living more like her people, would never happen.

Lightning looked back, trotting now in front of Dusty, lifting an ear, then turning his eyes to the trail.

"If I had listened and not followed Morgan, I wouldn't have watched friends die. Or maybe I would have anyway, on the other side. But you can't live in a what-if world. There are always choices, and you make them without knowing what's ahead."

The nights grew colder, but within a week Will arrived at Ute Pass. There was a steady stream of high-sided freight wagons going the other way along the narrow road, sometimes forcing them to stand aside and let them pass. After reaching the summit, the valley widened before them.

A rickety wooden sign proclaimed Georgetown, Colorado. Mountains towered on two sides, studded with evergreens. The town was a ramshackle combination of tents, frame buildings, and a few brick structures. The smell of pines gave way to the stench of burning coal, steam engines, and dung. The sides of the hills and the stream had slag heaps from the mining. The streets of the town were mud holes with deep wagon ruts. Will worried a little about Lightning coming into town, lest he tangle with the dogs roaming the streets, but he seemed to stay close to Will and the horses.

Searching the signs on the buildings, Will found the livery and the sound of a hammer on an anvil. The blacksmith was a large black man wearing a shirt with no sleeves, absorbed in his craft. Will had to walk around in front of him to get his attention after tying the horses and Lightning to a post.

"Excuse me, can I ask you a question?"

The blacksmith looked up and laid down his hammer with a sigh. "I guess so, seeing you already interrupted me. What is it?"

"I'd like to stable my horses, and I'm looking for someone: man name of Robert Crump. About six foot two, limps with a wooden foot, brown hair and eyes, Kentucky accent. Have you seen him around or know where I can find him? Or maybe where the Tiger Mine is?"

The blacksmith furrowed his brow. "Who wants to know?"

"Me—that is, Will Crump. I'm his son. I got a letter asking me to come."

The blacksmith picked up his hammer and pounded

a few more strokes on the blade he was making. Will began to wonder if he would answer, then the man paused, as though making a decision.

"Guess you'll find out anyway—you won't like the answer. Your pa, he's probably down to the Lucky Strike Saloon. He's there most every day. I didn't recognize you at first. Must be the beard. 'Course I only seen you a short time, and that was years ago. I'm Ned, Luther's father-in-law. Your pa, Robert, he's different than you remember. He's down there drunk almost every day when he can get the money for whiskey. The Tiger Mine went belly-up a few months ago. He lost everything."

Will took that in. "How? How is that possible? His letter sounded so hopeful. It is good to see you again, Ned. You know Pa. How could he do that? He never drank before the war."

"Fortunes are made and lost here every day. Everyone thinks they'll be the one to strike it rich. He was like that when Luther and I came here, after a time in Kansas. He took your ma's death real hard. Grief does funny things to a man. Some men take risks. Some men fall and don't get up. I guess your pa is a little of both."

"I need to find him. Is there a place for the horses

and maybe a hotel?"

"Corral's down yonder. Don't have enough stalls for indoor boarding. Two bits a day or ten bits a week, in advance. The hotel's called Aunt Mae's, three doors down from the saloon. Being Robert's son, don't imagine you're looking for the whorehouse, but the town's got that too."

"Aunt Mae's will do just fine. Much obliged. Is Luther here too?"

"No, he drives the stage and sometimes a freight wagon from the railhead in Kansas. He stops every few weeks. He's due back soon."

Will paid and tended to the horses, then he shouldered the pack, grabbed his rifle, and walked to see what he could find.

***

After checking in at the hotel and making sure his possessions would be secure, Will walked back to the saloon, rifle in hand in case of trouble, Lightning trotting at his heels. Will gripped the stock of the rifle behind the trigger. He stopped at the door and gazed into the dim interior, along the bar with spittoons next to the brass footrail. Two bartenders with bow ties, black vests, and white aprons stood behind the polished mahogany bar, turned to look at him, then resumed wiping the counter. The long narrow room was lined with tables on the left side, and miners grouped around playing poker and nursing beers.

Making a decision, he pushed the double doors open and went up to the bar. He scanned the room, looking for potential danger. He didn't see anyone familiar at the tables. The room had light from one candelabra and the fading afternoon sun from the front window. Satisfied there was no trouble, he ordered a five-cent beer.

"Barkeep, you know most of the fellas that come in here?"

The black-mustached barkeeper poured the beer into the tilted glass, minimizing the foam, and snapped out, "Sure, why d'ya want to know?"

"Just looking for somebody."

"Ain't we all, *compadre*. But some guys here don't want to be found."

Will laid a half dollar on the bar. "Would that help your memory?"

The barkeep pocketed it before his partner could see. "It might. Got a name and a description?"

"His name's Robert Crump, tall, missing a foot. Brown hair, Kentucky accent."

"Easiest half dollar I ever made—that's him, slumped in the corner over there. Ain't woke up yet from last night's bender. Boss lets him sleep it off sometimes."

Will tipped his hat, grabbed his beer, and moved to the corner. He wouldn't have known this wreck of a man: eyes sunken in and closed, brown beard with streaks of gray obscuring the face, all matted and tangled, wet with a little drool. Noticing the man had a missing foot, he reached a tentative hand and shook him. Will half expected to find a bird's nest in the beard. The smell of whiskey, body odor, and sour breath was overpowering.

"Pa? Pa, is that you?"

An eyelid cracked open as the mouth shut, and the man tried to focus. He wiped at the drool and pushed Will's hand away.

"I'm nobody's pa, nobody that would own me. My boy run off. Lemme be," came the slurred words. Turning his head toward the wall, he seemed to go back to sleep.

"Pa, it's me, Will. You wrote me a letter. I'm here."

The head turned back, brow furrowed, and both eyes opened.

"Will? I wrote that letter months ago. Thought you musta died up with the Indians."

"No. I'm here. I came to find you. Let me help you up."

"Lemme be. No use now. Mine's gone. Money's gone. Your ma's gone. Nothing left. Too late."

"It's never too late if you're breathing. I learned that in the war—and from you. C'mon."

Will put Robert's arm around his neck, put the other hand under Robert's belt, and lifted. The extra weight hurt his bad ankle, where the arrow had gone in during the incident with the Cheyenne and Dove months ago, but he was determined. Robert groaned and let loose a string of curses, but he didn't resist. Will had him standing, moving for the door.

Will called back to one of the miners, "Take the beer, on the house."

***

Late morning the next day, Will brought some coffee upstairs to his hotel room and rousted Robert.

"Time to face the music, Pa." He went over to the bed and dumped a small glass of water on his father's head.

Robert lashed out with an arm, causing the glass to fly and shatter while giving a deep guttural groan.

"What did you do that for? My head feels like it got hit by a rebel cannonball."

"Fair is fair. You did it to me enough times growing up. You need to sober up so we can talk. I'm not fifteen anymore, and whatever is going on with you isn't good. I'm grieving Ma too, plus a gal you don't even know about. I watched guys in the war solve their problems or get their fun with the bottle, and it never helped them one bit. After the trail yesterday and the way I felt, I was starting to want that beer, but when I saw you, it cured me. I'm not gonna be the drunk in the corner of a saloon, and I won't let you either. Have some coffee."

Robert grunted and reached for the coffee. An hour later, after washing his face in a basin and combing out his beard while Will watched, Robert began to seem normal.

"All right, you wanted me to come. I'm here. Tell me what's happened."

Robert set the cup down on a little table by the bed. He wouldn't look at Will and instead stared out the window.

"After you left, we ran a store, and it went well for a few months. Then your ma fell ill—ague—and she just got worse every day. We tried everything. Peter prayed, Albinia nursed, and we even gave her Dr. Bull's patent medicine. The doctor who came tried to lower the fever, but nothing helped. She sank until she was taking a gasping breath once in a minute."

Robert held his head in his hands, sobs shaking his shoulders. Will reached out a hand to comfort, but let it drop. Let his father have some dignity. Robert gained control.

"She died the next day, rasping and rattling— horrible to hear. I hadn't seen anything like it since the war. But it's different when it's your wife dying, and there's no way to fight. I just sat for hours, staring at nothing. Albinia and Julia tried to comfort me, but they had their own grief. I have to admit, I cursed you for leaving then. I could have used you. But no one knew for sure where you were. After a week, I couldn't stand it anymore. I sold the store, got on a horse, and pointed him west."

"I understand that, more than you know."

Robert stood, and began pacing. "I invested the money from the store in the Tiger Mine here; that's when I wrote to you. But it played out within a month. The guys I went in with were in debt for equipment and supplies. I lost everything. It felt like God had deserted me, and I had nothing. I swept floors and mucked stalls but couldn't get ahead. The prices here are crazy. I even lost my horse, so there was no way to go. Then I started drinking."

"Pa . . ."

"No, let me finish. It wasn't long before all I looked for was the next drink—and wished I could just die. That's how I got to be a drunk old cripple. And that's all I am now. Go away, and let me die."

"No. I won't. Albinia or Julia would crown you with a frying pan for talking like that, not to mention Ma," said Will, guilt tugging at his conscience for his recent thoughts of giving up. "I lost someone too, a girl you never knew. I won't lose you. You asked me to come, and you're stuck with me."

Will rose and hugged his father, refusing to be pushed aside.

***

The next day, Will stopped to look in on Dusty. Lightning had taken his customary place at the foot of Will's bed in the night after a brief snarling argument with the hotel clerk.

Will found Dusty well cared for and Ned at his forge. He hesitated, feet shuffling and hands in his pockets, not sure of his welcome. He cleared his throat between blows of the hammer.

Ned looked up, laid the hammer down, and wiped his hands on a towel.

"What can I do for you?"

"I'm just wondering, does Luther sometimes bring store goods in on the stage? You know, food-stuffs, cloth, tools . . ."

"Sometimes, when there isn't enough passenger traffic. Why?"

"Would he buy something I ordered through him?"

"Maybe. It depends."

"Any idea when the stage will come?"

"Heard a newcomer say it will arrive today. But with weather and Indians, you never know."

Will frowned, then tipped his hat and walked out into the sunshine. His brow furrowed, thinking. It was frustrating trying to pry information out of Ned, but he knew no one else at all. He dared not leave his pa for too long, lest Robert end up back at the Lucky Strike.

As he wandered toward the lone three-story brick building in town, he jolted out of his reverie when a thunder of horses headed toward him, and the sharp crack of a whip whistled through the air. The stagecoach rumbled past, and Will saw a black driver. Will followed the stage until it stopped, horses steaming and blowing, in front of the station.

The driver turned and hopped down to help the passengers. Will waited, then stepped forward when the baggage was unloaded from the roof of the stage.

Will turned to the driver, ignoring the passengers. "Luther? Is that you?"

Eyes wide with surprise, Luther turned. "Do I know you?"

"I'm Will Crump, Albinia's brother. We met back in Indiana some years ago."

"Well, Mr. Crump, it has been a while. Your beard makes you look different. What brings you to Colorado?"

"My pa is here, not doing too well. I have a business proposition for you if you'd let me buy you dinner."

Luther threw down some more luggage. "Not sure why I should listen to anyone who wore the gray, but for Albinia's sake I will. Ain't but one place serves colored in town: Auntie Mae's."

"That's where I'm staying. Meet you there after the horses are stabled?"

"All right."

Will hurried back to the hotel, hoping his pa would still be there sleeping.

Back at Auntie Mae's, after Will roused Robert, who had found a small amount of whiskey somewhere, they headed down to the dining room to wait.

Will ordered beef stew for all of them and laid out his plan to Luther. "My pa and I need to make money to start up somewhere else. We are willing to work, but as Pa has discovered, the mines are not reliable. I have a small amount of cash from the sale of some horses. I propose that we become partners. You take my capital—I trust you for Albinia's sake—and buy trade goods back east to sell here for higher prices. I will hunt and get meat for the restaurants around here. We split the profits. When there's enough, we'll open a small store. Pa has experience with that. We sell for high but not unfair prices. If there's a loss due to Indians or weather, it hits us all the same. I say we can get richer selling to the miners than mining the dirt. What do you think?"

Luther considered, fingers tapping on the table. "I'm not saying yes or no, but why couldn't I just do that myself, let Ned sell stuff for me? Why should I take your money?"

Robert spoke up, "You're not taking our money,

we're helping each other. Mark can help in the store. If I appear to be the owner, white folk will buy. If you were to do it on your own, some whites wouldn't shop there. It's stupid, but that's the way it is."

"I have to leave with the stage in the morning. It doesn't leave us much time," said Luther.

"Then you'll do it?" asked Will.

"I'll give it a try."

"Great! Then after we eat, let's go shopping, look at who has what and how much they charge. Let's talk to Auntie Mae and some of the other establishments."

After the meal, they agreed to split up, talking to people all over town. Will took the saloon and bordello district, to keep Robert away from there. Robert took the main business district. Luther would try the hotels, bathhouses, and restaurants. As he walked, Will kept an eye out for unused buildings or lots that might make a location for a store. Wandering into the Lucky Strike, he asked the barkeep about what supplies the saloon might need, what they were paying for whiskey and beer, and how much they sold in a week, explaining that he wanted to help them make their business better.

As Will talked, a cowboy at the end of the bar pushed back his slouch hat, revealing silver hair, deep-set eyes under eyebrows that stuck out like a canyon overhang, a strong nose, intense black eyes, and a graying bushy beard. He seemed to take an unusual interest in the conversation, making Will nervous. When Will finished with the barkeep, the cowboy approached.

"Couldn't help but overhear. You sound like a man with a business head. Buy you a drink?"

"I don't drink much sir. But sure, a beer. I have to keep moving soon, though."

"Not much of a drinker myself. A man needs his wits about him. Know anything about cattle or farming?"

"Some," Will said, his back stiff and his guard up. "Why?"

"Name's Charlie Goodnight. You may have heard of me. I own a few spreads in Texas and New Mexico Territory and down near Pueblo. I'm looking for smart, hungry young men. Fight in the war, did you?"

"Yes." Will's guard went up higher. His beer arrived, and he gave it a tentative sip.

"Gray or blue?"

"Gray, but that's not how I think now."

"Lots of good men lost in that tussle. I was gray

myself. Know anything about Indians?"

"A little. Spent the last two years with the Shoshone."

Goodnight drummed his fingers and seemed to reach a decision. He handed Will a silver dollar with a triangle cut out of it. "I fought Comanche for years. Now I fight beside them as a Texas Ranger. If you ever decide to come near Pueblo here in Colorado or Texas, over around Dallas, look me up. I'd have a job for you. Give that dollar to any of my foremen. They'll recognize it."

"If you've got a place near Pueblo, do you need meat for your hands? I was a sharpshooter in the war. I'm doing some hunting to supply local restaurants and businesses. Any interest?"

"As long as you're not shooting my cattle. Bison, deer, and elk are all welcome," said Charlie.

"All right, I'll look you up."

"On the Arkansas River, just west of Pueblo."

"Much obliged."

Will had never heard of him but figured since they were looking for work and for a new place, once they built up their savings Dallas might work as well as any. Will finished his beer and continued canvassing merchants.

Back at the hotel, he met up with his pa and Luther. Luther shook his head, shoulders slumped. He seemed discouraged and angry.

"Storekeepers wouldn't talk to me, most of 'em. I bring their mail, their goods anyhow, but not a one trusts me to do orders."

Robert rubbed the stubble on his chin. "I couldn't get much either. Guess my reputation as the town drunk doesn't help much. One told me he thought I'd spend it on whiskey."

"That's why we have to work together. I have a little start-up capital and can talk business. Luther hauls the goods on the stage, paying the stage company freight charge unless they let him take some stuff for free. He knows the country. And, Pa, you know how to run the store—you've done it before. Together we can make the miners' gold and silver flow into our pockets and never lift a pickax."

Robert said, "I hope you're right, son."

"I'll do three runs," Luther said. "If we make a profit, I'll keep going. Otherwise, I'll find a different way. I got a wife and family to support."

The Founding

***

The next morning, Will found his pa's bed empty. Where could Robert be at this early hour? Will shrugged into his clothes, worry growing in his belly and crowding out the desire for breakfast. He'd like to think that Robert had gone out to find a quiet place to pray, but there was another possible explanation. Maybe he'd gotten up while Will was asleep and gone out drinking. Will felt his pants pocket and found the coins missing. With a deep sigh, he buckled his gun belt and decided to look for his wayward father.

He went first to the livery and found Luther, both to ask for information and to give Luther a list of things to buy and bring back for sale.

"Ain't seen Robert this morning." Luther looked the list over. "Gonna be tough getting all this for forty dollars." He tipped his hat back, scratching his head. "Don't forget, we gotta pay the stage company to transport this stuff. And find room on the stage."

"I know," said Will, "but I think there's enough demand here. Just make the best deal you can."

"It'll be at least two weeks before I'm back, assuming no bad weather."

"We'll be here. You think some of the places in town might buy fresh meat?"

"I s'pect so, but you might have to go far out to find game."

"Good luck, Luther, and prayers for you. Travel safe."

"I'll do that. If you find Robert, tell him this partnership got no room for wasting money on being drunk." Luther turned to help passengers onto the stage and load their trunks on top, then climbed to the driver's box, slapped the reins, and with a loud "Hyah!" and a cloud of dust, thundered out of town.

Will continued his search. The Lucky Strike looked closed and empty. The dining room at Auntie Mae's had several patrons, but no Robert. Will had an idea. Going up to their room, he got Robert's spare shirt and had Lightning smell it. Untying him, Will encouraged the dog to seek.

Lighting bounded down the stairs and stopped outside Auntie Mae's, sniffing the boardwalk. As Will had feared, the dog headed toward the saloon district, but down a different street than the Lucky Strike. After searching three saloons, they found Robert sitting with a cane chair tipped back on the boardwalk, bottle in hand. Lightning barked and danced around the chair, almost knocking it over.

Will wasn't sure how to approach him, so he said, "C'mon, Pa. We're going hunting."

"What if I don't feel like it? In case you forgot, I'm the pa."

Will twisted his mouth into a frown and said, "I didn't forget. When you lose the bottle and start acting like my pa again, I'll remember better. You said it yourself: you have a reputation as the town drunk. We've got five dollars left after what you stole from me. You're not spending it on whiskey. We need to rent or build a store and get it ready, and we need food in the meantime. Hunting is the best way; you used to be good at it."

Robert let the chair crash to the boardwalk, shoved him aside, and stomped into the saloon.

Will shook his head. Life was simpler with the Shoshone.

***

Two weeks passed. Robert was drunk more than he was sober. He'd gone back to sweeping out stores, cleaning out stalls for whiskey. He stayed out until dawn, coming back to sleep it off. Will was ready to abandon the whole venture and let Robert sink, but pride and love for his father wouldn't let him. How could Robert run a store if he was sloshed every night? How could Will function if he couldn't sleep for worrying about him? He had nothing. Again, he looked into the dark abyss of grief and saw how he could become like Robert—but who would save them both?

Morning no longer had any joy in it. If Robert was there, he stank and snored loud enough to vibrate the walls. If he was gone, Will worried that he'd fallen into the river or drunk himself to death this time. Will prayed for him but saw no change in his behavior. Lighting grew adept at finding his new hiding places and the liquor bottles stashed in Auntie Mae's.

Will was about to give up, and then Dove came to

him in a dream. She wasn't sick, she was vibrant and alive. When he told her to stay, she shook her head and put a finger to her lips.

"Listen, I don't have long. You must live, Will. Father God gave you a beautiful world. One day we'll see each other again, but it will be different. Live, love, laugh, and enjoy the world you are in. There is always hope."

Will reached for her, but she was gone.

***

Two days later, Luther brought in the first order of goods, and they sold within a day. Ignoring Robert for a time, Will built a store, sawing the lumber himself, and continued to supply restaurants and residents with meat using his shooting skills. It gave him something to do and dulled the pain of missing Dove.

Robert came hunting with him once or twice but often was too drunk to hit anything. Most of the time they passed each other, not speaking, and Will quit trying. He despaired over knowing what to do with his pa.

Luther stayed in town longer than normal while he and Ned repaired wheels and tires on the stage.

Will took the opportunity to get to know Luther better, hearing about his escape from the Clay plantation, the Underground Railroad, slave catchers, and the expulsion from Indiana. They sat together in Auntie Mae's, which raised a few eyebrows.

"So once you got to Leavenworth and continued blacksmithing, how'd you end up here?" asked Will.

"After a year, we were out of work again. The fella that owned the shop up and moved. We could have tried to start on our own, but with the railroad it seemed we'd be better off farther west. Ruth, though, she didn't want to move. With a new baby and another on the way, she thought I should take a job driving the stagecoach. Might let me scout out where we want to locate permanently. I began making the run from Leavenworth to Denver, then up to the mining towns."

"Railroads changing things for sure. I wonder if it'll go through Denver or farther north," said Will.

"Looks like Cheyenne first, but who knows? I'm hoping by the time it gets to Denver to have land of my own."

"I'm beginning to think that way too. Railroads mean new towns. Bound to be opportunities."

"Maybe, but not so many for black folks. 'Less maybe we start our own town." Luther shook his head.

"Seems like we both have dreams and need to

get this store working. Pa isn't much help right now. What do you say we take on some help?"

"Ned's son Mark could do some, and Ned's wife Katy could help, but what about the white folk?"

"Bound to be someone in town who needs work. Or if Pa starts behaving, they could do it together."

***

When Will arrived back at Auntie Mae's for the evening meal, he saw his father on the porch, leaning back in a wooden chair, about to take another drink from a whiskey bottle.

Something snapped in Will, and without thinking he drew his Colt revolver, sighted, and shattered the bottle, sending glass and whiskey everywhere.

Robert ducked in surprise, then jumped to his feet.

"What the hell do you think you're—"

That's as far as he got before Will's fist hit his face. He staggered backward, falling as his missing foot threw him off-balance.

"I'm sick of your excuses. Either stand up and be a man, like you taught me, or take a swing at me. If you're going to drink yourself to death, I don't want to be here to watch. I'll be back after supper ends. Either get changed, sober, and serious about living or I'll pull out tomorrow. I came here to help you. Let's see you help yourself."

Will was breathing hard as Robert stared at him. He turned back toward the store and strode away.

When he cooled off, after hammering many nails,

and returned to Auntie Mae's, the lamps were low in the dining room, but at one table sat his pa, well dressed and shaved. Seeing Will come in, Auntie Mae told him, "I saved supper for you. There's a pot of coffee. I'll leave you two alone to talk."

Will went to the table and sat down. He felt he should apologize, but the words wouldn't come. Instead, he waited.

Robert looked down at his coffee cup and stammered, "Son, you're right. I haven't been fair to you, and I haven't been myself. I told you in the beginning, I'm just a drunk cripple now, and you should leave me. I don't deserve anything else. If you want to go, I wouldn't blame you."

Robert shuffled his feet and took a long drink of coffee. "I thought about what you said. I hope you can forgive me. I don't want to hurt you or Ned and Luther. Can we try again? I won't touch a drop of alcohol, and I'll pull my weight as a partner."

***

Two weeks passed. Will finished an apartment over the store. Robert moved into it while Will stayed at Auntie Mae's. Robert stuck to his word about keeping clear of alcohol. Will watched over him but said little. After their blowup, he thought it best to be casual, as if nothing much had happened. Robert said no more than necessary, drifting like a shadow around Will, as though afraid talking might trigger another storm.

"Pa, I want you to start working in the store. You know how to organize, order, and make nice with the men while making sure they don't give Mark trouble. Mark is going to help with the heavy stuff, loading and unloading wagons, sweeping up, and keeping the store in order. I told him to tell me the first time he smells you drunk."

Robert frowned and rolled his eyes. "Not necessary."

"Maybe not, but you have to show me. Any problem with Mark helping out?"

"Guess not."

"Good. With y'all doing the store, it will let me concentrate on hunting and keeping the books. I'll start

supplying Goodnight with meat as well as the businesses here. If all goes well, I might get Ned to build a couple of freight wagons and hire some extra drivers. We
could be ready to buy land elsewhere within a year."

"I don't know, Will. The future isn't clear to me.
One day at a time." He held out a glass of water so Will
could see his hands. They trembled, but not enough to
spill the water. "I'm concentrating on this for now, and
reading my Bible—kinda got away from that."

"One day at a time is good enough for me." Will
smiled and extended a hand, which Robert shook.

***

Will hunted, far and wide, accompanied by Lightning. He brought meat for hungry miners and cowhands. Once in a while, he donated a deer to the needy. He made sure to take Sundays off and be in church with Robert. He dropped into the store unexpectedly, at different times of day, but always found everything in order. Mark was a marvelous help and a hard worker. Now that he was sober, Robert showed a flair for the window displays and talking with the miners, as well as the occasional female customers. Will was pleased with his progress but watchful.

"Mark, I'm going to try being gone a few days. I need to take a shipment down to Goodnight's ranch. It's about four days' round trip. If Pa starts drinking, get your pa to help and tie him up until he's sober. I hope you won't have trouble."

"All right, Will. The store's going good. It'd be a shame to lose it. Can't say as I mind a few coins in my pocket either. Sure a lot easier than shoeing horses."

Ned had built a new freight wagon and bought two draft horses to pull it. They'd agreed to split the profits two ways, half for Ned and his family and half for Will and Robert. Will shot and butchered the meat, giving Robert and Mark the hides to tan and sell. Ned took care of feed for the horses and kept the wagon in repair.

The trail through the mountains past Mount Rosa was narrow, winding, and treacherous. Will used wide spots in the road to rest the horses and to gaze in wonder at the snow-capped peaks, fields of wildflowers, and mountain sheep. After weeks of town life, everything smelled fresh and new: the perfume of grass, the clove scent of alpine avens, and the air washed by rain. Will was glad the trail had a chance to dry from the last rainstorm. He got the team moving again, eyes glued to the corkscrew track over the mountains. He hoped he didn't meet anyone coming the other way, as backing down it wasn't something he would relish. He hoped to make the town of Como by nightfall but had to keep moving with only short rests to avoid the meat spoiling.

After almost two days, he was in flatter country around Pueblo. He crossed the Arkansas River on a wooden bridge, wheels scraping and the bridge complaining at the load, and saw a cabin and corral. Horses milled about, restless in the corral, some saddled. A man had steer hides drying on the fence as he scraped them. When he saw Will, he ran to open the corral gate, mounted, and took off, leaving Will to scratch his head at what had caused the rapid departure. Will stopped the team, set the brake, and wandered close to the corral, calling out to see if anyone was in the cabin. No one answered. Will looped the reins over the brake and went over to look at the hides, one hand on the butt of his revolver. The wind raised dust and a sign creaked, making him nervous. The hides all bore the same brand. Looking further, he saw a stack of steer heads in the creek, all with ears removed to prevent identification. It struck him as odd, and he resolved to mention it to Charlie when they met. He found one of the ears and took it with him.

With no reason to stay, he mounted the wagon box and drove on. Arriving at the Goodnight ranch the next day, a foreman asked his business and directed him to Charlie, saying he'd take care of unloading the meat.

"Will! Good to see you. Any trouble?"

"No—just one curious thing. Back up the river on this side, I found a cabin. There was a fella scraping hides. He took off like a shot as soon as he saw me and didn't come back. It looked like about fifty head they were butchering and tanning. Hides all had this same brand." He took out the ear and showed it to Charlie, who whistled and then let out a string of curses.

"That's my brand! We've had some trouble with rustlers up that way, but with thousands of acres to patrol, we can't be everywhere. I'm much obliged. When you've rested and slept, perhaps tomorrow you'll show me where you found these. Me and my Sharps would like a conversation with those thieves."

"Rustlers? So not your men?"

"Nope."

The next day, Will and Charlie retraced his steps to the bridge across the Arkansas. The hides were gone, and the cabin was deserted.

"Figger they headed for Denver to sell the hides?"

"Seems likely. I see other wagon tracks here besides yours, and they head off east on the other side of the bridge," said Charlie. "With the wagon, I don't know how many of them there are. But I hate to take time to go back to the ranch for help. If I don't catch them with the hides, I'll have no proof."

"I'll come with you," offered Will.

"Might be some shooting. You all right with that?"

For an answer, Will drew his pistol, sighted a pine cone on a tree at about fifty yards, and fired. The pine cone splintered in all directions "I think I'll manage."

Charlie grinned. "Let's look in the barn and see if they left a saddle. If not, I'll ride one of your draft horses bareback, and you can ride my horse."

As luck would have it, there was a large saddle in the barn. Will unhitched the horses, leaving one in a stall so he'd be out of sight, and saddled the other. Charlie took the lead as the better tracker, and Will scanned the ridges, looking for a possible ambush or horse tracks going off the trail in another direction. They followed the wagon track through scrub pine and granite buttes. Will wondered if the rustlers might abandon the hides if he and Charlie got too close, or would they fight?

Charlie held up a hand, palm flat, then motioned to the right. Will saw a small game trail and figured Charlie wanted him to follow it. He split off, heart hammering, ears perked to listen for danger. He tried to remember everything Bridger and Dove had taught him about following a trail. He saw a few horse tracks. The horses had worn shoes, indicating probable white men.

Will wished for Dusty instead of this noisy, plodding draft horse, but it couldn't be helped. He hadn't brought Dusty since he was hauling meat for Charlie's ranch. As he reached a point where another trail split off, he saw light ahead, perhaps a clearing, and heard the repeated call of a kestrel. Was Charlie trying to warn him? Will pulled up, dismounted, and tied the horse to a tree. He went forward on hands and knees until he was in the clearing, then slithered like a snake up to the edge of a twenty-foot drop. Looking across the ravine, he caught a flash of sunlight on a gun barrel. He made out Charlie behind a rock. A little farther up the trail, smoke rose from the trees, and Will could hear faint voices. Looking over at Charlie, he saw him motion to go around the voices and come back, driving the men toward him. Will prayed and then snuck back to his horse, which he led back on the trail until they could pass unobserved in the trees.

When they were on the other side of the party, Will repeated the kestrel sound he'd heard before. Then he heard Charlie yell at the men to drop their guns and come out in the open. Will fired three shots in the air with his revolver and reloaded fast from his cartridge belt. He mounted, and moved forward, watching for any movement. He heard a shot from Charlie's direction and then saw a man running toward him, gun raised.

Will laid low on the horse and fired, aiming at the belly. The man dropped but then rose, unhurt, and fired again. This time Will took no chances, aiming higher and to the left. The man screamed, clutched his right shoulder, and dropped the gun, staggering a few steps. Another man came behind, but seeing his friend fall, he turned and ran toward Charlie. Will raised his gun but couldn't fire before a man dropped from a tree and pulled him off his horse.

Will was trapped as the heavier man pinned him to the earth. His heart hammered in panic. His pistol was three feet away. The stench of sweat and whiskey from his black-bearded antagonist, mixed with the smell of his own fear, deprived him of movement. The man's rotten teeth showed as he let Will's arm loose to grab a knife. The stab came downward, but Will caught the wrist in time to slow it. The knife inched closer. Will raised his legs, grabbing the man's head and twisting. His foe fell off, and Will rolled, grabbing the pistol. Two shots hit the assailant at the same time, one from Will and one from Charlie. The man lay still, but Charlie kept his rifle pointed at him.

Will groaned and stood, looking to see if others were around. His horse had wandered off some distance.

"I'll get my horse and keep my eyes open. Thanks for getting him. He was too much for me."

"Are you hurt?"

"Just my pride. I was too eager to move forward."

"Let's make sure we have all of them, then look for the hides."

Will and Charlie scouted the area and found four men, all dead. They collected the hides and marked the location with cairns for the Pueblo sheriff. They loaded the bodies into the thieves' wagon and hitched the draft horse Will was riding to it, returning to the Goodnight ranch.

Chapter 2

Kansas City, Missouri, 1867

Julia Crump Johannsen checked her hair in the mirror, repaired her makeup, then went into the kitchen to go over the menu again with the cook. Tonight they were hosting Senator Samuel Pomeroy, who was also president of the Atchison, Topeka, and Santa Fe Railway, and Jay Gould, the railroad financier from New York. Julia and her mother-in-law Kirsten Johannsen fussed and bustled over the table settings and arrangements. Kirsten reviewed the seating order for the guests with the serving maids one more time. Everything must be perfect. With Hiram's blessing, she had invested in some shares of the AT&SF during the war and then soon after a new venture building a bridge across the Missouri River. Now, however, he had reservations.

Since Hiram had resumed control of the steamship line, there had been successes with steamboats reaching the upper Mississippi and Missouri rivers, even to Dakota. Hiram was beginning to doubt the need for expansion into railroads. Julia had persuaded him to invite Pomeroy and Gould to at least listen to their ideas.

"I hope this doesn't all blow up in our faces," said her mother-in-law, Kirsten. "You pushed Hiram into this. We've always done well enough with steamboats. My husband built this business. I stood by him through all the lean times and the panic of '57. What does a farm girl like you know of business? It's a wonder we didn't go bankrupt with you in charge during the war."

Julia clenched her handkerchief, wanting to explode. Her lips tightened into a thin line. She wanted to scream that if she hadn't taken over, Kirsten would have spent them into poverty. Instead, she replied with controlled emotion. "I push Hiram into nothing. He prays and makes up his own mind. Sometimes I offer suggestions, and he listens. Like keeping the ships neutral to prevent them from being targets for both Union and Confederate batteries in the war."

Kirsten made a noise in her throat but did not reply. Julia smiled grimly, claiming victory, and moved on with dinner preparations.

Hiram bustled in, and Julia noticed his frown and bunched eyebrows. She saw her nervousness reflected in him. This meeting would determine whether they should invest heavily in railroads.

"Julia, dearest, is everything ready?"

"Yes, I think so. I had your mother make inquiries as to the favorite foods of Pomeroy and his wife, Martha, as well as Mr. Gould and his wife, Helen."

"Good, good! You know how much this could mean to us."

"Yes, I think we're both nervous. We have a big decision here—whether to invest more or not. And whether to go in with Gould, Pomeroy, or both."

"If you're right about the railroads, we need partners; we haven't the capital to do it ourselves. If railroads overtake steamships and we haven't made allies, we could be in trouble. I'm not convinced, but I do know that these men are ruthless and powerful. Even spiteful. If they wish, they could do us great harm. They don't need us, we need them. We are in a delicate position negotiating. Our main asset is to reduce their risk by taking it on ourselves. They will be the controlling partners. We need to be careful. They could help us or ruin us."

"I know, it's just that Gould has a habit of turning on his partners. Remember what he did with the Erie Railroad."

"Yes, but it won't help to worry about them. Instead, pray. And help Mama with the women. The wives may not write the bank drafts, but their influence on their husbands could be substantial. Both men are still newlyweds. You need to make friends with the wives."

"I'll do my best. But I do think we need to be in railroads, whether these men help us or not."

Hiram grinned. "Nothing like a wife who insists on speaking her mind. Good thing you're beautiful too," he said, kissing her.

She smiled, enjoying his attention. "Now about that wifely influence . . ." she teased.

"Save me!" Hiram said with mock terror.

***

The Pomeroys arrived first, in a fine carriage, but with only a footman and a groom. Hiram greeted them.

"Good evening, Senator. And this must be your lovely wife. Please come into the parlor. I'm sure our other guests will arrive soon, and dinner will be ready shortly. And may I present my wife, Julia, and my mother Mrs. Kirsten Johannsen?"

"Evening, Johannsen, ladies. Figured Gould would be late just to show how important he is."

Hiram just smiled. Julia stepped into the awkward moment.

"Mrs. Pomeroy, I understand you are interested in flowers. Would you care to see our rose garden? There are some fine specimens in bloom just now. We can leave the men to their business until dinner is ready."

"Sounds splendid, Mrs. Johannsen."

The ladies moved out to the garden. Julia hated not knowing what was being said inside, but she knew that Hiram was right: her role was to cultivate the wife.

"I understand you are recently married, Mrs. Pomeroy."

"Yes, Mr. Pomeroy and I wed only about a year ago. His first wife died during the war. He's been much occupied with getting the railroad started. So much politics. And the Indian troubles."

"Indian troubles?"

"Oh, you know, not actual battles, but working toward a new treaty since the original treaty fell through without getting the land for the railroad. A real opportunity, I'm told. Convincing the savages to give up without a fight. So much better for them. Their only option, really."

"I suppose so."

"I've warned Hiram about the Indian troubles," said Kirsten. "Never had that problem on the rivers."

"It's something to be aware of, but the army will force them on to reservations. Then the mission schools will make Christians of them—isn't that what the Bible teaches us to do? And, of course, they'll learn to dress decently and how to farm. No more running about slaughtering people. I'm sure you've heard of the Moffit massacre?"

"Well, no. I'm from Kentucky, lately of Cincinnati. I have small experience in Indian matters," said Julia.

"If you're going to be in this railroad business,

you'd better learn. I'm from Boston myself, but I've been learning. The Moffit brothers settled in Kansas just over a year ago. They built a home, trying to make a go of it, though the farmland is rather poor due to lack of water. Within a few months, the Indians came and murdered them all."

Julia raised her eyebrows and moved a hand to her mouth. "What was the reason?"

"They are heathen savages—they need no reason. They must be moved, civilized. If not, then as our General Sherman said, 'The more Indians we can kill this year, the fewer we will need to kill the next.'"

She continued, "The railroads will bring settlers, ranchers, and commerce. I heard one scout say, 'Kill every buffalo you can! Every buffalo dead is an Indian gone.'"

"Perhaps I'm naïve, but where is the love of Christ in that?" Julia asked.

"If they would accept Christ, farm, dress like white men, and follow our ways, there would be no problem. We could accept them as brothers. Alas, they will not. They cling to the murderous ways of their forefathers."

"Exactly right!" said Kirsten.

Julia wanted to ask more questions or even object.

However, she kept in mind Hiram's plea to cultivate the wives, not offend them.

"That is most interesting. I shall have to make further inquiries. Shall we look at the new roses I've planted? I hope you'll find them beautiful."

***

The Goulds arrived, and dinner was served. Julia was still nervous but hopeful as she saw Hiram laughing and joking with the men. Business would wait until later when the men took their brandy in the parlor. Julia listened with half an ear to the men's conversation as they took one another's measure, trying to pay attention to Helen Gould's description of current New York fashions. Kirsten finished eating, and finding she was out of her depth, said she had a headache and retreated upstairs.

"They've done something with skirts that makes sense—to keep long skirts from dragging on the ground when walking, they've fastened cords at intervals to the inside of the skirt. The skirt can then be raised from the ground to the desired height, and the cords are tied around the waist. That might be of particular value here, where there are no paved streets."

"And I hear they're flattening the front of skirts while extending the back for next year," said Mrs. Pomeroy. "That is not sensible! But I suppose we'll all have to follow along or be thought old-fashioned."

Julia was bored but managed to get through most of the dinner without appearing too distracted. In the parlor afterward, she resisted convention and stayed by Hiram's side, more or less forcing the other ladies to do the same.

Pomeroy spoke first. "We must mobilize the financing now. President Johnson is weak and distracted, not a force. Congress is weary of the war and wants to expand westward. This opportunity in Missouri and Kansas is too good to ignore. Land for just over a dollar an acre. We can bring immigrants by the hundreds. And think of the business in cattle coming up from Texas and Oklahoma."

Hiram said, "But why rails? We already have rivers, many of them navigable for smaller steamships. No construction cost and little maintenance. And no trouble with Indians."

"Get with the times, man," Gould said impatiently. "Rail doesn't require rivers, just a flat, open country. We've already laid track from Leavenworth to Abilene. Expansion is unlimited. Even mountains can be overcome, as we've done in New York. A train can carry several times the freight of a boat and with more profit. Labor is cheap—lots of new immigrants looking for land and jobs. In California, they've got Chinese coming in to work on the railroad. And in New York, if I put up a sign in Five Points for jobs, I'd have no lack. If you're not in this, say so. It only wants capital. I'm extending you this offer as a courtesy, in memory of your father. The venture will go forward with or without you."

Pomeroy chimed in, "Settlers want to move west. Cattle from Texas can be transported to the East. Why, by the time the cattle make it to the Missouri River on a boat or cattle drive, they've lost half their weight—and value. With rails, the profits are limitless. Once we move the Indians, which the army will tend to, nothing stands in our way. Certainly not steamboats."

"And just think," said Mrs. Gould, "New York will only be a few days away by train, even from Kansas. Have you ever been to New York, Mrs. Johannsen?"

"No, I've not had that pleasure," said Julia. "My family was much involved in the war. We've not had the leisure to travel."

"Then you must come and visit us at some point. I could show you the sights and introduce you to important people."

Julia noted the condescension in the remark but did not bristle.

"All very well," said Mr. Gould. "And now if you ladies will excuse us, we have business to discuss."

Thus dismissed, the ladies moved to the veranda, and Julia heard no more.

***

After their guests left, Hiram and Julia sat in the parlor.

"What do you think of our proposed partners, dearest?" said Hiram.

"I think one is a rattlesnake, the other a wolf. If we get in with them, we'll either be poisoned, devoured, or ruined. I know it was my idea, but having met them confirms my worst fears."

"And yet what choice do we have? You said that railroads are the future. Steamboats can go west and north on the Mississippi and Missouri, but what about farther west or south to Texas? We haven't the capital to strike out on our own with a railroad. We can join with these or watch our shipping slowly dwindle. You can't go by the river to California."

Julia sighed. "I know. I just have a bad feeling about working with those two."

Kirsten appeared, and announced, "I cannot understand you working with these men. Railroads are unnecessary. Since I know you won't listen to me, I will take the steamboat in the morning back to Cincinnati." She sniffed and returned upstairs, without waiting for a reply.

Julia looked at the ceiling a moment and then turned back to Hiram.

Hiram drummed the table with his thumbs, forehead creased. It was easier driving spikes for railroad ties than doing all these negotiations. He reached for Julia's hand.

"So how do you catch a wolf?" he asked.

"Distract it and then shoot."

"Maybe we can't shoot him, but what if we distract him? Let's play along. They are pushing the east-to-west line. There isn't anything out there except the uncertain possibility of gold. The east-west line is worthless without a bridge across the Missouri River. I know everyone says it can't be done, but that little company you invested in is trying to build the Hannibal Bridge with that designer Octave Chanute. What if we get Gould looking west, and with Pomeroy we help make the bridge and move south to where the cattle are—Texas, New Mexico, maybe a connection to New Orleans? We can at least *avoid* the wolf while we keep an eye on the rattlesnake. We could generate enough money to help finish a line to Santa Fe across north Texas. Once the bridge is finished, Gould might have to pay us to get his trains over the river. And maybe . . .

maybe the snake will bite the wolf."

Julia withdrew her hand, but her eyes sparkled with excitement.

"Do you think we could pull it off? If we canceled the order for our next boat and sold one or two . . ." she speculated.

"Then we can finish the bridge and maybe lay track south to Lawrence. Or move just a little west and make new railheads for cattle as we go, getting closer to Texas," said Hiram.

Hiram stood, lit the lamp, and kissed Julia on the forehead. "I love you, and I love working with you."

He sat again, head near hers as they looked at maps and chattered together late into the night.

Chapter 3

Abilene, Kansas, 1868

Julia swore at the newspaper she was reading—more delays and more debates over the railroad, both in Congress and in the Kansas legislature. They'd already run roughshod over the Indian tribes, lied, and deceived to get funding, so why couldn't they get on with it? Gould may have gone north with the Union Pacific, but he was always circling like a buzzard around a kill. When she and Hiram decided not to throw in their lot with him, they knew he would be a fierce competitor. What if he just bided his time and bought out their southern branch when other investors hesitated?

Hiram had been gone a lot, seeking more investors, but

promises of investment could fade faster than a Kansas winter sunset. Success was not yet assured.

Just a week ago, she'd watched as the first locomotive and four cars crossed the bridge over the Missouri River. The brilliant railroad bridge design that allowed trains to cross and their steamboats to proceed upriver had worked. When the train was across, the bridge span had swung to the side, taking only two minutes, and their *Ohio Zephyr* steamship had crossed in the open space.

Fidgeting, she put on a bonnet and decided to go down to the end of the tracks just outside Abilene to see what was happening. Even though this was a rough cow town of boardwalks, saloons, and bordellos, not safe for ladies, in her impatience she didn't wait for the groom, hitched the buggy herself, and drove in a whirlwind of dust to the rail construction site. The hot, dry wind whipped her hair into disarray despite her bonnet, and sand coated her outer skirt.

She found Thomas Peter, the chief engineer, expressing his loud and profane opinion of how the crew was operating.

"You're a flapdoodle at home and no better here with a hammer! A bigger group of zounderkites I've never seen! Here, give me that! If you can't drive a spike straight,

I'll show you how it's done."

Peter laid aside his waistcoat, grabbed a sledge-hammer, and drove three spikes into the rail in a few minutes.

"Now it's your turn. We have to lay track south faster than a jackrabbit and be south of the Kaw River by Christmas. If you can't do it right, find another job. We've no time to do it over!"

Julia motioned, and he took back his coat, walking over to her.

"Pardon my language, Mrs. Johannsen, I didn't see you over there. These numbskulls have Irish heads as thick as their brogue. What may I do for you?"

"Just what you're doing, Mr. Peter. If I could drive the spikes, I'd join you. I'm wondering what the holdup is and whether you've seen Pomeroy about."

"Hasn't Mr. Johannsen told you? Pomeroy has gone back to Cincinnati, then to DC. Something about selling his portion of the railroad."

"What? No one told me."

Julia flushed, and not from the heat. What else was Hiram not telling her?

"I see. Thank you, Mr. Peter. And what news of the line south from Topeka?"

"Just put out an order to hire five hundred workers. Senator Ross is presiding over pictures today of the start of construction."

Julia fought to keep her anger from boiling over. It wasn't the engineer's fault. She pulled her eyebrows together and scowled. She brushed aside an errant curl and, in a voice that would have cut diamonds, said, "If you see Mr. Johannsen, please inform him that I am looking for him."

"Yes, ma'am."

"Good day, Mr. Peter." Julia turned to her buggy, not waiting for an offer of help to mount. As she drove home, she fumed. "If he tells me I shouldn't worry my pretty little head . . ."

***

When she arrived at their rented house, Julia asked the maid to draw her a bath, but not a hot one. A nice cool soak would be good preparation for talking to Hiram. What good was it for her to endure the frontier if they weren't going to operate as a team? She might as well be back in Cincinnati, suffering with Mama Kirsten. Maybe he'd just been busy. They hadn't had much time together of late. That was no excuse, though, she decided, for making major decisions and leaving her in the dark.

"Emily!"

"Yes, Mrs. Johannsen?"

"Please send a girl with a note for Mrs. Pomeroy. I desire to call upon her. And don't bother about dinner for either Mr. Johannsen or me. When you clean up here, you may go home."

"Yes, ma'am."

Julia stepped out of the tub, dried herself, and began to dress without a maid's help. A glance in the mirror made her wince—her hair looked like Medusa's. She almost regretted sending Emily home, but then she thought of the time long ago, primping for the dance at her uncle's when she'd met Hiram. She'd done everything herself then; she could do it now. With Pomeroy selling the major part of his stake in the railroad, she needn't worry too much about cultivating his wife—and good riddance. No, she was after information, not friendship.

***

A boy knocked at the door, and Julia received a note saying that Mrs. Pomeroy was home today and would see her.

Julia arranged her hair and selected a teal morning dress with brass buttons down the front, a bow with brass buckles on each sleeve, a pocket with tassels, a matching scalloped hem and collar, and a high-necked ruff. After satisfying herself in the mirror, she walked to the livery and asked them to hitch a buggy for her.

Arriving at the Pomeroy house, she set the brake on the buggy. When no servant emerged, she picked up her skirts and descended from the buggy, her determination overcoming her nervousness. The white frame house with a broad front porch and Corinthian columns was far beyond Julia's usual sphere, and she tried not to gape at the ornate lamppost, doorknob, and other decorations.

She knocked, and a black servant answered and escorted her to the drawing room, passing a staircase to the second floor and a grand piano in the foyer.

Martha rose to greet her, setting aside her sewing. "Julia, how lovely to see you. Society is so limited here. I hope you are well? John, please bring us tea."

"I am well, though it has been lonely with Hiram absent so often on railroad business. I understand Samuel is traveling also?"

"Yes, poor dear. His health is none too good, and the stress of all the railroad business has taxed him. He's gone back east to see if he can sell our interest in the railroad to other investors while still retaining some control. Of course, I don't pay much attention to men's business, but I believe he's talking with the investment firm of Dodge and Lord."

"How interesting! Did he mention anything else?"

"Oh, you know, just some boring details about hiring more men and ordering more rails. And something about the Pottawatomie Indians having to move now that the army is forcing them off their land. Nothing important," said Martha.

"Did he say why he would sell?"

"I suppose it's his health. Or some political trouble in Washington. I leave such details to him."

When Julia returned home, the front porch lamp was lit, and she could see Hiram on the porch swing, probably furious after arriving home to a dark house with no supper and no word. Served him right, she thought. The very idea of permitting the sale of a major stake in the railroad without her still set her boiling.

"Good evening, Hiram. I hope your day went well."

He stood, clutching one arm of the porch swing as though to snap it in half.

"Why weren't you here? And not even a word. I might have looked over half the town for you."

"You might have, but you didn't, did you? I had no idea when to expect you home. You didn't tell me. I've been visiting Mrs. Pomeroy, who seems better informed on many issues than I am. You did tell me to cultivate the wives, did you not? Of course, we needn't worry about Mrs. Gould anymore, and it appears not much for Mrs. Pomeroy either. When were you planning to tell me?"

"Now, Julia, you must understand . . ."

"What is it I must understand? You think me incapable of understanding anything."

"No, it's just . . . bills have been mounting and not

much income. I didn't want you to worry your pretty little head."

When she heard that, she exploded. "My pretty little head! Is that what you think of me? I know as much as you do about this company, and you know it!" She drew her eyebrows together and glared at him, eyes shooting flames. She wanted to slap him. Her hurt and anger threatened to overwhelm her. She would *not* cry! She threw her umbrella at him, point first, hitting a shin.

"Ow! What was that for?"

"My pretty little head ran the company for three years. I think I can be trusted to know about a potential sale that affects everything. But if you think not, then my heavens! How can I even be trusted with shopping and getting your meals? I might just forget altogether!"

"I don't like your tone. See here—"

"No, you see here! I am in this godforsaken cow town with drunks, gunfights, heat, and bugs instead of our comfortable home in Cincinnati to be with you and to help with the railroad, which was my pretty little head's idea! Instead of a partnership, you think you're a one-man show. I have to find out from Mr. Peter that we're hiring five hundred for the southern line. Visiting Martha Pomeroy, I couldn't ask for more details without appearing a fool. She did tell me that her husband swindled the Pottawatomie out of the best farmland in Kansas under threat of army intervention."

Hiram's shoulders drooped, and his head lowered in surrender. "I'm sorry. I only meant to save you from worry."

"Don't patronize me. We're in this together, remember? For richer or poorer, or whatever it was in that Swedish marriage ceremony. I know how to read a balance sheet. If we're in trouble, we share it. If we triumph, we share that."

"You're right, of course. The truth is the railroad is almost bankrupt. Without new investors, we could lose everything. There's a chance now that we've made it to Abilene that the profits from shipping cattle will begin to pay off the bills. I haven't sold. I just gave Pomeroy the chance to reduce his stake so we can take on new partners. We need the cash to keep expanding, to build the line south to Texas. You said Pomeroy and Gould were a snake and a wolf—without more cash, the wolf would take everything, and at pennies on the dollar. To keep expanding, we just ordered a new locomotive."

"Another thing you didn't tell me. Look, I am neither a child nor an idiot. Perhaps some women cannot comprehend business, though I expect most know more than their husbands think. You know well that I can handle it. Let me help you fight off Gould. Let's pray together and counsel together as we used to. I don't want to run things, I just want to be a part of the business. Don't let it tear us apart."

Hiram turned away a moment and then said, "I am sorry. I've let business pressure drive us apart. You've been a tremendous help to the business, with ideas, energy, and bookkeeping. I don't know how I would do it without you. I was wrong and presumptuous. Will you forgive me?"

Julia debated but felt the steam go out of her with his unexpected apology. She knew what it cost him. "I forgive you."

"Let's work together, starting now," Hiram said.

Once inside, they embraced each other and met for a long kiss.

***

The next morning, Julia stretched sleepily, looking over at Hiram snoring away. He should be up and attending to business, but after their three-hour lovemaking session, she hadn't the heart to wake him. She was tired herself. She should have been angrier with him, but he always managed to look sheepish, like a little boy with his hand caught in the cookie jar. Truthfully, after these years of marriage, he still took her breath away and filled her with longing. His strength and forcefulness made her feel safe, and well, last night he had been nothing like a little boy!

He stirred and moaned, and she traced the line of his jaw with her index finger, feeling the stubble of two days' beard. They hadn't woken up together alone, without servants, in more than a month. Often Hiram had some business or other and took coffee and a pastry out the door with a quick kiss goodbye. It felt like a luxury to sleep until seven and wake up together. She started to pull her hand away, but he grabbed her wrist lightly and held it until his eyes opened and met hers. Smiling, she shook free.

"No more of that this morning. We have work to do."

He moaned again and then smiled at her. "Yes, partner, whatever you say."

They were up and eating breakfast on the porch when Emily came, apologetic for being late, and brought a note for Julia.

"Don't worry, we enjoyed our morning," Julia said, smiling at Hiram. "Who is the note from?"

"Telegraph office. It doesn't say. It just asks if you or Mr. Hiram could meet the noon stage."

They looked at each other, questioning, and Hiram shrugged. "I have a shipment coming in on the train. Could you, Julia?"

"Yes, I can manage to stop by there. I'll get some shopping done as well."

Julia stood and began helping Emily clear away breakfast. Once the dishes were inside and Hiram was out the door, she checked herself in the mirror, grabbed a bonnet, and set out for the stage depot.

When she arrived, Julia sat on the bench in front of the depot and the dry-goods store. She fidgeted, tapping her fingers on the bench arm. It wasn't the best part of town, close to the jail and the saloon. She hoped no trouble would break out. It was early for that, at least. The noon stage was westbound, coming from Leavenworth. She couldn't imagine who could be on it or why she was to meet them. She had knitting with her, in case the stage was late, but found it hard to concentrate, her curiosity growing by the minute. A thought occurred to her that sent her heart down into her shoes: What if it was Mama Kirsten, surprising them from Cincinnati? It wasn't that she hated her mother-in-law, but . . . didn't she and Hiram have enough to work out already?

She heard the rumble of hooves and saw the cloud of dust as the stagecoach approached.

"Abilene!" called out the driver as it rolled to a stop. Julia looked up, startled at the voice and the face to match it—Luther!

The lathered horses pulled to a stop, looking over at the water trough, sides heaving, snorts and a whinny breaking the hot stillness. Luther climbed down, smiling and tipping his hat to Julia, and opened the door to the coach. One little girl about three years old didn't wait to be helped and clambered down from the stage onto the boardwalk. A boy, much younger, seemed determined to match his sister, but couldn't quite make it. Luther laughed, picking him up and helping him down, the resemblance between the two obvious. Last of all, a very pregnant Ruth slowly slid over and put her feet out, but Luther caught her under the arms and gently lifted her to the boardwalk, giving her a brief hug.

"You keep growing and I won't be able to reach

around," said Luther.

"You keep opening your mouth, you might get very thin!" she teased.

Julia put away her knitting and came over to them. Should she hug them or offer a hand or . . . It had been so long she wasn't sure of her welcome. Luther turned to take care of the horses.

Ruth solved her dilemma by opening her arms wide and embracing her.

"Julia, after that ride, it's surely good to see a friendly face. Is there a place a girl can wash up?"

"Absolutely! Y'all come along to our place. Are you here for a while?"

"Until Luther decides where we're going permanent. He's got to go on to Colorado, but me and the children stay here for now."

Julia looked down and saw the boy drawing in the dirt.

"And who do we have here?"

"The little one, he's Matthew, but we just call him Matt." She pulled the girl into a hug. "And this is our oldest, Lindy. She got more energy than three racehorses in spring."

Julia squatted to their level. "Hello, Matt and Lindy.

You may call me Aunt Julia or Mrs. Johannsen, but that's quite a mouthful. I'm glad to know you."

Ruth beamed. "We won't impose, we'll find a place in town that takes colored."

"No, you won't. You'll stay with us as long as you want. What about Olivia?"

"Olivia's still helping your sister with the colored school. So far the white folks haven't bothered her, but she may come west soon. You heard that Luther's mother, Jemima, passed?"

"Yes. I'm sorry about that. She was very brave."

Luther returned from taking care of the horses. "That last bout of fever, Mama just wasn't strong enough anymore," he said.

"Well, you're all out west now. We're glad to have you. It will be fun to have children about since Hiram and I don't have our own."

"Won't be permanent," said Luther. "Just till we find the right place to settle. I'll be glad when I can stop driving this stage between Leavenworth and Colorado and have a farm and a blacksmith shop. I heard tell of other black folks in Leavenworth looking to start fresh out west, near the railroad. And some from back in Kentucky looking to come too 'cause of all the laws cooking against black folks."

"You're more than welcome however long it is. Ruth, let's get you and the little ones settled, and I'll have Emily get Luther some food for the trip."

Luther left early the next morning, having arranged to have another man continue the stage to Colorado while he drove the company's eastbound stage back to Leavenworth. This gave him a night off to see Ruth and the children settled.

Julia decided to offer Ruth employment, both at the railroad office and helping Emily.

"I know you have your hands full with the children, and I know there may be days when you are too tired or not feeling well enough to work, but if you'd like, I can offer you a job helping Emily here at the house and helping me in the railroad office. I know you are good with numbers. You needn't work any day that you feel poorly."

Ruth considered, then smiled. "That's generous, Julia. I accept."

"Emily can watch your children when you're in the office. I know some won't approve of a pregnant woman, let alone a black woman, in the office, but I don't care. And when you're here, you can teach your children. In a few months, a colored school is supposed to open, but it hasn't started yet."

Lindy was listening and spoke up. "Auntie Julia, you mean I can go to school?"

Julia kneeled to her height, not caring about the dust on her dress. "Not yet, Lindy, but soon. Until then, I will get some picture books and a slate for you, and some dolls. Would you like that?"

"Oh yes, ma'am! Thank you!"

"When I was a little girl, I had to walk a long way to get to school, even in the winter. Your mama is so smart you won't have to do that—she can teach you. Then later this year, the school here in town will have other colored girls you can play with. Now run along while I talk to your mother."

"Yes, ma'am. And thank you for my room."

When Lindy skipped off to play, Julia turned to Ruth again. "You're probably aware, but just in case . . . Abilene is still a rough cow town, especially when a new drive comes up to the railroad. Sheriff Tom Smith is a good man and tries to keep the peace; you have nothing to fear from him. But a woman walking alone in town, especially a colored woman, is taking a risk. I usually carry a derringer or have one of the men come with me. I'll have our groom drive you wherever you want to go—that way men won't think you are another soiled dove. The town has plenty of them, poor girls."

Julia motioned her to sit down and poured tea for them.

"That's nice of you, but don't worry. I know my place and how to stay out of trouble. You're being much nicer to me than you have to be. I am a little worried about when my time comes. With Lindy and Matt, Jemima was there. Begging your pardon, but you haven't any children, so I am wondering if there is a good midwife in town. Luther doesn't always think of these things."

"Yes, a woman named Mary. She was a nurse in the war. She rotates between here and Salina. It's all very new. Why, two years ago this wasn't a town, just a few huts and a saloon. It's growing every day."

Ruth sipped her tea, and the worry lines on her forehead relaxed.

"It's a comfort to know that I won't be alone. But will she take colored?"

Julia laughed, and Ruth frowned. "Forgive me, you wouldn't know. But yes, she takes colored Not only that, she trained colored to be nurses in the war. You'll be in good hands as long as she is here. You should visit. She has a clinic on Buckeye Avenue next to the seminary. Let her know when you're due."

Ruth rubbed her belly and grinned. "All right, I will do

just that!

Julia let Ruth and the children settle into their rooms. It was a good thing she and Hiram had rented a big house with extra room. When Hiram arrived home from the office, she and Emily were making supper. Ruth hadn't come back down, no doubt exhausted from her trip.

"I'm going to the end of the track tomorrow," Hiram said. "New men are starting, and I need to look them over."

"Should I come?" asked Julia.

"You could, but unless you can swing a sledgehammer, you'd probably distract the men more than help. Let them get used to the work before we shock them with a lady boss."

Julia glanced over and decided he was serious. "All right. I have plenty to do with the books and getting Ruth settled. She's going to help out in the office some, if that's all right."

"That will be welcome—then I can see more of you when I get back." Hiram smiled and drew her into an embrace.

***

April 1868

Hiram decided that setting an example would do well for the workers. He discovered that his foreman, Leonard Blood, was inexperienced. He took the train with Leonard and the chief engineer Tom Peter, to the end of the track for the southern branch.

The assembled road crew was a motley bunch—blacks, Irish, a few Chinese, and more than a dozen who looked like they knew more about a whiskey bottle than a pick and shovel.

"All right, gentlemen, it's time to earn your wages. Our quota is a mile of track each day for the first week, then a mile and a half a day until we reach the Big Osage River. We've two locomotives, the Holliday and the Burnside, hauling materials and men from Kansas City, a hundred men mining coal at Carbondale, and another crew with lumber hauled on wagons out in front of you, building camps where you lay your heads at night."

Hiram looked at the men, some restless, some almost laughing.

"If you can't keep up, you're no use to us. We start at

sunup, and we work to dark. Each crew gets one day off, though on your day off you may need to work while the main crew eats lunch. Any man who shows up drunk is fired. Any questions?"

"D'ye think we're daft? Or maybe oxen? No man can keep that pace."

Hiram mounted a box and addressed the men. "I can. Gould's men up north on the UP are, and so are the Chinese in the west. If you don't want the work, leave now. The rest of you, grab some rails, and those assigned as graders, get to your horse teams. Tom, let's show them how it's done."

Graders flattened the prairie and followed the surveyors' instructions. Tom and Hiram helped lay crossties and rails on top. Hiram rarely required more than three strokes of a hammer to drive in a spike, and the astonished hands followed quickly.

After a time, they developed a system where a crew laid a section of track and then levered it sideways until it fitted with the previous section before the spikes were driven clear through into the ground.

Another crew would be ahead, laying out the oaken ties at correct intervals, which Tom checked, while another group lifted the fifty-five-pound iron rails into place. Tom showed them how to cut rails and ties for a switch so that cars could be moved off to a siding.

By day's end, they had laid almost two miles of track along the surveyed route and sent men ahead to identify places that would need more pick-and-shovel work for the new hands coming the next day. The Atchison, Topeka, and Santa Fe was moving south.

Tom and Hiram stood together at the side, watching the crews work, Leonard Blood leading them. Hiram wiped the sweat away with a handkerchief, thinking Julia would give him hell for ruining a good suit. The wind gusted weeds, dust, and the faint sound of a song from farther down the tracks from the black workers. Not to be outdone, the Irish group commenced a round of singing, "It's work all day for damn sure pay on the Atchison, Topeka, and Santa Fe." The rhythmic pounding of the hammers and the occasional curse in Gaelic, Chinese, or Italian was hypnotic as the silver rails slithered across the prairie like a rattlesnake on the hunt.

A group of horsemen topped a rise to the southwest and moved back out of sight before Hiram could identify them. The sight made him uneasy. Could it be Indians? He'd better post a guard.

***

Hiram had time to think during the train trip back to Abilene. Tom was a good engineer and a good manager— not afraid of hard work. Yet how could Hiram adequately supervise and make decisions for both the northern and southern lines of the railroad at once? And someone still had to pay attention to the steamboats that paid their bills. Maybe it was time to abandon the northern line to Gould and concentrate on getting to Santa Fe via Texas.

If he and Julia truly worked together as partners, could they beat Gould? The heat and the blowing dust didn't help his mood. Fatigue caught up with him, and he nodded as the car rocked along, dozing slightly until it stopped with a jerk. Awakened, he wondered if there was a problem with the engine and was about to go see when he looked out the window. It was obvious why the train had stopped: it was surrounded by thousands of buffalo as far as the eye could see. At the edge of the herd, he could see Indians galloping around the herd and the train, using lances and bows to kill the bison that got too far from the herd's protection. He had no idea what tribe it might be and hoped they would soon leave. The herd split to go around the train, which was only five cars long, bringing the Indians closer. The loud blast of the engine's whistle spooked the herd, and they broke into a run, pursued by the Indians. Hiram watched in amazement—he'd never seen so many animals before in one place. The *thwock* of an arrow embedding in the seat next to him brought him to his senses, and he dropped to the floor, motioning Tom to do the same. Maybe if the Indians couldn't see them, they would pass. The herd continued to thunder past, shaking the ground. Why hadn't he brought a rifle?

When it had been quiet for a time, the train began to move again. Hiram pushed himself up and ventured a look out the window. There was nothing but prairie and a few dead bison. Carrion birds were circling in the blue Kansas sky overhead.

"That was close!" Hiram said to Tom. "Have you ever seen the like?"

"Only once, but I was on horseback and didn't get too close. It's less common to see such a large herd these days."

"What about the Indians?"

"I've seen them in the distance. You might have noticed them back at Topeka. They leave us alone most often, but there have been attacks."

"I think we should be ready. Pomeroy underestimates their rage at having their way of life disrupted.

Crews should have guards."

"Not a bad idea. Maybe some from the former Kansas militia, looking for work."

"I was just thinking about whether my wife could help manage the work on the southern line. Seeing this, I am even less sure."

"Begging your pardon, Mr. Johannsen, you know her best. But Mrs. Johannsen seems to be a formidable woman, both charming and tough. She told me about being in the Confederate prison. I think she might be just the person you need there. I can't be everywhere at once. I can appoint a junior engineer to advise her."

Hiram remembered the bruise from the umbrella point and decided that maybe Tom was right—perhaps Julia could be his eyes and ears on the south line.

***

The train lurched to a stop.

What this time? Hiram wondered. There was nothing obvious. He went forward from the passenger car to the coal car and shouted to the engineer.

"Why are we stopped?"

"Out of water. The boiler has to get filled from the river over there since we don't have a water tower. It'll take an hour to get up steam again. May as well stretch your legs."

Hiram's mouth set in a thin line. This would never do. Passengers would not tolerate it. He made a note to have a water tower built at the first opportunity. He passed the time by planning with Tom the next stage of construction. He looked up when the train lurched forward. The landscape passed fast at first, but as the train came to a hill it went slower and slower until it stopped. After a few minutes, it reversed, chugging back down the hill.

"Tom, what in creation? We can't run a railroad like this."

"I'll have to get crews out here to make the rise not as steep. Otherwise, we'll never keep a schedule. I'm sorry, Mr. Johannsen, we miscalculated what the engine could do."

After backing a mile, and crossing the river, the train stopped. Clawing their way forward again, the wheels screamed on the rails, sparks flying, as the engineer came to full throttle. Faster, faster, until the shaking in the cars made Hiram grab a pole to avoid falling out of his seat. The train came to the hill just after they crossed the Wakarusa River, and this time, though it slowed to a walking pace, the momentum was enough to carry it over the hill. Though pleased, Hiram's grip on the pole didn't slacken. Muscles tense, he knew this section would have to be rebuilt. They didn't have time or resources for mistakes.

***

Julia was tallying the recent railroad profits when the telegram boy knocked. Tearing it open, she read,

Hiram,

Regret to inform you your mother suffered a heart attack. She did not survive. Please advise your wishes.

Sympathy,

Albinia

Stunned, Julia let the paper fall into her lap. It shouldn't be a surprise, Kirsten wasn't young. Their relations hadn't often been cordial. Kirsten had disapproved of her taking charge and was always jealous. Yet it was a loss and would be worse for Hiram. She found a tear escaping from her eyes, and dabbed it away with a handkerchief. Kirsten had been like the river, always there, always flowing and strong. She'd been patient with Julia not having a grandchild.

Julia called out, "Emily? Ruth?"

When they came in, she showed them the telegram.

"I'm sure Hiram will want to return to Cincinnati for

the funeral. I will do what he wants, but I don't see how we can both go with the current state of the railroad. I must travel south to watch over the progress to Burlingame. Can you manage here without us for a while? Or it may be that Hiram will want Emily to travel with him to arrange receptions in Cincinnati."

Ruth extended a hand to Julia, and Emily hugged her. "Whatever you need, you can count on us," said Ruth.

"If Mr. Hiram wants me to go to Cincinnati, may we hire Luther's sister, Olivia, to stand in for me? I'm sure Albinia could spare her from the school for a time," said Emily.

"An excellent idea. If Hiram approves, I will put that in the answer to Albinia. Emily, will you go and find Hiram? Tell him I need him at home urgently, but don't tell him about the telegram. I want to do that myself. Ruth, let's get lunch together and pack some suitcases. Hiram will likely want to leave on the next train east. I may be gone for as long as a few months, depending on how construction progresses. Ruth, if anything changes with you and Luther, do send a telegram. The Emporia office will know where to find me."

Emily said, "What shall I say when he asks why? Begging your pardon, but interrupting him in the middle of the day, he's likely to be impatient."

"Tell him I have news about the steamship line, and we must talk. It's true, for all that."

Emily curtsied and left Ruth with Julia to make preparations.

Chapter 4

Georgetown, Colorado, January 1869

Will waited on another customer in the store, worried at Robert's tardiness. Why hadn't he been here to open? Will wanted to get started with the freight wagon to the railhead and pick up new supplies. Luther was still driving the stage, but it wouldn't be for much longer. Already the railhead in Julesburg was beginning to replace the stage, both for passengers and freight. Mark bustled in, checking shelves and display cases.

"Seen my pa today?"

"No."

Will groaned. He couldn't be drinking again, could he? "I'd better go find him."

Determined to think the best of Pa, he went out the back

of the store and climbed the stairs to the little apartment he'd built. It saved money over living at Auntie Mae's and gave Robert more privacy, which, up to now, he'd earned. But when he knocked, there was no answer. He waited and then opened the door.

The interior was well-ordered, clean, and smelled like pine oil. Robert wasn't there. Will took off his slouch hat and scratched his head. If Robert were sick, he'd be there. This place didn't look or smell like the home of someone who had been drinking.

Where could he be? Will decided to check with Ned and see if his pa had taken a horse or buggy somewhere. Maybe he should stop in at Auntie Mae's in case Robert had grown tired of his own cooking. The chill in the air and a look at the sky confirmed that it wasn't a day to be out or far from shelter. A snow sky, Dove would have called it. The town seemed to sense the coming storm.

Auntie Mae's had one or two miners nursing hangovers with coffee and eggs, but no sign of Robert. Ned confirmed that Robert had paid for a horse for the morning and had ridden out toward Silver Plume. At least Will didn't have to make the rounds of the saloons. He saddled Dusty and followed.

He figured he might see an elk and come back for the meat after the storm, but he should get his town-dwelling father back to safety. Lightning stayed with Ned these days more often than not, but Will decided to bring him along.

The snow began when he was less than a mile out of town, falling in soft, wet flakes, as though some capricious giant were throwing cotton balls from the sky. Will prayed as he rode, hoping to find Robert before the cotton balls became ice balls.

He followed Clear Creek and reached the point where a tributary came in from the east. Horse tracks led along the water's edge. He followed, and after about five minutes he saw one of Ned's horses tied to a tree. Pa must be around here somewhere. Lightning looked up at Will. Will dismounted and began searching up the little creek. Lightning bounded through the snow, getting far enough ahead that Will had to follow by sound of Lightning crashing through the woods rather than sight. Tracks were soon filled in as the fluffy white blanket covered everything. What could Pa be doing out in this mess? After a few minutes of stumbling over rocks and downed tree limbs, getting his boots wet when the ice gave way, Will found Lightning barking and sniffing over the legs of a form lying in the snow, covered with rock, not moving.

"Pa! Pa, it's Will. Are you hurt?" Will began digging, moving rock, working his way toward the head of the figure in the snow. Once the rocks and snow were removed, he could see a gash on Robert's head. Robert was still breathing. The cold had stopped the flow of blood. There must have been a small avalanche.

Will scooped some water from the stream and poured it over his pa's face, washing away the blood. He picked up his head, and Robert's eyes fluttered open.

"Pa, where does it hurt? Anywhere besides your head? Talk to me."

Robert groaned and tried to lift his head farther, but he fell back.

"Where am I?"

"You're in the middle of a snowstorm by Silver Plume. We need to get you warm. If I help, can you sit up? We have to get out of this storm."

"I can try."

Robert moved his elbows back and pushed up. Will put a hand under his back and slowly pushed up until Robert was sitting.

"How's that?"

"The world is spinning a bit."

"That's a nasty bump on your head. What are you doing

out here?"

"I didn't want to tell you yet until I was sure, but . . . I found gold."

"Pa, not that again. Remember the Tiger Mine?"

"I know, but there really is gold here. I found it on the creek—nuggets waiting to be picked up. I've been working it a little at a time."

"Well, it won't be worth anything if you're frozen stiff."

Will pulled Robert's arm around his shoulder and helped him to his feet. Stumbling and picking his way around boulders, he helped Robert back to his horse and then got him mounted. He led the horse back to Dusty.

"Hold on, I'll lead you."

Robert slumped forward on the neck of the horse but stayed on. Will mounted and led the horse all the way back to the store. When they arrived, Will got Mark to help him carry Robert up to the apartment.

"Mark, will you go ask Doc Adams to come by? I'll feel better if someone checks him out."

"I'll have to close the store while I'm gone, but I shouldn't be long."

Will stoked the fire in the potbellied stove and got a wet cloth to wipe Robert's head. He set out a pot to boil water and a cup with willow bark.

Mark returned with the doctor, then left to re-open the store.

"Good afternoon, Mr. Crump. I understand your father has a bump on the head?"

Robert spoke up, "If you call a mountain falling on me a bump on the head, that's about right."

"Plenty of that around here," said Doctor Adams. After poking and prodding at Robert, he said, "You need bed rest for a day, but not more than that. Take it easy, but move around. Your son has the right idea here with the willow bark tea."

He turned to Will. "Keep his feet warm and keep him quiet. Absolutely no alcohol. In a day or so, get him up and walking. If he has too many dizzy spells, back off and let him rest more. I'll look in on him in a couple of days. Unless something changes, he should be all right."

"Thanks, Doc, much obliged. I s'pect the snow will keep us indoors."

Will thought Robert was sleeping, but then he opened his eyes.

"All right, if you're up to it, tell me about this gold."

"Did you get the poke off my horse?"

"Yes. And I saw the nuggets. You'll want them assayed, I expect."

"Yes. Do you see what this means? I've been working the site during my time off. Haven't filed yet, but if the assay turns out good . . ."

"You're thinking you're rich. Pa, haven't you seen enough around here with the Tiger and all the others? Boom one week and bust the next. By the time you buy the equipment to work the claim, you're not just broke, but in debt."

"But what if—"

"That's what they all say, you know that. If the assay is good, we should file and sell the claim. Then we can get some land and some cows, have something solid and sustainable," said Will. "What did your partners in the Tiger say?"

"It was always, 'Another month and we'll be rich.'"

"Let's get this assayed and then decide what to do. Meanwhile, think about the fact that you almost got yourself killed for yellow rocks."

***

Will made sure to file the claim on the same day. The assay report took two weeks to come back and showed gold, but only a quarter pure, mixed with copper.

Will and Robert were talking it over when a knock came at the door of Robert's upstairs apartment over the store.

"Who is it?" said Robert.

"Name's Yancy Roberts. I come with a message from Charlie Goodnight. Said to deliver it to Will Crump, personal."

"Come ahead," said Will, standing aside for him to enter.

"Charlie is starting some new ventures. He's perfected his breed of cattle at the Pueblo ranch and wants to start herds in Texas, where the grass is better and open range is more plentiful. He's planning a drive for spring and needs good men. He wanted me to come and ask for you personally."

Will looked at Robert. "What do you say, Pa? If we sell the claim, we could get land down there."

"Charlie also said to tell you that you can have four head to start your herd if you come on the drive. And he expects the railroad to be in Denver by next fall. That might impact your freight business and your store."

"Will Charlie come on the drive himself?"

"That's the plan. Just be warned—nobody can outwork Charlie, and he expects hands to keep up. He must think well of you to invite you like this."

"Can I give you an answer tomorrow? I need to talk it over with Pa and our partners in the store."

"All right. But I need to head back to Pueblo by the day after tomorrow."

***

Luther wondered at Will's message to meet at Auntie Mae's but decided he and Ned should do as asked. They took a table and ordered the stew. When Will entered, Luther could tell by his serious expression that something was in the air.

"Thanks for meeting me here," said Will. "I'm sure you've heard by now of the new claim Pa filed in Silver Plume. What you may not know is that we've decided to sell rather than work it. You've been good partners, and we'll leave the remaining stock in the store to you. Pa and I plan to strike out for Texas."

"I knew you'd move on at some point," said Luther. "The railroad keeps getting closer, and it's moving faster than we expected. We probably won't stay either. Ruth is after me to find a place to settle. Ned and I have been talking about Topeka. With the two railroad lines intersecting there, it seems like there would be a lot of traffic."

Ned said, "Your brother-in-law offered us jobs there, making parts for the railroad, but with the freedom to set up a shop and work for anyone we choose at the same time. It seems a fair offer. We'll see what Mark wants to do. He might stay and keep the store. He's built a good relationship with the customers."

When Luther approached his brother-in-law Mark the next morning, he felt sure of what he was going to do, but he didn't know how to present it. He knew what Jemima would have said: pray.

"Mark, I got somethin' to talk to you about. Will came to your pa and me last night and said he and Robert are pulling out, heading for Texas with Charlie Goodnight. He's leaving the store to us."

Mark's eyebrows came together, and he slumped into a chair, holding his head.

"You mean they running out on us 'cause they got the gold."

"I wasn't thinking that way. You know how your sister been pushing me to be with her, not running back and forth between here and the railroad. The last trip, the railroad was almost knocking on our door—sometimes they make ten miles in a day. The stage and the freight business are gonna dry up by the end of the year. Your pa and I are thinking of going back east, maybe Topeka. Will's brother-in-law offered us railroad jobs."

"What about being on our own? Look where depending on white folks got us!"

"Mark, you got to be real. When the railroad comes, no more freight hauling. No more stagecoach. Goods will be a lot more plentiful and cheaper. White folk gonna buy from whites, not us."

"It's not fair."

"No, it isn't. But thank the Lord no one is burning you out or tying you to a tree. You got a choice. You're of age—you can come with us, or stay."

Ned walked in, and said, "Luther been telling you about last night? You know they ain't hardly any colored here in Colorado Territory. The railroad gonna bring a flood of white folks. It will change things, probably not for the better."

"I don't believe you," said Mark, stamping the ground. Luther could see tears threatening to escape the corners of his eyes. "I've worked hard on this store. Will has hardly been here. Robert knows the business, but I've done more of the work. They're leaving it to us—to me! I finally have somethin' of my own."

Luther laid a hand on his shoulder, but he shook it off. He looked at Ned, who shrugged.

"Have it your way, son," said Ned. "Just remember, we always have a place for you."

By the beginning of May, Ned, Luther, and the rest of the family packed the freight wagon, and headed east, leaving Mark in Georgetown.

***

May 1869

Will and Robert sold the claim, netting five hundred dollars in gold. Will felt he should leave some of the money to Mark to help him get by, but Mark politely refused.

The problem of how to keep their profits from the store and the claim safe on the trip to Texas bothered Will considerably. They had two thousand in gold dust from the store and freight business. He decided to deposit most of the money with the First National Bank in Denver, with assurances that he could access the money when needed to buy land.

Charlie was offering them a spot on his new ranch near Dallas until they could get established on their own, and Will planned to take it. He knew that moving cattle over six hundred miles of mountains and deserts through Indian territory and bandits was not a guaranteed success, and he didn't want to risk having the gold with him. Banks, however, were not without risk: they got robbed and sometimes failed. Will didn't like it, but putting the money in a bank seemed safest.

They arrived at Charlie's Pueblo ranch in the middle of

the month. The last snow was only two weeks behind them. They'd camp for the night and meet the other hands.

Charlie greeted them. "Will! Good to see you again. Glad you decided to accept my offer. And this is your father? Good to meet you, sir. I assume Will has told you the rules of the drive—absolutely no alcohol between here and Dallas."

"Good to meet you as well, and no problem with the rules. I imagine we'll need to keep our wits about us unless the Comanche are sleeping," said Robert.

"And they rarely are off guard. Like any man, they love a good steak. Yancy will show you your spots in the bunkhouse for tonight. Sleep well. We leave at dawn tomorrow."

***

Will and Robert had never done a drive before. Charlie placed them as outriders on opposite edges of the herd. The more experienced hands were either at the front or the back of the herd. At the front, the men were called "pointers," and their job was to guide the lead cows and head off any stampede. At the back, the hands kept the stragglers known as the "drags" moving to prevent the herd from stringing out in a line from Pueblo to Raton. The two groups kept the cows evenly spaced so that there was no more than half a mile from the leaders to the last. Will pulled his bandana high over his nose to avoid breathing dust and cattle dung. Dusty and Lightning ambled alongside the herd, Lightning nipping at the heels of any cow that got adventurous. They were to keep the cows close together, bunched, the edges of the herd about forty yards apart. The early spring morning had a blue bowl of a sky without a cloud as the sun pushed its way above the horizon, illuminating the path south toward Raton Pass.

Will felt peaceful. Riding a horse into the unknown was what he'd done most of his adult life. The road ahead to Texas seemed full of promise. He reflected that God brought people into your life at just the right time. Charlie seemed like a gift—only eight years older than Will, but listening to him was an education. Charlie was a man of dreams who turned them into actions. Will decided he'd spent too much time on regrets in his own life and not enough enjoying the moment and looking forward. The cows lowed and complained their way down the trail. Gazing across the herd, he tried to see if he could make out Pa through the dust. It was early in the season yet, and a spring snowstorm wasn't out of the question, but today the crisp morning was a delight. Will guessed it might be fifty degrees.

It seemed there was always something moving him on: the war, prison, an attempt to find peace, the love of a woman, the need to care for his Pa. Where was God leading him? He only knew that digging in the dirt and lusting after gold wasn't where he should be.

The whistles and calls of the other cowboys combined with the hypnotic plodding of the cows as they climbed south following the river toward Trinidad. They should reach it by the third day and then begin the hard climb to the top of Raton. At about eleven o'clock, they stopped to let the cattle graze. When the cows began to lay down, the hands got them on their feet and moving again.

Around the campfire in the evening, Will and Robert listened to the other cowboys' tales and reminiscences. Some had made the journey with Charlie before.

One hand with a red beard told of being separated from the herd and surrounded by Comanches, escaping by night. Another told of a sudden snowstorm, leaving them without grass for days. The cook pulled out a harmonica and played a lively tune. Then Charlie gave assignments for the next day. The pointers and the drag crew never changed, but the rest rotated along the edge of the herd and switched sides each day.

"We'll try to cover twelve miles a day, except when we get to Horsehead Crossing in Texas. At that point, the cattle will have been without water for three days. As soon as they smell the river, there's no holding them back. We'll try to control the stampede, but don't risk your life," said Charlie. "For you new men, don't take your boots off, keep your horse hobbled nearby, and don't touch anyone without talking to them first. Keep your pistol and rifle in easy reach. Now let's get some sleep, except for you on the first watch."

Will grew used to the routine, day in, day out. Occasionally a cow became too weak to continue, and they had a steak that night. More often the fare was beans and flapjacks.

Will spread his bedroll near Robert. They looked up at an infinite night sky spread with diamonds.

"Pa, it's a new moon tonight—look at all the stars!"

"It's something all right. But it also means that cattle thieves can move unseen. Best sleep while you can. They'll wake us around midnight. My pocket watch said it got light at about five this morning."

***

June 1869

Mile after weary mile, they traveled. Will and Dusty moved up and down the line of cattle, pushing them together to keep the herd line narrow enough. Lightning came in very handy at the pass, nipping heels, moving them on up the narrow trail and down the other side. Once they were over Raton Pass, Charlie called a halt for two days. There was enough forage for the cattle. Charlie wanted to scout a new route rather than following south along the Pecos and cut off miles by following the Red River. The scouts would assess the water level in the river as well as the mood of the Comanche, Kiowa, and other tribes along the route. The main risks in trying something new were being closer to Indian Territory and the weather.

Will used the break to hunt and bring meat for the drive, which was salted and stored in the barrels they had emptied thus far. Late on the second day, as the sun sank low, the temperature began to drop, and the scouts returned.

After the cook gave the men some coffee and hard tack, they sat to talk.

"Charlie, the river is good—a few low places, but mostly three to five feet and getting deeper."

"The cattle could cross without trouble?" asked Charlie

"Yes, so long as nothing spooks them."

"What about Indians?"

"Saw a few Kiowa, didn't feel like risking a conversation. Heard rumors of Comanche. Could be they saw us, but we didn't see them."

"I guess we had to expect that, whether we went south or not. What do you think? Should we turn east or go the old way?"

"Well, boss, it's always a guess, but I'll bet my pay that we can make it going east and save two weeks."

Charlie grinned. "All right, you're on. If we make it and save two weeks, double your pay. If we don't . . ."

"If we don't, it won't matter, the buzzards will have us on the prairie."

Will and Robert bedded down, catching a few hours of sleep before their watch. Will pulled a blanket around him, thinking it was pretty crazy to need a blanket in Texas in June. He was so tired after the long day herding cattle he dropped into a deep sleep.

He woke at a crack of lightning that filled the sky. Rain hit his face, small drops and then a downpour. Everyone was up, putting on rain slickers and mounting up. Will cursed his luck at first, then prayed, "Lord protect us from this storm."

"Never seen anything like this," said Robert, looking at the swirling dark clouds.

Will couldn't see any stars, only blackness. The wind tore at him, like a beast trying to rip his flesh. From the edge of the eastern horizon came a roar of wind, hail, and sand. The sky split again with lightning, and the cattle began to move, bellowing in terror.

"Move those cows now! Get them into draws, canyons, arroyos—any low place. Keep them together as much as you can," Charlie yelled into the tempest. "If they run, turn them south. Storm's out of the north and east. I think it's a twister!"

The wind and driving rain pummeled the men and the herd. Lightning howled in fear and then followed Dusty as Will pushed twenty or so cows into an arroyo to escape the tempest. There was no way to talk; every few minutes, the lightning would illuminate enough to see Charlie giving frantic hand signals, like those used in the war. The wind sounded like the cannons at Shiloh. Will felt fear clenching in his gut, and it occurred to him that the water could rush down the arroyo and trap them, but he trusted God and Charlie—staying out of the wind as much as possible was preferable. The cows kept moving down the narrow draw, seeking escape, but there was no way to get away from the tempest.

Hailstones began striking them, like pebbles at first, then marble-sized. The herd bawled in protest and began to run, up onto the plain, out of the arroyos and depressions, running anywhere to escape the sting of the ice falling from the sky. The drovers pressed the cows to the right and south until they formed a whirling circle, not unlike the funnel cloud they could see in the distance. Every few minutes, a few would try and break loose, but Will and Lightning drove them back into the circle.

After a time, the storm moved on by them. The wind dropped, the rain turned to a drizzle, and no more hail fell. Men and animals were exhausted. The dawn showed the herd scattered. Will groaned. He wanted to crawl into a cave and sleep, but there were no caves, no dry places, no trees or roofs. He hadn't ridden this long without sleep since the war. He looked around and saw Lightning sprawled by a boulder. Robert had dismounted and seemed in a daze. Where was Charlie?

"Pa, let's ask someone what to do. I know the herd needs to regroup. Charlie has to be somewhere, and he knows how to do it," said Will.

"All right. It's just that I'm so tired. I've never seen a storm like that. I guess it's a blessing no trees were flying through the air."

When they got to the front of the herd, they asked a drover, "So now what? Where's Charlie, and what do we do next?"

The man spat a long stream of tobacco juice and said, "Charlie is riding like a madman through every gulch and dip around here with a couple of the other hands. They'll drive the cattle this way, try to collect them into a herd again."

"What can we do to help?"

"Search east and south in gullies and washes. Work together. When you find cows, move 'em back here—we'll be here to keep them. If you hear gunshots, come back this way in a hurry. Bring whatever cows you can, but leave 'em if you can't get them moving together. Charlie'll aim to have the herd back by tomorrow so we can move east."

"All right. You game, Pa?"

"Don't see much choice. The sooner we get the cows back, the sooner we can rest. Let's ride."

They agreed to ride about thirty yards apart, searching. Lighting stayed in front and ten yards to the right. Within half an hour, they found a group of twenty in a depression they couldn't see until they were almost on them. They herded them back toward the pointers and saw Charlie and another hand coming in with a group of fifty. Will and Robert turned and went searching for more, leaving theirs with the pointers.

Will got so thirsty he was ready to quit, but there were always more cows. He wiped away the sweat from his forehead—the temperature was back to Texas summer heat. His back ached, and he felt ready to fall out of his saddle. Twice he stopped to let Dusty drink and graze, but only for a few minutes. As the sun reached the western horizon, Charlie called a halt.

"I reckon we've got them—only fifty head missing. No sense in losing men in the dark. Get some sleep. Yancy and I will take the first watch. Tomorrow we're back on the trail."

The next day, they successfully made it to the Red River and followed it east.

"Will, good job during the storm. I knew I could count on you. We'll dip a little south to avoid the canyon. I don't want to get the herd lost in there, and at times the Comanche have a village there."

"I hope there won't be more storms like that," said Will.

Charlie chuckled. "Oh, no more than a few every year."

They followed the river for the next three weeks, then

cut south to Charlie's old trail, the Goodnight-Loving trail. Everyone was alert, anticipating Indian trouble, but aside from two or three head lost to nighttime raids, the Indians left them alone. Will looked forward to celebrating the fourth of July in a town: Dallas.

***

September 1869

Will and Robert bunked at Charlie's ranch east of Dallas for a time. It had been an atypical cattle drive since the object was not to sell the cattle, but to establish a herd. Will had seen the Herefords before at the Clay plantation in Kentucky, but not often in the west. Will wondered how they would do compared to the tough Longhorns he was used to.

Charlie came by the bunkhouse one morning. "Will, I'm giving you this bull and three cows to start your herd. That's your wages for the drive. I hope they will do well for you. You and Robert were a big help on the drive, for beginners."

"It was an education."

"Not one I care to repeat, begging your pardon," said Robert. "Storekeeping and straight farming suit me better."

Charlie laughed. "Not everyone is suited to the long hours in the saddle. Tell you what, I'll show you a few things here—there's a patch of land, almost four hundred acres, for sale southeast of the center of town on Lancaster Road. Go see my friend David King at the bank. He can help you with a land purchase and recommend a place for a store. You're welcome to graze these cattle here until you get situated."

"Thanks, Charlie. We'll do that."

***

Will hesitated—he never liked banks. It was like telling a thief where your money was hidden. He knew he needed to transfer the money from Colorado, and he didn't know the lands around here. Friendly and knowledgeable advice would be welcome. He opened the doors and walked past the islands of desks to the teller windows, glass behind iron bars on a long mahogany counter. Two of the three windows were busy, so he went to the one with no customers.

"Yes?" said the young woman behind the window.

Will looked around, nervous. When he looked at the clerk again, he had to work to keep his jaw from dropping.

"Miss King? Mary King? Am I right?"

She looked up and brightened. "Will Crump! I'm flattered that you still recognize an old maid like me. Where have you come from?"

"You sell yourself short, ma'am. I came in with a cattle drive run by Charlie Goodnight. Pa and I are thinking of settling around here. Charlie recommended that I talk to your father about land and a possible store location. I need to transfer funds from the First National Bank in Denver to get started." He handed her the bank receipt.

"I suppose chatting will have to wait, and business has to be done. I'll tell Father."

Will waited while she went to the back and returned.

"Father says he'll wire Denver tonight. We should have an answer by morning. The actual transfer may take a few weeks. But we can let you draft on it once Denver answers, up to the amount on the receipt."

"I have some paper and coins also. I'll only keep out about fifty dollars."

"Very well. I'll write you a receipt for two thousand three hundred twenty-three dollars, the amount on the Denver receipt plus your cash. The cash is available anytime."

"How about you? Are you available anytime?"

"Mr. Crump!" said Mary, blushing but smiling. "Whatever do you mean?"

"I mean I'd like to know you better. We didn't have much chance in Indiana, and I was in a whole different world then. You can see I'm a man of means. Father and I did well in gold country. I don't know the town well, but is there a respectable place a fella can take a beautiful lady to dinner? If the lady agrees, of course."

"I think it's my father who has to agree, even for an outing."

Will's face fell. "Oh, if you'd rather not . . ."

"I didn't say that, silly. I may be . . . well, embarrassingly old, but Father still has the last word when it comes to gentleman callers. I'll talk to Mother and see if she can persuade Father to invite you to our place for dinner. You can talk to him, get to know him, and then he may let you call."

"All right. I guess I've been out of civilization for a time. You may remember my father, Robert Crump. He is going to start a general store—we'll be partners. We're bunking at Charlie's ranch."

"I think I know where that is. Anyway, enough to get a message there."

"I'll look forward to hearing from you, Mary."

Chapter 5

Dallas, September 1869

Will waited for two days, hoping for word from Mary. It had been a long time since Dove's death, and while the memories still ached, he knew he couldn't mourn her forever. Mary was pretty, had a sharp mind, and seemed interested. He knew he wasn't getting younger—most fellows his age were married. With any luck, he would soon have a ranch, which might make him a better catch.

A messenger came to the bunkhouse. He'd begun to think Mary was toying with him, but here it was, hope in a note.

Dear Mr. Crump,

I'm glad to inform you that the telegram from your bank has arrived. The transfer is in progress. Also, my father will send a note inviting you to Sunday dinner tomorrow after he and Mother re-turn from church. Please answer promptly. Father hates it when people are late.

Your friend,
Miss Mary King

Not an hour later, another missive came from her father with the promised invitation. Will answered immediately.

He went to a barber and got a haircut and shave.

Robert grinned when he saw him. "Sprucing up for the lady, eh?"

"I know, it's probably stupid," Will said sheepishly. "She's already seen me. Won't likely matter."

"Don't be too sure. A lady appreciates it when you take trouble for her."

"I worry about her father the most."

"As do most young men—and with reason. I tried to be protective of my girls, but for the most part they went their own way. From what I remember of Mary, she probably will give him no peace until he does as she wants."

Will rented a buggy rather than riding Dusty, intending to arrive precisely at two o'clock, as the invitation said. On the drive to the Kings' house, he began to wonder, should he start attending a church here? He'd gotten out of the habit of formal churchgoing with the war, prison, and then being in the wild. Would they expect it of him? What did he want himself? He still read the Bible and talked to God. Wasn't that enough? He hoped to have a stake with Pa in the store and a ranch, but he'd become something of a rolling stone, moving from this place to that, never sinking in roots. Would he be here long enough to matter? Tying up the horse as he arrived, he supposed it might depend on what happened with Mary. She certainly was lively and interesting.

Hat in hand, he climbed the steps of the large white frame house with a broad porch and knocked. A woman answered the door but was too well-dressed to be a servant.

"Mrs. King?" asked Will.

"Yes, I am Mrs. Ann King. And you must be Mr. Crump. Welcome. I'm glad to meet you. Mary has told me a great deal about you, and we remember your sister Albinia fondly. Come in. I have a few touches left before dinner is ready. Why don't you join David and Mary in the parlor?"

"Thank you, ma'am, and thanks for having me."

Will fumbled the bowler hat with nerves, uncertain whether to put it back on or keep holding it. He wasn't used to such formal occasions.

"Mr. Crump, delighted to have you here. Won't you sit down? Mary has been fidgeting all morning."

"Father!"

David King grinned. "Father's privilege, teasing daughters. I recall meeting you and your father in Indiana."

"Yes, sir. Thank you for having me. It was a pleasant surprise to encounter your family here."

"I can imagine. Mary said something about gold prospecting. I do hope gambling isn't something you do regularly."

Will fumbled his glass, almost spilling it. Despite his uncertainty about Dallas as a permanent home, he didn't want to do anything to jeopardize his suit with Mary's father.

"No, sir. I spent two years building a business in Colorado and filed a claim, but we sold it almost immediately. My pa and I want to start a general store here in Dallas, and I hope to purchase land around here for cattle."

"Have you ever ranched before?"

"No. It is a risk, but so is getting up in the morning. I've been learning the business from Charlie Goodnight. Gold prospecting was a chance to move up getting a ranch by years. My pa found the gold; I simply convinced him to sell. Land prices are going up—I'm sure as a banker you can appreciate that. My brother-in-law is working to bring the railroad down from the north. They'll be here soon, and that will connect Dallas to Kansas City and the east."

"Hmm, so you're looking to do business. I'm impressed. Your interest in Mary is commendable, but I don't want to see her tied to a man with poor prospects."

"Father! Will you please stop talking about me as though I'm not here or as if I'm one of your business deals? I like Will, and I haven't been shy about it because I don't believe in the silly coquettish games people play. But I am a woman, not a child, and I can make my own mind known."

"And likely will, I'm sure," said David ruefully. "Forgive—"

"Not to be rude sir, but Mary's forthrightness is part of why I like her. My mother was very quiet and didn't speak her mind much, God rest her soul. But I know there were times she would have liked to say more, and if she had, much sorrow could have been avoided."

Mrs. King came in and interrupted the talk. "Dinner is ready, if you would all care to join."

The dinner passed uneventfully until dessert. The maid was bringing in the coffee when a tremendous clap of thunder made them all jump. Coffee went everywhere, including Will's lap.

When they recovered, Mrs. King looked stricken. All pretense of formality was shattered. Mary and Will looked at each other and burst out laughing, breaking the tension. Mary got up and helped the poor maid clean up.

"I apologize, Mr. Crump, I don't know what to say," said Ann.

"No need, Mrs. King. After months on a cattle drive through a tornado and driving rain, a little spilled coffee is nothing. Don't even think about it."

"You must let us clean your suit for you."

"As I said, no need. I probably won't wear it again soon—unless you and Mr. King decide to allow Mary to accompany me to the Cattlemen's Dance next week."

Mary looked up from where she was helping the maid wipe coffee off the rug. A flash of lightning showed the surprise on her face in the candlelight. She looked over at her father, who shrugged.

"Why not? We'll look forward to seeing you again, Mr. Crump."

"Thank you, sir. And if the rain lets up, might Mary and I take a short walk?"

"I'm sure her maid wouldn't mind accompanying you,"

said Ann.

***

Will was glad the storm had passed. The streets were muddy, but little else remained of the tempest. The moon rose in the twilight as Mary came out of her house. Will offered an arm, which she accepted. Miranda, her maid, followed at a discreet distance. They stayed on the boardwalk to avoid the mud, strolling north in no particular hurry. Stars began to come out, with Cassiopeia peeking above the horizon, as nature's lamplighter made his rounds, strolling around the heavens until a thousand points of light twinkled back at them. The silence could have been awkward, but it wasn't, as each wandered in their thoughts.

Mary broke the silence. "What will you do now?"

"I will shop for some land, a good place to raise cattle, and help Pa set up a store."

"Is that all?"

"I don't know, except wanting to know you better. War taught me not to look too far ahead. Right now, being in this moment with you, the moonlight on your hair, that beautiful blue dress with pink flowers, it's all I want. I can't see farther than the horizon. What about you?"

"I confess I'm not sure either. Thank you for asking Father for this time—and the dance. It just feels right. I didn't know how well you even remembered me. Indiana was such a long time ago, and I spent a lot of time with Peter."

"Was there ever anything between you?"

"Romance? Oh, perhaps a small spark— when we were kids back in Pennsylvania. A girl dreams when she's twelve. But we were like siblings and seemed headed in different directions. Then Albinia came along. She's perfect for him. Do you hear from her?"

"Not much. She's busy with school, her babies, and Peter. Olivia brought some news. Did you know she's with Hiram and Julia now? Luther has moved to Kansas, working on the railroad."

"No, I haven't heard from Albinia. I suppose it was that suspicion that I was romantic about Peter. I regret that. I'm not very restrained in my behavior at times," Mary said with a nervous laugh.

"You needn't worry. It makes you delightful. I wonder that you haven't a string of suitors, or do you?"

"I shouldn't tell you, but frankly, no. There was a young man once, but he died at Gettysburg."

"I'm sorry. I lost a lot of friends in the war."

"As did almost everyone. It's one of the reasons I abhor violence. My parents were originally from the Society of Friends, Quakers, you might call them. There are no

Quaker meetings here in Dallas, so Father goes to First Baptist. Nevertheless, I believe in settling disputes without fighting. There's almost always a peaceful way."

Will's brow furrowed, drawing his eyebrows together. He was silent a moment, twirling his hat in his hands. Would his tendency to solve problems with a gun be a problem for them? But the thought of losing this new chance made his stomach clench.

Making a decision, he said, "I'm glad to know that. Seems like a fella wouldn't have to worry about being clobbered with a frying pan!" He turned to her and grinned, hoping she would smile.

"That's true," and she did smile. "But too much starch in the shirts can be an effective remedy."

They turned back toward the King house, not wanting to venture out onto the open prairie at night. Turning up the boardwalk to her door, Will wondered how best to express what he felt. Being with Mary excited him in a way he hadn't felt for years. He didn't want to ruin anything. He clasped both her hands, facing her.

"Mary, I don't know how best to thank you. You've been a beautiful and charming companion. I hope this was the first of many evenings together."

He searched her brown eyes and saw matching stars.

"I've enjoyed your company, Will. I look forward to the dance next week."

***

The day for the Cattlemen's Dance arrived, and Will made sure to be bathed and shaved. He'd gotten the suit cleaned and found prairie verbena and scarlet sage by the river for a bouquet. Will wondered if he would dance well enough—he hadn't done the quadrille in years. He hoped for more polka and waltzing.

Mary had told Will they would meet at the Crutchfield Hotel, where the dance was being held. Will was disappointed since he'd hoped to talk her father into letting them buggy ride afterward, but he said nothing. He didn't want to seem too forward.

He arrived early, surprised to find other early birds already there.

Will took a moment to look out across the Trinity River, breathe in the evening air, and try to relax. He admitted to himself that he cared more about how the evening turned out than was warranted for their short acquaintance.

Once inside, Will got directions to the ballroom and turned down the waiter's offer of a drink. The fiddler, the pianist, and the cellist had already begun to play light music to entertain the early arrivals.

The strains of the "Nightingale Polka" soon had him tapping his feet. He sat at one of the tables, watching for the Kings as each person entered the hall.

After half an hour, when the room was mostly full of buzzing couples of mixed ages, Will saw Mary, David, and Ann King enter. Mary's head swiveled about looking for him. He rose and walked toward her with a smile, giving her the flowers.

"Oh, how lovely! Thank you. Mother, will you take these for me? Ask a waiter to put them in a vase on our table."

Will couldn't take his eyes off her. He tried not to whistle. She wore a light green outer skirt over a gold-and-brown-striped shirtwaist and underskirt, a green belt emphasizing a tiny waist.

"You look absolutely beautiful. Mr. and Mrs. King, thank you for allowing Mary to come and for your company," said Will.

"Happy to come, my boy," said David. "Gives us old ones an excuse to get out."

"Good to see you, Will," said Ann. Looking at her husband, she said, "We shall have a marvelous time—with one condition."

Will's heart sank, thinking she would impose some

restriction on contact with Mary.

"Yes, my dear?" said David.

"Absolutely no business!"

Will smiled to hide his relief.

"You have my word, ma'am. Shall we sit?"

He signaled a waiter, who came and took their orders. He noticed none of the Kings ordered alcohol and abstained as well.

"Haven't they done a marvelous job rebuilding here after the fire, Father?"

"Yes, yes, indeed. Quite an upgrade from the original log structure that was here a year ago. I daresay nothing finer in St. Louis, and it rivals some in the east."

"Do you have ambitions to go back east, sir?" asked Will.

"No, not really. I like this town. It's vibrant, alive, and growing. Why, when the railroad comes from the north . . ." said David. Will caught a warning glance from Ann, and David appeared to shorten his remark. "We'll all be happy," he finished. "I did promise not to talk business. But I wanted to let you know I found a parcel of land I think would be perfect for you. It's four hundred forty acres. Perhaps we could look at it next Sunday afternoon? If the purchase goes through, you could have a cabin built before winter."

Will smiled. "That would be great! I'll keep working for Charlie until we make a crop next summer and get a store running, but it would be good to have my own place for the winter."

They continued small talk through the meal, and then a caller at the front of the hall announced, "It's time for the dance! Gentlemen, grab your partners, and let's go."

Mary looked over at Will and blushed as he offered his arm. They formed an octet for the quadrille with Ann and David and two other couples. Will kept his eyes on Mary as much as possible and hated to surrender her to the next partner as they worked their way around the circle. She wore gloves, so there was no skin contact when their hands met, but the light in her eyes said that she was as excited as he was.

When the dance finished, Will took both her hands and gazed into her eyes. "I've been thinking so much about you, about how I wanted tonight to be. I wish we could float away together."

"Perhaps after the dance," whispered Mary as the band struck up a lively polka. Mary picked up her skirt with one hand and placed her other on Will's shoulder as they whirled about the floor. They were laughing and out of breath. When the polka finished, the musicians took a short break and then played a waltz. It was a new one, "The Blue Danube." Will and Mary watched at first, but he offered her a hand, and they began. She was graceful, knew how to pirouette, and Will took his cues from the other men, even doing a lift here and there. His heart beat rapidly with the exercise and the feel of her. It was only a few minutes, but it seemed frozen in time.

Another young man attempted to cut in on a later dance, but Mary claimed to be indisposed and went to find the privy. When she returned, she went to her father, whispered something to him, pointing at her maid, Miranda, in the corner, and then came back to Will. They'd been dancing for two hours according to the large clock at the head of the hall.

"Will, I spoke to Father. What do you say to a buggy ride? He said you could drive ours. Miranda can ride in the back."

"I would love that! I'm out of breath, and it's a full moon tonight. It should be easy to see. As long as we stay on the east side, we should be safe."

Once outside, the livery man brought the Kings' buggy and helped the ladies get in. The moon looked like a huge yellow ball peeking above the horizon, so close it seemed to Will that he could simply step from the earth onto its surface. They drove at a slow walk along Broadway, with Will looking at Mary and the river. Miranda was in the back seat. Will thought she was pretending to be invisible.

"Wasn't that a fun dance? I can't remember when I've enjoyed one so much!" said Mary.

"You're a very good dancer! I'm rather out of practice."

"You did quite well for a cowpoke soldier. I hope we can do it again."

"I'd like to do it over and over, forever. You're the most beautiful woman. Dancing with you is like being in a dream."

"It is exciting dancing with you. I enjoy getting all prettied up, like any girl. But I also enjoy less formal times, getting away from it all," she said as they turned the corner to the right down Cochran Street. "I like fishing and long walks."

Will pulled the buggy over by a tree. They were both quiet a moment, then Will asked, "Would you care to walk now? We could go down toward the river."

"That would be delightful," said Mary.

"Oh dear," said Miranda. "I'm afraid I haven't brought the right shoes for it. Would it be acceptable if I stay at the top of the path—not too far back, mind?" Miranda gave a conspiratorial wink.

Mary smiled. "Why yes, I think that would work."

Will helped the ladies down, set the brake, and tied the buggy to the tree. He showed Mary a narrow path that led toward the water. Miranda stayed at the top of the path. About ten yards down, the land sloped more steeply toward the river, and Will offered his arm for balance, which Mary accepted.

"I love the quiet of the night," she said. "I know some are afraid of the dark, but to me, it speaks of hidden possibilities, magical times to come. And looking at the stars never fails to show me the wonder of God."

"It makes you feel special, like God took the trouble to design all that just for us to look at."

She stumbled a little, her head dropping to his shoulder. He caught her, turning her toward him. Miranda was out of sight, though not out of earshot. Her head tilted back, and he lightly held her arms a moment, looking at the moonlight on her hair and into her eyes. He moved closer and bent to kiss her, first lightly and then, when she responded, with more urgency. He let go of her arms and embraced her. Her arms encircled his neck. He kissed her quick and light several times and then returned to a deep kiss until they were breathless. He released her, and her head dipped, but she still kept her hands on his shoulders.

"I suppose we should get back," Will said, "or Miranda will think we've fallen in."

Mary chuckled. "No need to worry. She won't tell anyone. We have an understanding. But we do have Father's buggy, and he can't go home until we return."

"When can I see you again? Your father mentioned going to see the land after church. Could you come? Maybe we could ride around the property together."

"I'll ask Father, but I can't imagine he would refuse. If he agrees, I could bring a picnic lunch—and challenge you to a race!"

"A race? That wouldn't be fair. Dusty has never been beaten. And besides, what would your father say?"

"Father suffers from the disease of many fathers: underestimating their daughters."

***

Will set out from the First Baptist Church toward his potential ranch off Lancaster Road, going to meet Mary and David. As his banker, David would act as the agent for the property sale. Dusty was full of energy, prancing in the cool morning air. A northern mockingbird whistled and scolded as he passed, following a path where someone had planted trees. Lightning chased squirrels ahead of him but always came back, as if to ask what was taking him so long.

Will held Dusty to an easy trot. He wondered if the land would be everything he needed. He saw good water in Five Mile Creek and grass waving in the light breeze. A few bison were visible in the distance. He hoped the acreage would be enough for the long term. He'd concentrate on building a corral, a barn, a cabin, and fencing, planning to bring his cattle from Goodnight's in the spring.

He saw David waiting where the two creeks came together, just as promised.

"Hello, Will. A fine afternoon for a ride."

"Yes, sir, it is. Is Mary coming? I had hoped to show the land to her."

"She's here and has already seen it. She's waiting over the rise until we conclude business," said David.

Will looked around, assessing the property. "This land looks very fertile."

"I've talked to the owner. As I said, it's a four-hundred-forty-acre parcel with clear markers for boundaries. The grass is good this year. The Five Mile Creek, as it is called, is really about fifteen miles long and empties into the Trinity. Because of the water, there are some trees, for a wind break. On this side of Dallas, there's not so much trouble with Kiowa or other tribes."

Will looked around, following the motion of a red-tailed hawk in the air, distracted with thinking about Mary.

Coming back to the conversation, he asked, "What about drought?"

"It can happen, of course. But the creek has never been known to go completely dry. That will save a lot of well digging."

"How much are they asking, and why are they

selling?"

"He's selling for eleven dollars an acre. That's pretty high, but good grazing land like this is worth it. His wife decided it isn't civilized enough for her here and wants to go back to Philadelphia. Can you imagine?"

Will whistled. "No, I can't. This land looks perfect to me. How long to seal a deal?"

"If you're agreeable, we can sign papers tomorrow and let you get started building. The deed will get registered at the courthouse and then in Austin."

"That's wonderful! I didn't expect it so fast. By the way, I wanted to ask you—would it be all right to take Mary to the Metropolitan Restaurant later this week?"

"I think so. She's very fond of you, and so are we. It will be interesting to see what you make of this place and how you survive the winter."

"I guess I've got my work set for me. I'll leave it to Lightning to count the jackrabbits."

"No doubt he will. But I'm sure you would like to ride the boundaries of the land before we sign."

"Yes, sir."

"If you go just over that rise and turn east toward

the creek, Mary is waiting for you. She wanted to surprise you with having seen the land. We rode it yesterday, and I think she'd be happy to show it to you. I'll be along presently."

"You'd be all right with us riding out together?"

"You have my blessing."

Will put Dusty into a lope, with Lightning following, and found Mary waiting under a shade tree, ready to ride. He looked approvingly at her slim form in a burgundy riding habit and black boots. Will tied Lightning to a tree to keep him out of the food.

"Are you willing to race?" she challenged. My horse, Printer, is one of the fastest in Texas and has won several races. Father won't let me ride him in a real race, always hires a jockey. But Printer and I, we have an understanding. If I give a certain signal, he takes off like the wind. I'll race you to the branch in the creek. Then we'll ride the property line, rest, and eat. What do you say?"

"I say Dusty's never been beaten. But let's make it interesting. If I win, you sew curtains for my cabin and help me decorate."

"And if I win, and Father approves, you take me to a fancy meal next week."

Will grinned since he'd already arranged to do just that.

But she wouldn't win, he knew it. Should he go easy on her?

"What about your father? He'll never keep up."

Mary laughed. "Don't you know? That's the idea!"

Without another word, Printer leaped forward. Taken by surprise, Will was two lengths behind when he kicked Dusty. Mary looked back for a moment, laughing, hair streaming out behind her, then bent forward over Printer's neck. The weight shift triggered something, and it was as though Printer had spread wings. Will kicked Dusty again and watched the ground carefully for rocks, gopher holes, or other obstacles. It reminded him of some of the rides in the war, except then there were Federals shooting at him. Faster, faster—the prairie flew by, and his eyes watered from the wind. How could Mary ride like this?

They reached a point where a trail split off, and Dusty hesitated a step, asking if Will wanted him to turn. Will pushed his heels in on both sides, and Dusty stayed straight, leaping ahead. They were up to Printer's rear, then his flanks and Mary's dress billowed over almost in front of Dusty's eyes, but he didn't falter or stumble. On they flew, now Dusty's nose up even with Printer's withers. Will saw the log coming and leaned forward into Dusty's jump. Flecks of foam flew backward from both horses as the prairie resounded from the thunder of hooves. Stay focused, Will told himself. No time to worry about anything else. There was only him, Dusty, and this horse that ran like a winged creature next to him. What if there was a gully? No, focus! Dusty's nose was even with Printer's ears. Will leaned even lower, urging Dusty on. He could feel how tired the horse was. They'd been riding almost a mile, he judged. Up ahead, he could see water. Was that the creek branch? It must be. But Mary didn't slow down. They pounded on ten yards, twenty—the creek was coming at breakneck speed, and beyond, rocks and logs. Just when he thought she meant to jump it, Mary pulled up to a sliding stop. Will reacted a second later but twisted Dusty's head to the side to give them more room, stopping at the edge, pebbles splashing into the creek. Both horses stood with sides heaving. They dismounted.

"I won!" said Mary.

"By a neck. Where did you learn to ride like that?"

"I've been on a horse since I could walk. Hold my reins?"

She re-pinned her hair, laughing. "You know, I hear the roast turkey at the Metropolitan is amazing!"

"I think I've been set up," joked Will. "But that was a bet I couldn't lose—I get to be with you either way."

They fell into step side by side. "You never cease to surprise me," said Will.

Mary laughed. "Then we won't be bored. If you want someone proper and conventional, you've got the wrong girl."

"What do you want out of life, Mary?"

"Right now? A bath and that picnic basket!" she teased. She looked over and softened. "A home. A family. A place to sink roots, with someone I love."

They walked in silence, each lost in thought. Mary turned and said, "Thank you for a lovely afternoon. I've had so much fun! I loved the dance and the walk by the river with you, but I also love to ride fast. You make me feel alive and valued. You aren't always telling me what I can't do."

Will tied the horses to a tree and invited her to sit on a rock. She did, trying to smooth her skirts, and then laughed at herself.

"I must look a fright."

"To me, you look like an angel. One who has been flying upside down, but an angel nonetheless." Will smiled.

He looked into her eyes and saw warmth and desire. He put a finger under her chin, tilting her head up, and slowly kissed her. When she responded, he took her in his arms and kissed her harder. She held on tight, and Will rested his head next to her neck.

They separated, and after a leisurely lunch, Will said, "We'd better mount up if we're going to make it around the perimeter. And let your father catch up to us."

He cupped his hands and let her step into them, giving her a leg up to mount.

"All right, but not too soon, I hope. Father doesn't worry much about my safety when I'm riding. He says Printer could outrun 'the devil hisself.'"

"He might at that. The creek's warm; let's let them drink a little, then ride along the property lines."

They completed the circuit, noticing the low amount of clover and the beauty of the wildflowers, then road toward the creek fork. They could see David in the distance, as if he had been following discreetly.

Will found a place that was in a low spot near the fork with a few trees.

"What do you think, Mary? Put the cabin here?"

"Seems like a good spot. The little hill on the north side will protect from the wind in the winter; being open to the south will provide a cooling breeze for the rest of the year. The creek will give water, and there are some flat places to the east for the barn and corral. Yes, I think this would do nicely for you."

Will hesitated, then said, "It would also do well for raising a family. I love children." He wondered if Mary was thinking similarly. "It might do well for you too, if you were interested."

"I . . . I think I might like that," said Mary.

When passing behind a small grove of trees, they risked a quick kiss without dismounting, agreeing to meet after church on Sunday.

***

November 1869, Dallas, Will

Will and Robert rode through town, checking buildings and looking for a prospective store. Though Will was open to building one, with all the work needed at the new ranch, and winter closing in, he figured it best to rent a place.

"I want to get the store up and running fast. If I act now, I can cash in on people buying Christmas presents," said Robert. "It's too late for trade from farmers; most won't be looking to buy much before spring."

A few wagons creaked past, and they were getting closer to the Trinity River.

"What about this place?" said Will, motioning at an empty building on the corner of Commerce and Austin Street. "Needs some fixing up—probably got damaged in the fire."

"It does have an upstairs for storage and maybe an apartment. I suppose I could hire some help to get it fixed. Wonder if the owner would sell rather than rent?" said Robert.

"Don't forget you have to stock it. Why not rent for a

while and see how it goes? You could negotiate any improvements to be taken off the purchase later. And Hiram tells me that the railroad may come very close to here."

"Seems like a fine idea."

They inquired and were able to engage the building for five dollars a month, provided repairs were made, with an option to buy in a year. Will asked around and got four former Confederate Masons with some disabilities to work in exchange for food.

Once he got Robert settled, Will attended to building a cabin on the ranch and spent time with Mary. He didn't see Robert much during the next month since he opted to sleep in a tent at the ranch and Robert moved into the apartment above the store. When he came to visit, a large sign on the false front frame building proclaimed the *Crump General Store ~ Everything for Everybody*. The building shone. The front and interior were cleaned, and all burnt lumber was replaced. The store had glass windows on both sides of the door, one displaying women's dresses and the other showing tools and foodstuffs. Someone must be helping Pa with marketing—he'd never shown such flair. He even had a patent medicine section, featuring Dromgoole's English Female Bitters and Dover's Powder to sell to those afraid of the yellow fever epidemic.

When Will entered, Robert was busy with a customer, an older woman in calico with gray hair topped by a bonnet with ribbons trailing behind. Will stood at a discreet distance until their business concluded, then moved toward Robert.

"Will! It's wonderful to see you. Well, what do you think?"

"I'm amazed! I can't believe what you've done with the place. Is business good?"

"Indeed it is, growing all the time, though there's competition from the new Luckenbach and Johnson stores. Your investment helped to get things stocked."

"Maybe I'll have to do some shopping myself. I need something for Mary for Christmas."

Robert grinned. "Good idea. If you think of something soon, I could order it from St. Louis. And maybe I should get some mistletoe for the doorway?"

"A fellow could get in trouble with that," joked Will. "But it might be popular."

Chapter 6

Topeka, June 1870

Luther prepared to travel. He was working on the Kansas Pacific and AT&SF railroads. Ned and his family had moved east with them. Ruth and the children had joined them since no one needed them in Abilene, with Hiram and Julia moving south to Fort Worth. Topeka wasn't lively, but there was steady work. Now that the railroad had moved west and south, Abilene began settling down, and Topeka got wilder Luther didn't like the "end of rails" cow town atmosphere, which was now Topeka, but it was closer to the work. He was often called to one end of the tracks or the other to supervise a crew or a difficult repair. It allowed him to spy out the land, looking for where he might want to settle now that land was readily available. He wasn't ready to strike out on his own and risk something like the Kidder massacre, but he wanted to scout out likely places. It wasn't safe yet. The Cheyenne were none too happy about the railroad. It brought his mind to the current problem: rails were torn up down the line.

"Ruth, I may not be back until tomorrow. Depends on how messed up the rails are at Salt Creek. Could you pack me a cold supper? I recall the hotel there isn't friendly to colored. I'll likely have to sleep outside."

"I'll pack it. But I wish you weren't gone so much. Wasn't that partly why we moved to Topeka, so you'd be around? I worry about you traveling on the prairie. Daddy has a safe job in one place. Why can't we just help him? This ain't a bad place, even if it's mostly white."

"You know the reasons well as I do. I get extra pay, not just laborer pay, traveling for Hiram. He treats me as good as white. We got to save to get by. If we claim land, we can't expect a crop for one, maybe two years. We have to live, buy horses and food."

"But with Lindy being five and Matt three, they are growing up without their papa. Handling the house, little Lila and those two, along with taking in laundry—I'm plumb worn out most of the time. We need you around more."

Luther finished tying his boot and stood, taking her by the shoulders. "You are the most beautiful woman. How'd I marry a princess?"

"Don't you think you can sweet talk me into forgetting! Next week, I want you to ask for two days off, on top of Sunday. I'll telegraph Julia if you don't. And when you're here, I want you ALL here, not scratching in ledgers or sending messages. Otherwise, I might let *you* manage the laundry and the children and the cooking for a few days."

"All right," he grinned. "I s'pect they can spare me a bit to see my princess."

He kissed her, drawing her close and murmuring nonsense. She leaned into him. He thought he'd won when she laughed and shoved him away.

"You best get on. I gotta pack your food, you gotta saddle up, and we got no time or money for more children."

Luther reluctantly turned and went to saddle the horse. Matt appeared in the doorway, his eyes pleading. Luther laughed and said, "Come on, then. You can help."

Matt dropped his toy and ran to follow Luther. Luther shook his head and reflected on how life would have been for little Matt if he'd been born only a few years earlier. Lord willing, he would never know a master or a lash or be starved after pulling a bag after himself all day, harvesting in the fields. Sure, he would expect his children to work hard, but working for the Lord and themselves, not some white man.

He grabbed the saddle and handed Matt the bridle, helping him stand on a stool. After throwing the blanket and saddle over the horse and tying the lead to the hitching post, he showed Matt how to talk quietly to the horse, pulling gently on the lead until the head was low enough for him to reach, putting on the browband, and taking care with the ears. He encouraged Matt to apply slight pressure to the back of the mouth with his thumb and forefinger and watched as the horse accepted the bit. Then he let Matt attach the throat latch. He taught him about tightening the girth and the mustang's tendency to blow out his belly, leaving the girth too loose. Luther tapped the horse's front leg to lift it and then had Matt do it so Luther could cinch up tighter. When the horse was ready, Matt extended his arms skyward for Luther to pick him up. Luther thought of the time, then shook his head and swung his son high in the air to a chorus of giggles. Ruth appeared in the doorway, smiling, and caught Matt on his way down, handing Luther the saddlebag with his food.

"You let Papa go now. He's got to get to work. He's got to ride and then catch the train."

Matt clung to Ruth and then raised a hand to wave. "Bye, Papa."

Lindy, dressed as if ready for travel, raced out the door and grabbed Luther's hand. "Take me with you, Papa! I'm the oldest! Just this once. I'll help all I can. I'll tend the horse. I won't complain. I don't weigh much. Please!"

Her dark eyes pleaded. Luther noticed she'd braided her own hair and dressed sensibly. He looked up at Ruth, who shook her head.

"Not this time. Papa has to travel fast and light. I'll be back soon," said Luther.

"What about me, Papa?" cried Matt.

He bent down on one knee and looked Matt in the eye. "Now someone got to stay and take care of Mama. You be the man of the house. I know you can do that. She depends on you."

He gave Ruth a quick kiss and mounted, waving a hand back at them.

***

Luther rode with haste. Ruth was right—he hadn't been home enough for his children in the past months. He felt bad about leaving them behind.

He left the horse at the livery and got seated on the two-car train headed west. He wondered what he would find at Fossil Creek, what the trouble was.

When the train neared the station, it was approaching the middle of the day. He went into the depot, found the colored waiting area, and ate their simple meal.

"Where's the problem?" Luther asked the station master, Chambers.

"It's about two miles out west, the switch that goes to Pueblo. We need it fixed by nightfall when the train comes through. Take as many of the crew as you need, spare rails, spikes, hammers, and a crosstie or two—I don't know exactly what you might need."

"Yes, sir, Mr. Chambers."

"Just be back at dark. My wife won't wait for supper."

Luther smiled but thought, "He thinks a black man is too stupid to know what's needed to fix the rails, or how long it will take like I haven't been doing this for years already."

Luther gathered the needed supplies and three men. They took the handcar and a few Spencer rifles with cartridges that the railroad issued. After about two hours of hand cranking and taking turns, they topped a hill and looked down at the switch.

There was a group of about twenty Indians and horses surrounding the switch, with rails they'd pried up and then used as levers to move the track, hoping to force a derailment. The men on the car and the Indians at the bottom spied each other almost at the same moment. Four or five Indians leaped on their horses and began riding toward the railcar. Luther quickly assessed the odds and grabbed a handle, forcing the car back the way they had come. If they could pick up enough speed on the way down the hill, they might outrun their pursuers.

He pumped, muscles straining, hot wind blowing dust in his eyes, willing the car up the hill, and then not slacking on the other side.

"Harry!" he yelled. "You and John grab those Spencers! Lay flat, slow them down a little."

An arrow whizzed by his knee, sinking into the wooden platform of the pump. He heard whoops behind him but did not look back. A few arrows fell short as the car picked up speed downhill. Then he heard the crack of a rifle and the impact on metal—one of the Indians had a gun. He pulled down on the pump handle harder than ever, muscles screaming at him, and the man on the other side was hard-pressed to keep up. Another shot whistled overhead. He could see the depot now. Maybe the men there would help. Down, up, down up—two hundred yards to go. The Indians hadn't given up. One was almost alongside.

A woman stepped out of the depot, looking in the direction of the oncoming handcar.

"Take over!" he yelled at one of the men, abandoning the pump and grabbing a Spencer. He prayed it was loaded, levering a cartridge into place. As he aimed, he saw the Indian slump, falling off his horse, and then heard the rifle shot. He saw someone at the depot had fired, then several men began firing from behind barrels on the platform, and the Indians broke off their pursuit, turning back to the west.

Luther jumped from the car and ran to where the woman stood, looking terrified at the dead Indian. Probably Cheyenne, Luther judged, but his attention was on the woman to see if she was hurt. He stood sweating, chest heaving as he caught his breath, oblivious to the shouts of the men on the car and those at the depot. They were safe, and that was all that mattered.

The Founding

On return to the depot, Luther found that Chambers had telegraphed Fort Hays, and assuming that the lines hadn't been cut, the soldiers might give chase, though the result was doubtful. The Tenth Cavalry would be dispatched to stand guard while the railroad line was repaired, but not before the next day.

When the soldiers did come, Luther was surprised to see they were all black, except one white lieutenant. About fifteen troopers rode in carrying the Company F flag and another proclaiming them as Buffalo Soldiers. He stopped the sergeant in charge.

"Excuse me, why did the Indians attack?" asked Luther.

"Any number of reasons. The Indians don't like the railroad. They don't like people coming to take their land and destroy the game. Many have never seen a colored person, so you would be a prize to them. They want to stop the railroad, destroy it, and anyone who helps build it."

Luther frowned. "So we're all targets?"

"Yes. There are lots of folks, black and white, that want more land. The railroad's gonna get built whether we help or not," said the sergeant.

"All I want is some land for our family, a place where we can be free and enjoy what we work for without someone telling us what to do. Freedom, with no white folks in charge," said Luther.

The sergeant sighed. "That's all most of us want. There's enough land here for everyone. Back east in Kentucky, where I come from, the white men still make all the rules. The war got rid of slavery, but it didn't get rid of hate. Until we get the hate out of every person's heart, there will always be evil and one person treating another as if they own them."

"Everyone's looking for a place to stand," agreed Luther. "I'm looking for a place I can be my own person, work some land, and live in peace. That's what I hope for. Maybe if enough colored people come west, we can find our place."

***

Luther ate the food Ruth had prepared, sitting outside and watching the sun descend to the mountains in the west. He spread his bedroll on the ground near the depot, with his rifle nearby.

The following day, Luther again went out on the handcar with the men to repair the damaged tracks, this time under guard. He noticed the white officer doled out ammunition, ten rounds to each soldier, to be collected if not used.

Once the job was finished, he wasted no time catching the next train back to Topeka. Ruth was waiting at the station with the other children.

"Luther! It's in all the papers. Are you all right?" Ruth enfolded him in a hug.

Once they were back at their apartment, Luther and Ruth sent the children to their room to play.

"That was close, wasn't it?" said Ruth.

"My heart about burst when I saw that Indian alongside the handcar. I heard today they found two workers on the tracks farther west scalped and torn up."

"Luther, you got to get out of doing this. I can't lose

you."

"I know. Hiram's been good to us, but we still need to be on our own. And I got questions about taking Indian land. We can't follow the railroad to Texas anyhow. We're not going to a slave state. I know what the law says, but the law doesn't stop them from lynching, beating, and treating us like dirt. Just last year in Dallas, they burning houses and crops and beating and intimidating colored. Same thing back in Kentucky."

"Why not just stay here? You and Daddy can start a shop again."

"Might work. One white place is about as good as another, long as we stay clear of the big cities. I talked to one of the soldiers from Hays. He said they don't dare go out after dark, not because of Indians, but because of white people."

Ruth shook her head. "Aren't we ever going to be free?"

"Someday. Let's pray."

***

Topeka, 1871

Luther sighed, wiping his forehead and laying down his hammer. He and Ned had started a full-time shop again, corner of Fifth and Quincy, making wagons and farm tools and shoeing horses. They still took an occasional order from the railroad, but they were independent. The only problem was that there were nine blacksmith shops in Topeka, and only theirs was owned by blacks. Since only about ten percent of the population was black, the white folks—with the most money and trade—tended to go elsewhere. They were getting by, but it was frustrating to watch the large orders go to white blacksmiths, who didn't always produce better quality.

The one saving grace was that Lindy was able to attend school, a school that taught both black and white children.

Lindy came home from school and dropped into her father's shop as Luther was working on repairing a wagon.

"Papa! Can I show you what I wrote today?"

Luther stopped and smiled. "What is it? A story?"

"No, sir. I can't write stories yet, you know that. But I did copy the Lord's Prayer. See?"

She held out her slate. He could make out the words, even if the letters were a bit wobbly.

"That's real fine. You'll have to show Mama."
He handed it back to her, and when she reached to take it, he noticed dried blood from a cut on the back of her hand.

"What happened to your hand there?"

"It's nothin', Papa, really."

"It sure enough looks like somethin'! What happened?"

"I . . . I fell. Hit it on a rock, and it bled a little."

Luther could tell she was hiding something. The joy had left her eyes. Should he let it go?

Ruth came out, but Luther motioned her back.

He knelt next to Lindy and gently picked up the injured hand.

"You don't usually fall. Did somethin' happen? Did someone push you or chase you? You can tell me. It's all right."

He noticed then the dirt and grass stains on the back of her dress.

"The dress doesn't matter. We can fix it."

She started crying and fell into his arms.

"The white boys started making fun of me, asking me if I was there to learn to write, pick cotton, or clean up the school. Must be here to clean, one of them said, because black folk no good for anything else. They were all around me, and then they started throwing rocks, so I ran. Mostly they didn't hit me, but when I tripped and fell, they threw a sharp rock and it tore my hand. It bled some. I went back to the school, and the teacher bound it up with some petticoat lace until it stopped bleeding. She's real nice."

"Who? Who were they?" Luther demanded, furious.

"Oh please, Papa! Let it go."

"Luther!" said Ruth. "Listen to her. You can't make more trouble. It won't help. What if they run us out of town again?"

"Papa, I'm not hurt bad. And I do *so* want to go to school! Please don't make me stop." She hugged him with fierce energy as if all her being poured into the entreaty.

"All right, all right. But Mama or I gonna come pick you up from school from now on. We'll walk home together. Nobody going to hurt you with me there."

Lindy brightened. "Thank you, Papa! Thank you for understanding." She looked him in the eye. "You know, I can throw pretty good. Matt and I practice sometimes. You know I'd throw a rock back if it wouldn't cause more trouble. But what did the preacher say last Sunday about turning the other cheek? I guess that's what I have to do all the time."

Luther's heart ached, and his stomach clenched with anger. Suddenly the old scar on his back from the whipping when he was a boy burned and chafed.

He answered gently, "I suppose you're right, child. Now let's show Mama what you wrote and see if there's any of that chocolate cake left for my smart girl."

They walked into the house, Lindy in the middle, arms around each other.

Chapter 7

Fort Worth, 1872, Julia

Julia reviewed the reports from their engineers. The
AT&SF line was proceeding west and south faster than ex-
pected. They'd just reached Dodge City in Kansas. She had
suggested that she and Hiram move closer to the end of
tracks after the line founded Newton and pushed south to
Wichita. Since the goals were connecting with the line from
Galveston north to Dallas and building west to Santa Fe,
Julia persuaded Hiram to rent a house and offices in Fort
Worth, a tiny town west of Dallas. With good fortune, they
could link to the newly commissioned Texas and Pacific
Railway, giving two paths westward and a connection to
the sea in Galveston.

She looked around the combination office and resi-
dence with plank walls from boards shipped in by wagon.
One coal stove in the corner served for both heat and cook-

ing. Sometimes she asked herself what she was doing here. She could have been in their comfortable house in Cincinnati, but then she'd never see Hiram. Ladies' teas weren't really her idea of fun either. She enjoyed the challenges of the business, though right now it was worrisome that their steel supplier hadn't gotten back to her on their order of rails.

Hiram walked in.

"Have you heard from our Chicago supplier?" she asked him. "They're late with the next shipment of rails."

"Yes, just a few minutes ago. A telegram came. They aren't shipping them. Gould outbid us."

"But we have a contract!"

"It doesn't matter—they backed out. We'll have to find another source."

"That will take weeks. The men will be sitting idle, if we don't lose them altogether, and throw off the whole schedule."

"We can beg, but I doubt it will do any good. I smell Gould trying to bankrupt us."

"He *is* a wolf!" Julia slammed a decanter on the desk and let out a few unladylike words.

"I have an idea," said Hiram. "I've heard about a new mill in Joliet. They're making rails cheaper than the Chicago mill we've dealt with. Let's approach them."

"All right. Maybe if we're quiet about it, we can beat Gould at his own game. Let him have the Chicago rails and pay for the privilege while we save money at Joliet," said Julia. She put her hands together as if praying and smiled.

"Let's telegraph, and if it looks good, we can go together. It could be a short holiday for us. You've missed the big city, I think."

"Well, at least the shops. Can we stop at our house in Cincinnati? With the railroad, it wouldn't cost us too many extra days."

"I suppose it would be good to see home, but we can't stay for too long. The construction here is too important to leave to chance."

***

Hiram and Julia arrived in Joliet late in the evening, bone weary and ready for a hotel. They were to meet with a Joliet steel mill executive at noon the next day, Mr. Hugh Latimer. To solve the social dilemma that Julia presented by her presence, Mrs. Latimer would join them for lunch.

"I hope it isn't too inconvenient, having me at the meeting," said Julia.

"Nonsense. I want you there. If it puts them off-balance, so much the better. If Latimer has done his homework, he'll know that you aren't just decoration."

"We need these rails. It isn't a good negotiating position."

"This mill is new, only three years old. He needs the business. He'll still expect you to make nice with his wife and stay out of the actual negotiations. That's fine as far as it goes, but I want you to listen. You can catch his attitudes and weaknesses. And speak up if you think there's anything I am missing."

"I will. Mrs. Latimer, from all I can tell, is a young socialite from a rich family in Philadelphia. They've only been married five years. He didn't serve in the war and profited from munitions. The rumor in ladies' circles is that he's a philanderer."

"He likely won't try anything with his wife present. Mentioning mutual acquaintances might give us some leverage, though, assuming his wife doesn't know about his adventures."

"Or she may know, and resentment might make her willing to tell us things that would help us."

***

Hiram and Julia alighted from their rented carriage, and Julia gasped at the horrible smell, eyes stinging as she pulled a handkerchief from her reticule and placed it over her nose and mouth. The sky was dark with billowing clouds of smoke, and she had to pick her way through piles of dung and scrap, walking over a railroad track to get to the building where the sign proclaimed an office. She could tell Hiram was affected, as he uncharacteristically grasped her hand to hurry her along and get inside.

Once the door shut, they could feel the heat of the furnaces. Was Latimer trying to impress them with the size and efficiency of his plant or put them off-balance with discomfort? They could have met at a more comfortable place. Julia wondered if this was his revenge for having a woman at the meeting, an implicit message that women didn't belong there. If the meeting lasted until luncheon, perhaps she could suggest moving to the Tivoli across the river.

A young man met them and escorted them out of the bowels of hell up to Latimer's plush oak-lined office.

He rose to greet Hiram.

"Mr. Johannsen, pleased to meet you," he oozed, extending a hand. "And this must be the lovely Mrs. Johannsen. Pity about the steamboat business, but we must move forward. I hear you're expanding into Texas with the railroad. Great future there, I think."

Julia gazed around at the large flat desk, walnut bookshelves, and heavy curtains blocking out the factory landscape. Oil lamps were lit, even though it was daytime.

"Thank you, Mr. Latimer. We hear great things about your mill, and I'm impressed with the size of the enterprise in such a short time."

"Would you care to move next door? I believe my wife, Louise, is waiting, and there are some light refreshments."

"Lead on," said Julia. "I shall be happy to make her acquaintance."

They moved through a door to an adjoining room, furnished as a wealthy person's drawing room in a mansion, a great contrast to the belching mill outside.

A small dark-haired woman with a finely chiseled face, dressed in an elegant blue day dress, rose from her seat at the large circular table to greet them, and a waiter hovered discreetly in the background.

"Louise, this is Mr. and Mrs. Johannsen from Cincinnati and . . . Fort Worth, did you say?"

Hiram answered, "Yes, that's correct. Charmed, Mrs. Latimer."

"Pleased to meet you," she responded. "Was your journey pleasant?"

"Tiring, but travel always is. I confess I never expected such a pleasant place amid a factory," said Julia. She noticed Latimer's disrespect in using his wife's first name in public and the implied slight introducing her to Mrs. Latimer rather than the other way around.

When everyone was seated, with the men closer together at one end, the conversation split, the men discussing Grant's victory and Greeley's death and the ladies discussing Julia Grant and Victoria Woodhull, with Julia keeping an ear toward the men's conversation.

"What do you think of Mrs. Woodhull, Mrs. Latimer?"

"I don't follow politics much. I do think it is scandalous for a divorced woman to attempt to run for president. It would be senseless for any woman, but after a divorce?"

"It does seem a waste of time," Julia allowed. "Yet it does bring attention to the lack of women's rights. Greeley's attempt to smear her was cowardly."

"One mustn't speak ill of the dead. Did you see that Julia Grant ordered her gown from China? Imagine!"

"I did see that, but why not? With the railroad, she can have it in time for the inauguration. Are you and Mr. Latimer attending? I heard that Lucy Hayes and her husband are going, along with Mary Tomkins."

"I'm unsure at present, with the demands of the mill. I know Lucy and Mary slightly from an orphan's charity ball in Chicago before the fire last year. They say Lucy's husband, Rutherford, might be a future presidential candidate after Grant finishes this term. Mr. Latimer thinks highly of her."

"Indeed? I knew Lucy well in Cincinnati. I shall have to catch up with her."

Louise looked chagrined. "I've said too much, forgive me. Please don't mention Mr. Latimer to her. There was . . . a bit of unpleasantness, and I would consider it a favor if you didn't mention us to her."

"Of course. I was merely looking for a common acquaintance. Have you been much involved with rebuilding efforts in Chicago?"

"Only through the Catholic Orphan Society. Mr. Latimer helped secure a donation from the Ann Stewart Foundation for repairs after the fire."

"Ann Stewart, the bordello madame?"

"Oh dear, I've done it again, haven't I? Yes, but she's moved on, quite wealthy now, you know. And such a worthy cause."

"Yes, indeed," said Julia, filing away the information.

"Mrs. Johannsen?" Hiram interrupted their conversation. "What do you think of ten dollars apiece for twenty-foot rails, if we order four hundred at a time?"

Latimer chuckled. "Surely no need to involve the ladies."

Hiram cut him off. "Mrs. Johannsen and I run the business as a team. We consult each other on most things. Unusual, perhaps, but times are changing, as the ladies were discussing about Mrs. Woodhull." He turned back to Julia, eyebrow raised expectantly.

"Why, Mr. Latimer, your wife and I were just discussing your generosity and influence with the Catholic Orphan Society. Surely you could manage eight dollars per rail, which still leaves you a fifteen-percent profit if we agree to jointly donate the two-dollar difference to the orphans, keeping it anonymous? No need to mention how you came to be associated with the orphanage, just good works, of course. If you could guarantee delivery in two weeks, I could mention your assistance to General Buell on the Texas and Pacific. If Jay Gould is arrested, as the newspapers are suggesting, that could be significant for your business. The T&P will have quite an appetite for rails."

Latimer's eyebrows formed an upward V, and he turned slightly red, glaring at his wife and then quickly recovering.

"Ah yes . . . I suppose that would be . . . satisfactory. You are well informed, Mrs. Johannsen."

Julia smiled. "I try, even though I'm just a woman. An alliance could be profitable for both you and our firm."

Hiram pushed back his chair and stood, towering over Latimer. "If you'll draw up the papers and send them by our hotel, we can conclude our business. It's the Spicer Hotel on Jefferson, near the train depot. I'll leave a deposit with your clerk."

"It was a pleasure meeting you and doing business," said Julia. "Thank you, Mrs. Latimer, for your generous hospitality. Perhaps we'll meet again."

"I hope so, Mrs. Johannsen," she said with a smile. "I think it has been rewarding for both of us."

Within a month, the AT&SF was back on schedule, having received the rails from Joliet, along with a pretty thank-you note from Louisa Latimer.

***

September 1873

Hiram began his morning full of worry. While the AT&SF had reached Colorado, and the Kansas Pacific had linked with the Union Pacific earlier, they were now over four hundred thousand dollars in debt with no money to pay the interest. Like most of the railroads, they had floated bonds to pay for expansion. They were just short of linking with the Texas and Pacific after recovering from the near disaster of losing the rails contract a few months before. As he opened the morning newspaper, he saw that the stock market was in collapse, bonds were being called, and in the aftermath of the Franco-Prussian War, European investors were panicked. The streets of New York were lined with people pounding on the doors of banks, demanding their money. Jay Cooke, a large investor in their railroads, was bankrupt. Many railroads were going bankrupt. How would they pay their investors?

He ran a big hand through his hair. What could be done? The railroad lines were returning a good profit, but every penny and more went into expansion. Julia had done her part, though she was spending as the line moved south at a furious pace. He decided he must talk with her. Together they would overcome this new challenge.

Julia came bustling in, arms loaded with packages from her shopping trip.

He tried to smile as he made his way over to her. Fear gripped his heart. How would they manage? But she must know. Rich or poor, he'd always love his courageous, quick-thinking farm girl. He helped her stow the purchases. Then he abandoned caution and scooped her off her feet, whirling around as they used to in the early days, letting her feel his strength and protection. For now, he wanted there to be peace.

***

Julia wondered at Hiram's greeting—why this sudden joyous mood? It couldn't be good news, could it? She had read the morning papers; she knew about the panic. Was there something so awful he was covering up with this show of good cheer? Still, she supposed she shouldn't complain. His greeting was certainly boisterous enough. Maybe he had new financing? Or maybe, she thought, silly girl, he just wants to show how much he loves you?

"Hiram! You'd better put me down. People in the street can see us! They will talk."

"Let them. I don't care. I'm so tired of caring what the investors think, what the bank thinks, and what Gould thinks. It's been like walking a tightrope carrying a calf in each arm these past months. For once, I want to be with my wife and enjoy an evening. Let's escape to a hotel, just you and me."

"But why? What's happened?"

"No wifely curiosity until tomorrow. Today I want to enjoy you."

"All right," said Julia, whose curiosity was now larger than Texas.

She played along, sending Emily home.

She waited on him and rubbed his shoulders to relax

him. She called their groom, and had him make the buggy ready, and drive them to the best hotel in town. After a leisurely dinner with all his favorites, they went to their room.

Julia led him to their bed, poured wine, and waited.

"I know you said morning, but I'm bursting. What's wrong? I know you well enough that it isn't something good."

"You can't wait? All right, if you must. I wanted one happy night. We're broke. It's that serious and that simple. With the problems at Jay Cooke, and the run on banks, the Germans are calling in their notes—and we don't have money to pay them. We stand to lose everything, what's left of the steamship line, maybe even the house in Cincinnati. We're mortgaged to the hilt, and now the investors want their money. It isn't just the Kansas Pacific or the AT&SF, lots of railroads are going bankrupt."

"I know," Julia said simply. "I didn't want to break it to you when you seemed to be celebrating. I read the papers too, you know. It's not a surprise. I anticipated some trouble when I read about New York. I just made a deal here with the Dallas businessmen to bring the other spur we talked about here instead of to Corsicana. They'll pay one thousand hard cash."

"Yes, but it won't matter, though I love you for doing

that instead of diving into despair. We have to pay for the rails, the material, and the men to do it. Unless they'll pay in advance, we can't do it, not even thirty miles. All you wanted, in the beginning, was a rich man. That's what I no longer am."

"Hiram, we passed that point years ago. I love you because of who you are, not the money."

"But we have to come up with thousands we don't have or lose at least one of the lines. I expect Gould to swoop in with an offer at cents on the dollar anytime. After he cleared himself, avoiding arrest, from the Erie and the legal troubles, he's been more aggressive than ever. He'll buy up our bonds for almost nothing. After he holds all our debt, we'll be forced to give up control."

"Oh, Hiram! After all our work—there has to be a way out."

"My love, if you can find it, you're a genius. But this time I think we have lost. If we can keep our house in Cincinnati, we'll be fortunate. But even that is not certain. We're so close to connecting here. I took one risk too many. I failed you."

Julia looked at his defeated, slumping shoulders. He'd finally met something he couldn't muscle his way through. Without a word, she opened her arms and went to him, wrapping herself around him, holding tight. After a few minutes, she looked up, eyes wet with tears. "My poor, brave knight. You haven't failed at all. Even if we lose it all, our families started with nothing. We can rebuild."

***

December 1873

The news around the country grew worse by the day. Work stopped on the railroads, even though in Fort Worth they were a mere thirty miles from connecting. There was no money for rails, no money for workers, and no money for servants. Julia had to let Emily go, and they had to sell the houses in Abilene, Topeka, and Cincinnati and what was left of the steamboat business. As expected, Gould made them a ridiculous offer for the Kansas Pacific, and they were forced to accept.

Hiram read the newspaper and seemed to grow older with each page.

"Unemployment is now eight percent. I heard from Peters this morning; the workers we have left are threatening to strike because we haven't paid them. The only thing that keeps them with us is that there are no other jobs."

"I'm sure the weather matters too. I can't remember when the winter was this bad, even in Ohio. Snow, wind—you'd think we'd moved to Sweden." Julia bustled about clearing their meager breakfast. "There's plenty of workers coming in from Prussia, trying to escape after the war there, but there are no jobs for them. I feel sorry for them, but what can we do?"

"We cannot help them. We can barely help ourselves. If the workers strike, we can't mine coal or get it to market, much less move cattle."

"At least Will was able to buy his ranch, though how he'll keep the cattle alive I can't tell."

They looked at each other, faces creased in worry.

"We know how to farm, but it's too late this year for a crop. Robert would sell us food, but we'd have to buy on credit, take charity."

"We have to get enough to connect in Fort Worth. The freight revenue would be enough to see us until spring."

"Let's talk to the men. It's in their interest to finish."

Julia looked at her hands, red from the cold, roughened by laundry and hard work. She pulled off her emerald wedding ring, setting it on the table by Hiram.

"We'll sell it," she declared. "It's easily worth twenty thousand. You know I love you. I don't need a ring. We'll buy enough rails and crossties to finish the thirty miles and connect to the north. If Mr. King will extend us just a little credit, we might be able to get rolling again."

Hiram squeezed her hand. "I wouldn't ask you, but it might make the difference."

Chapter 8

December 1873, Dallas

Will took advantage of the crash. Even with his money in the King bank, he knew banks could fail. Local land was cheaper, and he took the opportunity to buy. He and Robert were living at his ranch. Robert had moved back in with him to save money on coal and heat. With the tough winter ahead, he hoped it would be enough. The store was foundering as people lost jobs and wanted to buy on credit. Will had finally stepped in and told Robert they could extend no further credit to anyone, except widows or orphans on a case-by-case basis. Even Charlie Goodnight couldn't help them, as he'd lost most of his land in Texas and Colorado. He sold fifty Hereford to Will for rock-bottom prices. Will's herd now numbered seventy. The gold and store profits from Colorado had sustained him thus far, even after buying the ranch. Will hadn't borrowed, operating on a cash basis, and wasn't in jeopardy, except for the vagaries of weather and keeping the cattle healthy.

Will built a sleigh and bought two draft horses that could pull it in the winter and a plow in the spring. He hitched the new horses to the sleigh and drove to town, planning to meet Mary at her house. In the past three years, he'd become a frequent visitor at the King household. He took Mary to the Baptist church, following her father's lead. They usually went to socials and other young couples' events, stealing private time when they could.

He whistled the new song "Home on the Range" as he drove, thinking that now he was home at last. He'd thought many times of asking for Mary's hand, but the uncertain economy made him wonder if the time was right. He decided to be patient rather than face a refusal. He knew David liked him, but David had expressed his concern for Mary's financial welfare. It was somewhat understandable — wealth could come and go, as he was seeing with Hiram and Julia. He'd been thinking of getting a special birthday gift for Mary. With money tight, he still wanted to get her something nice. He finally decided on some side-button boots, dark with gold trim, an ivory inlaid music box that played Pachelbel's Canon, and a necklace from Lange's Jewelry. He would give her the necklace now, and the other items at Christmas.

He did more shopping, thinking of Ann and David for Christmas. He found a hard rock maple cane stained dark with a golden wolf's head handle for David. He wandered down Main Street looking in shop windows, trying to find something for Ann.

As he walked past the Austin Clocks store, he saw the perfect thing for Ann: a white and gold porcelain pendulum clock that would look great on their mantelpiece. He went into the store, and the clock began chiming the hour. It sounded like bells from heaven. It even had angels with trumpets that circled in front while the chimes played. That was it, he would get that for Ann. He might have to shoot a bison and sell the meat to pay for the extravagance, but the Kings were worth it.

He stopped at the post office to get the mail and saw a letter from Albinia.

Dear Will,

I hope everyone there is well. The school is going to recess for a while, as funds are tight to continue. I thought I might come and visit and bring Lydia. What if we came at Christmas? We'd love to see both you and Pa. I know it's probably an imposition, and if it is a bad time, we can wait. Frankly, Lydia wants to move out there with you and Pa. She's twenty-four now and thinks her sister is bor-ing.

I think none of the young fellows here appeal to her. Let us know when you can.

> *Love, Albinia*

He thought it would be wonderful to have the whole family together for Christmas. By train, it would only take them three days to travel. He stopped at the telegraph office and sent a message for them to come, and invited Hiram and Julia in a separate telegram.

When he arrived at the King's house for Mary's birthday, he felt unaccountably nervous. He knew he would need David's approval for Mary to accept the necklace. He also knew it would begin to raise questions about why he hadn't yet formally proposed. Long courtships were less common than long engagements.

Miranda showed him into the parlor, where he found Ann and Mary waiting.

"Mary and Mrs. King, I would like to say how much I have enjoyed spending time with your family and the honor you bestow upon me by allowing me to continue courting. You have all grown in my regard, and I wish to give a small token in honor of Mary's birthday that might demonstrate my affection. May I?"

Will opened a velvet box and pushed it toward Mary. The opal necklace and gold chain sparkled in the light of the candles.

"Why, Mr. Crump! It's gorgeous. It's too much," said Ann.

"Will, you must have ordered the necklace from New York! Mother, may I accept it? And my birthstone—you remembered! I think it speaks of both our feelings."

"It's very generous. But, well, it's not my place to say." Ann looked unsure, her mouth pursed and eyebrows raised. "I suppose what I can do is accept it for Mary, temporarily, until her father has seen it. If he approves, then she may keep it."

Mary's eyes clouded, but her mouth stayed upturned. "It's the most beautiful necklace I've ever seen. Thank you."

Impulsively she reached out and covered his hand with hers, withdrawing it and coloring as her mother cleared her throat. Ann closed the box.

"Let me put this in the safe, and then perhaps Mr. Crump will allow me to serve us all some dessert to celebrate?"

"Thank you, Mrs. King."

"We do appreciate the care you've shown for Mary."

"Thank you, ma'am. Your family is a light to the community."

He exchanged glances with Mary as Ann summoned Miranda.

"If you'll excuse me, I'll tell Miranda to serve dessert in the dining room"

Mary mouthed, "I love you," before she left for the kitchen.

***

When Will arrived back at the cabin, he felt like he could touch the stars. Mary loved him, and the necklace had gone over well—he was sure David would let her receive it.

As a bonus, his sisters were coming! He wasn't sure of his reception with Lydia, but he could hardly wait to see Albinia. He might have to play peacemaker between her and Robert after him running off to the gold fields, but knowing Albinia, she would warm to him; after all, she was coming. Peace on earth, goodwill toward men - and women, he hoped.

He saw Pa chopping wood down by the creek. He hurried to get the horses settled and then walked down to where Pa swung the axe. He missed and set up the log again with a sigh. At fifty-nine, Pa was beginning to show his age. It was none too soon to mend fences in the family.

Will waited until the axe connected, splitting the log with a satisfying thud, and then spoke. "Pa! I got a letter. You'll never guess."

"Let's see . . . Basil Duke, your old regimental commander, is coming for a visit."

"No, much better than that. Albinia and Lydia are coming."

Robert dropped the axe and sat on an unsplit log.

"Here? For Christmas? I can't believe it."

"And I got a telegram from Julia and Hiram. They will be here too. The whole family will be together. Here's Albinia's letter, read for yourself. They want to see us, see right there?"

Robert broke into a grin. "My girls? Coming to see me? I've got five years' worth of Christmas in one. It's better than I deserve."

"We don't deserve anything, Pa, except another chance if we live long enough," said Will. "I hope we both have another chance with them."

***

A few days later, having gotten a return message from Albinia, Will rose early and went to the train station. He was expecting Albinia and Lydia on the ten o'clock train from Indiana through St. Louis. The train puffed in like an angry dragon, blowing fiery steam on anyone near the tracks. Will backed up as the hot spray landed on him, but then he peered back at the cars, looking for his sisters. After the wheels screeched to a halt, a boy ran to the passenger car entrance with wooden steps and placed them to aid the passengers leaving the train. Will saw a woman shrouded in brown velvet trimmed with fur and a floral hat that threatened to take wing in the strong Texas wind. As she turned her face toward him, he recognized Albinia, slim and beautiful despite her children. She took one elegant hand out of a muff, picking up her skirts and balancing on the car rail as she descended the wooden steps to the platform.

Will ran over to her.

"Albinia! It's so good to see you. Where's Lydia? Did you bring the children?"

They hugged, and she laughed at his breathless questions.

"Lydia is right here, you silly," said Lydia.

Will turned, and his eyes grew wide. "Is it really you? When did you get to be such a beauty?"

"Thank you . . . I think. It has been a few years, Will. Eight, to be precise. I'm not a little girl anymore."

"I should say not," he said as his eyes took in her svelte emerald velvet dress and hair in ringlets. "You'll be giving all the fellows here heart attacks."

"And you've gotten a little gray, I see. Just as scruffy as ever."

"A fella tries to give you a compliment, and that's the thanks I get."

Lydia smiled and opened her arms for a hug.

"Let's get you and your things into the buggy. I have hot bricks for your feet, and Pa's waiting for supper at the cabin. Though I won't mind if one of you takes over the cooking."

"Haven't even unpacked, and he wants to shove all the chores on us," joked Albinia.

"Typical man," said Lydia.

"To answer your other question, no, the children didn't come. Peter decided it would be too hard on them. I think he just wanted the chance to spoil them without me around. He couldn't leave the church at Christmas, of course. I can stay as much as two weeks, but we'll see how he is doing with the children. Thank heavens for telegrams and trains."

The porter rolled a cart of bags toward them.

"Only two weeks? Looks like you brought half of Indiana along. Typical women."

Lydia and Albinia looked at one another, grinned, and simultaneously clobbered him with their muffs.

After they were seated in the buggy, Will asked about Albinia's school for colored children. He debated how much to ask about Lydia's immediate plans. He wasn't quite sure what to do with this grown-up sister. When he'd last seen her, she'd awakened him from a nightmare about the war and he'd grabbed a pistol. He wondered if there was residual anger about him pointing a gun at her from that time. They hadn't been together in years, and he was unsure where to start with her. And what would her attitude toward Pa be? He'd left them to dig gold, become a drunk, and dishonored their family. Will decided to forge ahead.

"Lydia, if you don't mind my asking, what are your plans? I mean, you're very welcome here, but are you sure you want to be with a couple of old bachelors?"

"I want to see the country, spread my wings. Albinia has taught me to sew. Ever since Ma died and Pa left, I've felt at loose ends. I have a bit of money saved, I'm good with accounts and figures, and I want to try my hand at business. A girl can't just travel on her own. Julia and Hiram have come west, as well as you and Pa."

She shifted in her seat and flashed him an uncertain smile.

"Seeing Albinia's family has made me think I might like one of my own. Being an aunt is fun, but not like having your own children. None of the men in Madison interest me. At least here Pa can help introduce me."

"You do realize Pa isn't like he used to be? He's better than when I found him, but I still watch him carefully when it comes to drinking. He's always one bottle away from being the town drunk again."

"I'm not sure I agree, but even without Pa, there's you. Eligible young men are more likely to call with a successful father or brother to act as a broker. And I miss Pa."

"He'll be glad to hear that, but be aware, he may fail you. And would you trust me after what happened?"

"I've seen enough of what the war did to men. You weren't yourself. I've forgiven you."

Will felt a weight lift from his shoulders, the guilt of years. If she forgave him, perhaps he could begin to forgive himself. Maybe peace would really come this Christmas. Will reached over and squeezed her hand.

They reached the cabin, and he helped both women down. Robert must have heard the horses because the cabin door flung open and he came out to hug his daughters and help with the luggage. Will tended the horses, leading them to their stalls with grain, then went back to his family. As he looked at them in the warm cabin, his eyes grew moist. Family. It was more than a word—it was something he thought he might never have again.

The next day, Hiram and Julia arrived from Fort Worth. The family was complete.

***

Will had to use the sleigh to get his family to town. They squeezed in together, Robert driving. Hiram and Julia joined them, and the laughter never stopped as Hiram pretended to be *jultomte,* the Swedish version of Santa Claus, asking each of them what they wanted for Christmas.

"And you, little girl," said Hiram, turning to Julia, "I know what you want for Christmas, or you wouldn't have baked those gingerbread cookies . . ."

"Hiram!"

"I think your brother and sister want the same thing."

"Whatever do you mean, Hiram?" asked Albinia

"Why, babies, of course. In Sweden, gingerbread cookies are known to increase babies coming!"

Julia turned red, and the rest laughed.

"I think I'm safe," said Will. "Mary and I aren't married yet."

"Same here," said Lydia. "Now if Santa wants to wrap up a handsome young man, I'll be happy to unwrap him."

Hiram laughed. "I'll see what we can do. Meanwhile, we had best reform our manners, lest the Kings think us too coarse."

The sleigh pulled up at the King's house, festively decorated with garlands and candles in the windows. A groom took the horses, and the Crump family tumbled into the warmth of the house.

Ann came to greet them, with Mary discreetly in the background.

"Welcome, everyone! I haven't seen some of you for a very long time. Mrs. Johannsen, you look radiant—the weather brings out the blush in your complexion. Mrs. Jenkins is lovely as ever. And who is this? It can't be Lydia. You've grown into a beautiful young woman. Hiram, Robert, good to see you again. And of course, Will. Mary has been pacing for hours."

"I'm glad to see you all," said Mary, taking particular care, Will noticed, to include Albinia. "It's been such a long time since we've been together, and family is important. I hope we can all join in celebrating the birth of our Savior and rekindling our friendships. Won't you come and sit by the fire? There's hot cider and cakes."

Will noticed that Mary was wearing the necklace he had given her. His heart soared. When David came in, he shook Will's hand heartily and seemed unusually cheerful.

"I am extremely happy to see all of you. My, what a family! I'm afraid I didn't get to know you well in Indiana, but God has brought us all here. Mary, would you lead us in a few carols on the pianoforte?"

Mary played and sang the new *"What Child is This?"* song, and then repeated it for everyone. They sang several more carols until the maid came and announced dinner. David sat at the head of the table, with Mary on his left and Ann on his right. Will thought it a good sign that he was placed next to Mary.

David prayed, and then everyone began passing dishes. Two servants hovered in the background to assist as necessary.

"I understand you've been able to link up the railroad line from the north to the Texas and Pacific, Mr. Johannsen," said David.

"Yes, sir," said Hiram. "With the kind assistance of your bank, we can commence shipments this week. I think the community will appreciate the coal from the north with this hard winter."

"Excellent! It seems many other railroads did not fare as well. Our bank has been hard-pressed." David frowned and wiped his mouth with a napkin.

Hiram spoke again, "We're surviving, sir, but only just. Gould's control of the Missouri Pacific and the Texas and Pacific means that any freight bound for the Gulf or the west must pay his tariff, which is just short of ruinous." Hiram took another sip of cider. "I must say I don't want Santa to leave him even a bag of coal."

"He refuses to use local banks, always using the New Yorkers to finance. It certainly doesn't help either of us," David agreed.

Ann cleared her throat. "David, I'm sure the business is fascinating to some, but perhaps, as it's Christmas, it could be deferred to another time? I'm sure Lydia and Albinia, at least, have other topics of interest."

"Yes, yes, forgive me, my dear. How is your church and school, Mrs. Jenkins?"

"Peter has done wonders with it. The church now boasts three hundred members, about half of them black. The school has graduated forty, and two have gone on to Oberlin. Almost all the children can read and write and know the Twenty-Third Psalm. Olivia, Luther's sister, was a great help while she was there, but her family needed her. I understand they are in Topeka now."

"Yes," said Julia. "The railroad could no longer pay them. It may go hard with them this winter as so many lose their jobs. But horses always need new shoes, and farm equipment breaks, so I suppose they will make out all right."

The dinner progressed, and Ann suggested they take dessert in the parlor. Mary stayed to help and supervise the maids.

Will presented his gifts, and the Pachelbel canon tinkled in the parlor as the music box played. All the women admired Mary's new shoes. Mary had gotten Will a new pocketknife, and Robert a new stickpin. Albinia and Lydia had hand-embroidered scarves for the women, and pocket handkerchiefs for the men. Everyone seemed pleased.

After another hour of conversation and dessert, the Crumps began to take their leave.

"Merry Christmas to all!" said Will.

Mary followed them out to the veranda. Will lagged behind the others while Robert got the horses, which gave them a moment.

Mary gave him a quick hug. "I appreciate everything. I loved the necklace for my birthday, and today the shoes, and the music box. I love you, Will."

"I love you, Mary. Being with you was the only gift I needed, but I'll treasure the pocketknife."

***

Will insisted on driving the sleigh back to the farm. The family was full of Christmas cheer, singing, and laughing. No one seemed to notice him being quiet.

The clopping sound of the horse hooves on the icy road played a rhythm in his brain. Marriage...it was suddenly very real. Was that what Will wanted? Was he ready at last to settle down and find peace? The questions circled in his mind like two cats chasing each other around a table, scratching and hissing. He almost missed a landmark turn in the dim moonlight. He shook himself. What else? Why should he be afraid to be happy? Hadn't the time with Mary been wonderful? Everything had gone well, hadn't it?

By the next morning, his jitters hadn't abated.

"Will, what's wrong? It's Christmas, but you don't seem happy," said Robert. "Something bothering you?"

"I don't know. I should be happy, but I'm nervous. Mary told me that she loves me, and I told her the same. All seems well with her parents. Did you have questions before you married?"

"Not the first time. But the second, marrying your ma? I did wonder if I could handle it if something happened to her, like with my first wife."

"Maybe that's my problem. After losing Dove... How

did you get past it?"

"To tell the truth, I think being widowed hurt so much that I was looking for any way out. I knew marrying again was risking the same kind of pain, but your ma, well, I don't have to tell you how special she was. She gave me hope. I never thought I would outlive her. And when she died, obviously I didn't handle it very well. But I don't regret trying again, not a single minute of it. With Mary, from what I've seen, that girl loves you. If you love her, then you'd better fight for her. Get over your demons. Reach for hope and don't let go—the sooner, the better. When you've got your head right, talk to David. You wouldn't want to lose her, right?"

"No. But what if—"

"The time for *what if* is over. If you love the girl, if you think she's God's choice for you, get after her."

Lydia came in from outside.

"This looks serious. It's Christmas. Who died?"

"It's nothing, just some jitters about Mary," said Will.

"You can't be serious. You'd be an idiot to lose that woman," said Lydia.

"What if her father won't say yes? What if she won't?"

"Never mind *what if*, just do it. A girl can hardly resist a man who loves her and wants her forever."

"You think so? What if she heard about the gun incident? Mary hates guns."

"I'll never tell her. It's in the past. So? What are you waiting for?"

"You're probably right. Mary has shown nothing but love for me. I'm being silly."

***

Will prayed and thought and decided—it was time. He knew some couples had long engagements after accepting a proposal, but he and Mary had already been courting for over three years. He knew she loved him, but if there was to be a refusal, now was the time to find out. He stopped by Lange's jewelers again and picked out a ring. Then he headed purposefully to David's office.

Will had dressed in his best. He'd been less nervous at the battle of Shiloh. He figured he wouldn't be turned away at the bank since he was a depositor and his mission could be business, but it wasn't.

After sitting in an anteroom for half an hour, a clerk told him that Mr. King would see him. Thankfully Mary wasn't working that day. At least she wouldn't be curious.

Will entered the back office with frosted glass on the windows and waited to be acknowledged.

"Will, come in and have a seat. What can I do for you?"

"Well, sir, I'll get right to the point. I know you love your daughter. So do I. I have always been rather awkward with women, not knowing exactly what to do or say. I want

226

you and Mrs. King to know how much I value Mary and your family."

"I'd like to give this to Mary." He pulled out a small white velvet box and opened it to show a gold ring with a circular blue diamond in the center surrounded by small white diamonds. Will waited for a reaction, heart pounding.

"Impressive, young man. And not cheap. However, as your banker, I know you still have adequate funds. Is this an engagement ring? Hmm. This will take some thought and prayer. I think it best to take a little time and talk to Ann, without giving away your intentions. I think Mary has been expecting it."

David continued, "It's not as though you can buy my daughter or my regard, you understand. The main issue is your regard for her heart and how well you will protect her. Do I make myself clear?"

"Yes, sir. I will always protect her. If your decision is favorable, I would like to invite you all to the ranch for a meal and ice skating. I could propose and give her the ring then."

"I'll send word after I talk to Ann."

Will walked back to the livery, and rode Dusty home, alternating between fear and elation.

Within two days, Will received a message from David. He and Ann were giving their blessing and would come out to the ranch for the proposal. Will scurried to make arrangements, enlisting his sisters' aid. He wanted everything to be perfect. The pond was frozen solid. He'd laid in supplies of chocolate, and Lydia baked a few cakes.

The Kings arrived in their carriage, and Will welcomed them out of the cold. Lydia, Albinia, and Robert were already there, and the cabin buzzed with lively conversation. After an hour, he heard another horse and hurried out to meet the visitor.

"If you'd all join me outside with your ice skates, I've hired Amos here to fiddle while we skate," said Will.

"If I jig on your ice, I'll punch a hole in it," said Mary.

"I'll ask him to play slowly. Something like '*Laughing Eyes of Blue.*'"

"I don't know that one, but I'll try," said Mary.

They all moved outside, and as they glided on the ice, the fiddler began. Amos slowed the tempo, and the couples held hands while Albinia kept Robert company since he couldn't skate with his missing foot. Lydia spun and bobbed on the ice, with her imaginary partner, stopping as Will began to sing to Mary:

"I know a little maiden fair and young,

the most bewitching creature in the village.

Her face is like a garden of flowers new-sprung,

and she dwells within a little cottage.

There may be maidens just as fair,

with bright and winning ways,

but none have eyes so lovely,

such a sweet bewildering gaze.

Yes! She is a beauty, so loving kind, and true,

and the only girl to suit me, with laughing eyes of blue.

One day we're walking side by side,

I never can forget the look she gave me . . ."

Will looked Mary directly in the eye, then spun on the ice to a kneeling position, continuing to sing,

"Twas when I asked her would she be my bride,

She smiled and said . . ."

Will paused and looked up at Mary, holding out the ring he had purchased for her.

Mary put her hand in front of her mouth, surprised as he knelt before her. He put every ounce of love and longing he could into the gaze until she nodded. "With all my heart, Will." He stood and put the ring on her finger. It fit snugly, but not too tight. He opened his arms, and she melted into them, parents looking on smiling.

Everyone was excited about the engagement. Albinia decided her mission was complete, seeing her brother safely engaged. It was time to go home.

At the train station, Albinia turned to her sister.

"Are you sure you won't come, Lydia?"

"Yes, I'm settled on it. Maybe I will go back east again someday, but for now I want to stay with Pa and Will. I'll try my luck in Texas."

They embraced, and more hugs were exchanged with Will, Pa, and Mary, who had come to see her off.

"Remember me to Peter," said Mary, "and tell him how happy I am here."

"I will. Do come and see us if ever you can. Let us know when the wedding will be."

Albinia got on the train, and they waved until it pulled from   the   station.

Chapter 9

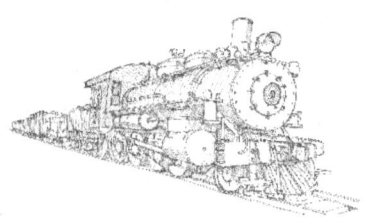

Topeka, September 1876

Luther wiped the sweat away from his head. The stifling heat beat down, and the forge glowed. He couldn't imagine autumn around the corner. Sighing, he picked up a hammer and worked on flattening the iron that was to be a mechanical corn planter. He'd heard about the design and had written to the patent office to get plans and a license. He was surprised to find the patent holder was another black man from forty years prior. They sure never had machines like this when he was at the Clay plantation in Kentucky. He turned the iron, pounded two more strokes, and saw a man in the doorway to the shop. He was about done with that piece anyway, so he plunged it into the water to cool, laid down the hammer, and cleaned his hands on his apron.

Luther walked over to the doorway, and in better light, he could see the man was black, with a triangular brand mark on his right cheek. The man wore a long black coat, even in the heat, a slouch hat, and a clerical collar.

"Afternoon, Reverend. What can I do for you?"

"I'm Reverend Simon Roundtree. Someone told me that you and your family here know most of the black folks around and that you're originally from Lexington, Kentucky."

Luther frowned and moved back toward the forge. "Somebody talks too much."

Luther picked up the hammer again and heated an iron bar in the forge.

"Is it true?"

Luther turned toward him. "Yes, sir, it is. But I don't much like talking about the slave days. I know we are free now, but I still look over my shoulder, 'specially round white folks. I have been betrayed by black folks too. My sister died because of it. Makes a man wary."

Simon pointed to his cheek. "Think I don't know? I understand that. But what if I told you that you got a chance to come to the Promised Land, to freedom, own your land, answer to nobody?"

Luther set the hammer down again. "I'm listening."

"I'm partners with a white man named William Hill. We're platting out a town in western Kansas. A colored town. I'm from Dry Lick, Kentucky, north of Lexington and Georgetown. I pastor the Mount Olivet church there."

Luther stroked his chin. "How many people has this town got?"

Simon said, "Well, ain't got any right now."

"And where is this town with nobody?"

"Almost fifty miles north of Fort Hays. And before you ask, thirty-five miles north of Ellis and the railroad. But the railroad is coming."

"I been out there. I worked the railroad. Ain't nothin' out there but a hell hole with jackrabbits in the summer and frozen wasteland in the winter."

"There may be nothin' there now, but think—a black town! We could start everything from scratch. Real freedom! And everything will change when the railroad comes through. Businesses, easy shipping for crops, and the land is good."

"Mm-hmm. I've wanted somethin' like that, but it sounds like freedom to starve. I hear you, but I can't see how it could succeed. For the railroad to come, you gotta raise money and pay for building a depot. There are no trees for wood. That's gonna take a lot of people."

"That's where you come in. I have families back in Lexington that will jump at the chance to get land. But they'll have to come on the train, not by wagon. They won't be able to bring much. A few will bring horses and plows, but not many. They'll need tools made—plows, planters, all kinds of farm equipment, just like what you're making there."

Luther chuckled. "And I s'pose these black families are flowing with cash to pay for all these things."

"No, no, they ain't. But God will provide, just like when Moses led the Israelites to the Promised Land."

Luther raised an eyebrow. "I seem to recall those Israelites near died of thirst and starvation, not to mention Egyptians. I read the Good Book. And I've fought the Cheyenne."

"Sure, the Israelites had to fight against a whole bunch of kings, but ain't we been fighting our whole lives? Fight the white man to keep your family together, to learn to read—that's how I got this!" He pointed at the brand on his face. "White man decided I got too smart for my own good, or at least for *his* good. Fighting for food, the right to walk down the street without someone saying, 'Hey, black boy, pick that up.' We didn't ask to come to this country, but we're here. We're full citizens by the law. Now we just got to make folks respect us and show what we can do. This black man gonna get free and work to enjoy all the good Lord gives. What about you?"

Luther considered, pounding a few strokes. "Folks here in Topeka sure don't respect a black man. Let's say me and my family go with you. What about this white man, this Hill fella? How do you know he ain't gonna just steal you blind, leave you in the wilderness with nothin'?"

"I do have papers for the land. Each family pays Hill five dollars for the land and opportunity. It's all the white folks had when they came to America and more than we've had in a century. If you come back with me to Lexington, just for a time, you can help convince families to come. You've been around there. You know what it's like. You can testify."

"Let me think it over. I'll talk to Ruth and my in-laws. My father-in-law is a blacksmith too Getting a little old, but he taught me everything I know. Come by the house for supper tomorrow." Luther picked up a pencil and scribbled the address, handing it to Simon. "They can meet you, and we can decide."

***

Luther strolled to his rented house that night, in no hurry to reach home.

"Lord, who is this man? Is he really your preacher? Is this You leading us? I need somethin', Lord. I swore I'd never go back to Kentucky again. My old master Jameson, who was also my pa—he's dead. He got what he deserved. Who do I even know there now?"

He kicked a rock down the dusty street, hands shoved in his pockets, brow lined with thought.

"I hear you, Lord. Like Isaac, you're saying, 'Don't take your family back there.' I won't. I couldn't bear for somethin' to happen to my children or Ruth. Ruth ain't never seen a slave state, just that rattlesnake that kidnapped us and what he did to my ma. She doesn't need to risk more. There's a lot of good white folks, like the Crumps, but there's a lot of bad ones. Even Hiram and Julia left us high and dry with no job. I worked hard to get this shop started, beginning again. Do I walk away from that? For what?"

The moon came out, but the wind picked up, blowing in more heat from the west. The clouds in that direction were dark, and a fork of lightning split the sky, thunder following a minute later. He'd best get home before the storm. Ruth might send someone looking for him. He stopped briefly at Ned's and asked Ned and Katy to come by after supper to talk.

Luther opened the door to bright noisy confusion at his own home and choruses of "Papa." It was his favorite part of the day, aside from snuggling with Ruth after the kids were asleep.

Supper was ready, one of Ruth's sweet potato casseroles. He listened with one ear to all the events of the day with Lindy and the other children, his mind still dwelling on the proposal from Reverend Roundtree. After clearing up and putting the children to bed, he heard Ned knock at the door.

"C'mon in! I think Ruth's got some coffee and corn fritters."

"Won't say no to that."

Ned and Katy sat at the table, coffee in hand.

"You got somethin' on your mind, son?"

"I do, and that's for sure. You know how we been moving around like a hound dog nobody wants since I got kicked out of Indiana. We're back to having a business here in Topeka—we're not getting rich, but we're getting by. A black gentleman, Reverend Simon Roundtree from Lexington, Kentucky, came to see me today. Seems he and a white man are starting a town in western Kansas—a town of black people, for black people. For five dollars a family, you get a share in the land and a chance to be free, with no white folks to control. He's looking for our help to recruit other black folks. He says the town is going to need black-smiths because when the people come from Kentucky on the train, they ain't gonna have the farm equipment with them that they need."

Luther took a swig of coffee and bit into a fritter, let-ting his words sit a spell, like an old woman with an arthrit-ic hip, rocking and thinking.

Ruth spoke first, "He wants all of us to up and move to this new town? Our children? Ma and Daddy?"

"That's what he says. But there's more—he wants me to go back to Lexington with him. He says this Kansas town is the Promised Land, and he wants me to come and witness to the folk in Kentucky. He thinks it's safe now."

Ned rubbed his chin. "And what do you think? You know we've had some trouble here in Topeka, people look-ing down on us, trying to make us leave. Would this just be giving in? If we've had that trouble here in a free state, how is it safe for you to go back to a state where you was a slave?"

"That's what I am thinking. But I have also been praying on it. The Lord just won't let it go. We talked about having our own place, maybe a black town. What if Round-tree is a Moses, leading our people to the Promised Land? It's not like Topeka has made us welcome."

Luther stood and paced as he talked, moving his hands to punctuate his words. "It ain't like they gonna put me in chains."

Katy spoke, "That's true, they can't do that. But the Klan might put a noose around your neck. They won't like black folk getting free. In the last year or so, the Klan has ridden every night over Kentucky county towns, spreading terror wherever they go by robbing, whipping, raping, and killing our people, just for being free and black. It was in the papers—a group in Frankfort sent a delegation to Congress."

"But don't you see? That's why black folks got to get out, to find their own place, away from the Klan. I know it sounds crazy, but what if there's a chance, a chance at real freedom? We got most of the money from Colorado still to help see us through. We're used to living with not much, good weather and bad. We've been here several years. We know freedom isn't going to happen here. Living on the Kansas plains couldn't be worse than that slave cabin on Jameson's plantation, could it?"

Ned shook his head doubtfully. "I can't speak to that. Let's pray and think on it. I'll trust you to do the right thing. If you go to Kentucky, I'll watch over Ruth and the children for you."

They bent their heads in prayer. When they finished, Luther and Ruth looked at each other and nodded.

"I think we should go. We have to give it a chance," said Ruth.

"I'll have to trust God and Roundtree that nothin' will happen to me in Kentucky. We have to persuade people to move and tell the whites to let our people go."

***

Luther endured the long train ride back to Lexington. It stirred mixed feelings. In some ways, it felt like coming home. Yet the memories of plantation life and the long escape journey, hiding and running to gain freedom, came back like a nightmare. It was hard to shake the feeling that he needed to hide.

Train travel was uncomfortable at best, but traveling as a black man, consigned to one car with hard board seats, a chamber pot, and no way to get food, made the journey more unpleasant. Many of the depots didn't even have a colored waiting room.

When Luther arrived at the Mount Olivet Baptist church the next morning, word must have spread that something unusual was happening. It seemed people had come from miles around. The white-framed churchyard had more buggies than he could count and twenty saddle horses tied to hitching posts. People of all ages were standing in little knots, talking. When Simon Roundtree dismounted and tied his buggy to a hitching post, it was like Moses parting the Red Sea. People moved back on both sides, creating an aisle to the door, with a chorus of respectful "Good Mornings."

Once he passed, everyone followed inside. Luther heard a few whisperings about who the young buck with Simon was. Simon smiled and greeted folks, stopping at this one and that, asking a question, and playing a game for a child to guess which hand held candy. Several parents greeted him with respect.

Being new, Luther took a seat near the back. When everyone in the crowded church was seated, Simon mounted the pulpit.

"Good morning!"

When the response was too light, he said, "I said good morning, y'all! Still asleep in your bed? Well wake up and praise the Lord! We got freedom to thank Him for!"

"That's right," responded the congregation.

"We got the time and the freedom to meet here, brothers and sisters, to praise and lift Him up! The Bible says in First Thessalonians 5:16-18: "Rejoice always, pray continually, give thanks in all circumstances; for this is God's will for you in Christ Jesus." Sister, will you come and lead us in a song?"

A pretty young black woman in a simple calico frock came forward and nodded to the woman at the organ, beginning a clapping rhythm and singing:

"In that great gettin' up mornin'

Fare ye well, fare ye well

In that great gettin' up mornin'

Fare ye well, fare ye well

In that great gettin' up mornin'

Fare ye well, fare ye well

In that great gettin' up mornin'

Fare ye well, fare ye well

When you see the moon a'bleedin

Fare ye well, fare ye well

When you hear the rumblin' thunder

Fare ye well, fare ye well . . ."

It was a new one for Luther, but he caught on, singing and clapping with the others. The joy was infectious.

Roundtree resumed his talk.

"The moon bleeding—we know that means the last times, according to Joel, right before we all go to heaven. Being with the Lord, now that's real freedom. But sometimes, down here on earth, the good Lord opens the doors and leads His people out, like Moses out of Egypt. Sometimes you got to get ready, like putting blood on the doors before the angel of death passes by."

"C'mon," said the congregation.

"Question is, when the Lord calls, are you gonna be

awake? Or you gonna be sleeping doing just like you always done? Are you gonna be faint of heart and turn back to slavery because you are afraid of what might happen?"

"No, sir, we ain't afraid," they said.

"That's good 'cause love drives out fear, and fear is the opposite of faith. How did the Israelites get across that Red Sea? Shaking in their boots?"

"No, sir! Singing and shouting, that's right!"

"God went before them, He open a way. Some want to turn back, but when that sea open, they go walking on through."

"Hallelujah!"

"I want y'all to hear me now—God's calling you today."

"C'mon."

"Right now, He's calling you to pick up your children and march out to freedom, out to the Promised Land in Kansas."

"Mm-hmm."

"I know you're thinking, Kansas? Ain't that like Nazareth? Ain't nothin' good ever come from there. But can you trust God if He's calling?"

"Sure can!"

"All right, then, the sermon's a little different today.

I've seen good farmland, nobody on it. Mr. Hill there," Simon pointed, and Hill stood with a little bow, "he will help any family that wants to go, get to a new town, a black town, in Kansas, with land all your own. No more paying the massa. No more giving up your hard-earned crops. You pay five dollars a family, once, and you own your land free and clear."

"Sounds good!"

"Do you like being Jim Crow? Do you want your children told they can't go to school or vote?"

"No!"

"Here's what you got to do—you pray. Yes, sir, I said pray! And you ask God about signing up to go to Kansas. One week from now, we gonna walk up to Sadieville and climb on the train to freedom. That's just an eleven-mile stroll. Think about doing that twenty years ago, with patrols on the roads! My family's going. Any questions, you can ask Mr. Hill here or my friend in the back, Luther. He's been there and is taking his family. Luther was on the Clay plantation before the war—he knows. May the Lord bless our journey."

There was a buzz in the crowd, and then someone started to sing.

"Oh, freedom, oh, freedom

Oh freedom over me
And before I'd be a slave
I'd be buried in my grave
And go home to my Lord and be free
Oh, freedom . . ."

Luther circulated among the people as the service broke up, answering questions. He gave truthful answers, not minimizing how hard life on the plains could be, but not wanting to discourage too many, he answered only what was asked.

By the end of the day, over three hundred had signed up with Hill, committing to travel west to the Kansas Promised Land.

Chapter 10

Fort Worth, 1876

Julia shoveled more coal into the potbellied stove and pulled her shawl tighter around her. Ice formed on the windows, inside and out. Julia thought about their financial limitations and the economy—how had they gotten so low? She and Hiram couldn't afford to keep the rented rooms at a comfortable temperature. In the last three years, more than eighty railroads had gone bankrupt. The Panic of 1873, they were calling it, but it wasn't over yet. They'd had to sell the remaining steamships for a song. It was hard to find buyers because the steamer traffic had given way to the railroads. With the railroads not operating at capacity, unemployment went as high as fourteen percent. No one had money to buy the goods they shipped. Nationwide deflation struck. They couldn't charge enough for freight to keep things going.

She needed to get the water heated for supper and hot coffee for Hiram when he came home. Her house gown had a few burned spots from tending the fire, but it couldn't be helped. Another train might come today on their newly constructed Fort Worth line, and if it did, coal would be more plentiful. She held her hands out to the stove to warm them and then set about cutting up the few potatoes they had to make soup. If they could only ship some cattle north, there would be enough money to pay the workers for another month. Hiram, bless him, had convinced new workers to toil without pay on the promise of payment at the end of the month. After all their years of prosperity, it was embarrassing to be so dependent on others.

She was wondering what to put with the potatoes when she heard a knock. Who would come to see her in the middle of the day? She hoped something hadn't happened to Hiram.

He swung a hammer these days more often than managing a crew. She wiped her hands on her apron, tucked an errant strand of hair into her bun, and answered the door.

"Lydia! How nice to see you. What brings you out this far? Come in out of the cold."

"Thank you, I was afraid my fingers would break off like icicles. It's only two hours to here on the train from Dallas."

Lydia came in and took a seat on the secondhand couch.

"I came to offer you some salt pork. Will slaughtered a pig recently, but there's too much for us to eat in a reasonable time. He thought you might want some."

Julia saw through the transparent lie, but she was grateful. "Thank you. It will liven up the soup I'm making. Hiram should be home in a few hours if you'd care to stay."

"Oh no, I wouldn't dream of imposing. But I do have some news. Normally I'd tell Albinia, but she's so far away . . ."

"Good news, I hope. I've had an oversupply of the other kind of late."

"Yes, good news. I've met a young man, George Sceafors. I never thought I would, but he's ever so handsome and kind. And he makes me laugh! He's a butcher, but he has three shops, and his business is growing, even in this economy. After all, people still have to eat."

"Did Pa introduce you?"

"Yes, in a way. Pa and Will wanted to feature fresh meat at the store, so they hired George to butcher cows and pigs. I met him at the store."

"Seems love is in the air, with Will and Mary's wedding coming up, and now you have heart anxiety. Sounds like a good solid man. I'm happy for you."

"I've never quite felt this way. I can't stop thinking about him, wondering what he's doing now, whether he might come to the store, or whether I can find an excuse to see him."

Julia smiled for the first time in weeks. "I envy you. It wasn't like that so much for Hiram and me. We love each other now, but in the beginning . . . I just wanted a rich man, and he seemed to care for me. It felt more like a business deal than a romance, except for that magical picnic Hiram put together. Now we're finding out about that 'richer or poorer' part of our wedding vows. At least I think that was in there somewhere—it was all in Swedish."

"That must have been confusing. The main reason for my visit is that George is wondering if you and Hiram would be willing to try one of those new refrigerated train cars to ship meat to other cities. It would help him expand his market. He would buy the first one, and if it's a success, you could go halves on two more. All the risk would be his to start with."

"I don't know what to say. We have so little now. We're barely hanging on to the railroad. I'll have to talk with Hiram and get some figures on the cost of the cars, as well as understand more about how this refrigeration works."

"You know more about business than I do, but George seems to think that instead of shipping the cows, which can lose weight, get sick, and have to be fed, you can just ship the already butchered meat, as long as it can be kept fresh. The cars are well-insulated and packed with ice. He seems to think even New York or Boston would be possible."

"Smart and handsome too, eh? When's the wedding?"

Lydia turned scarlet. "Don't be silly, Julia. We're just friends at this point. I hardly know him."

"Does Pa like him?"

"They do seem to get along well, except he's Methodist."

"Shouldn't pose a problem. And I don't believe the *just friends* part for a minute. In the old days, I would have thrown a grand dinner and invited you two."

"It's not necessary. Besides, he'll be traveling to Detroit

soon to look at the new cars."

"Well, bless you, Sister! He sounds divine, and thank you for thinking of us."

"Shall I have him come round, maybe meet Hiram, when he returns?"

"Yes, please."

"Well, I must be getting back to the farm before the storm blows in."

"Thank you for caring and coming. Not a short trip from Dallas. It means a great deal to me. I haven't always treated you well, being a bossy older sister."

Julia could see Lydia's face struggle between tears and laughter. The tears won out.

"You were always a rock when I needed one. When Albinia was in jail and when Ma was sick, you were some-one I could count on. When I was difficult, you told me so—and I needed it. With Ma not here anymore, I know if I need someone, you're always there."

Lydia came round the table, and Julia stood. The sisters hugged, and in their embrace, the years they had been sepa-rated melted away.

Julia shifted uncomfortably, taking another drink of water as she and Hiram sat at their Lone Star restaurant table. She wondered what Lydia's beau would be like, whether he would measure up, or whether her sister's love had given her unrealistic hopes.

"What do you think, Hiram? Is this going to be worth it?"

"I don't know, dearest. But I can't see that we have anything to lose by listening."

George and Lydia arrived at the restaurant, looking around for Hiram and Julia. Lydia spotted them and waved.

George was medium height, balding in front, with black hair and a mustache, slightly plump, with laugh lines at the corners of his eyes, a head taller than Lydia. Julia thought him handsome, though middle-aged.

"Julia, Hiram, this is George Sceafors, the friend I told you about. He wanted to meet you and explain his idea for shipping meat to eastern markets."

"Pleased to meet you, sir," said Hiram, standing and shaking his hand. "We're very interested in this idea."

"And anxious to meet the gentleman that Lydia has gushed about," said Julia.

"Julia! Pay no attention to my sister, she only wants the details," said Lydia, blushing.

George smiled, and everyone was seated.

"Thank you for meeting with me. Your sister is a lovely young woman, Mrs. Johannsen. I hope to talk more with your father soon, so that we may improve our acquaintance. Do any of you like oysters? I hope you will try some from the menu here today. I was able to arrange a shipment in my one refrigerated car from Baltimore here to the Lone Star. But it is difficult to find railroads that will allow the car, I have discovered. That is why I think a partnership could be beneficial to both of us."

"Difficult? How?" asked Julia.

George smiled and turned toward her. "Lydia has told me of your business acumen, Mrs. Johannsen—quite admirable in a woman. I will be open with you: I approached Gould's Missouri-Texas line first, but they are unwilling. I discovered other railroads that have invested too much in building stockyards, and loading and offloading facilities for cattle—that would all be unnecessary if the idea of refrigerated cars took hold. They hope to prevent it by not allowing the cars to attach to their trains. I heard some of your difficulties and decided to risk throwing my lot in with you if you are willing. I need railroad partners. You need beef and the means to get it to market."

"You express my thinking exactly, sir," said Hiram. "But how do these cars work?"

"The one I have is on the Hammond design, a compartment at the top of the car and on both ends, it's packed with ice, and the walls are four inches thick, insulated. The current design hangs the carcasses in the air and lets the cold flow around them. The ice lasts up to four hundred miles, depending on conditions, and then is replenished from warehouses along the route. Mr. Swift of the Chicago stockyards and Swift Meat Company has also been interested, and with his investment, we are experimenting with other methods that would allow the meat to be in layers on the floor. There was one unfortunate incident in the early experiments where a car derailed due to the weight of the meat swinging on the hooks. I believe we've solved that with ballast, but the Swift idea would allow a tighter pack and higher profits. And it is naturally colder on the floor of the car."

"It sounds genius but complicated," said Julia.

"Not really," said George. "There will be refinements, but the basic idea is the same as your icebox."

"And our investment is simply to allow the cars to hook up to our trains?"

"Initially, yes. You can become more involved by taking a stake in the cars and the profits as you begin to see the benefits. The risk is primarily mine. We can work out a discount freight schedule and timetable."

Julia and Hiram looked at each other with barely suppressed excitement. Lydia's smirk of pride all but broadcast, "I told you so."

"Mr. Sceafors—" began Hiram.

"George, call me George. If we're to be in business together, formality is unnecessary."

"And I am Hiram. George, we accept. And thank you for coming to us. We admit we are looking for an escape from Gould's ever-tightening noose. A business independent of him, outside his control, is exactly what we need."

The waiter came.

"Have you decided on your orders?"

George looked around, and Hiram nodded.

"I think we'll all have some of those marvelous Baltimore oysters that came in on the train," said George.

***

Hiram gazed at the warehouse with satisfaction. The meat scheme with Lydia and her beau was bringing new life to their business, much-needed capital. Sceafors had brokered a partnership with George Hammond in Detroit. Hammond held the patent for the railroad cars, Sceafors supplied the beef, and with the new capital, Hiram supplied the rolling stock and the railroad routes. They had a business outside the clutches of Jay Gould—at least for the moment. Hiram was meeting with Gould today, under a flag of truce, to negotiate. Gould had invited him, saying he had a proposal.

The Panic still gripped the country, but people had to eat, and it seemed they had an appetite for Texas beef. The warehouse had cold rooms that preserved the beef, and with refrigerated cars, people in Boston could be enjoying Hammond steaks within a few days of the time of slaughter. The business was booming.

Julia handled renting the warehouse. Hiram thought it fitting that she be in charge, cutting Lydia in on the profits since she had brought the meat business potential to their attention and provided the connection to Sceafors.

That left the problem of their struggling railroad interests. Hiram would have loved to get revenge on Gould for his ruthless business style which had led to Hiram losing the Kansas Pacific, but it would be suicide. Gould was too big, and an all-out war would bankrupt them. Gould had the lawyers, the connections, and, even after the Credit Mobilier scandal, access to more capital than they could muster. Hiram and Julia would have to deal. After selling out of the Kansas Pacific, he and Julia were left with an interest in the AT&SF. Recently, after paying down debts, he'd taken a part in the "Katy," as the Missouri, Kansas, and Texas Railway was known. Connecting to the AT&SF gave the new line a solid connection to the east. The AT&SF wasn't on solid ground yet, but it was headed there. Hiram was still nervous, and his meeting with Gould today was very different from the one in Kansas City years ago.

He straightened his tie and went out to his horse. Julia had not been invited to this meeting. Gould had made it clear that it was business, men only. Hiram hadn't recovered enough financially to have a carriage and a driver. Julia insisted on economizing until they were sure of solid growth. They'd prayed together this morning before he left, feeling like the lamb headed for the slaughter.

Mounted, he rode the two miles to Gould's ranch house, a temporary office for the tycoon. Even in his short time there, Gould had erected a stone fence with wrought-iron gates sporting a large golden *G* in the center, a message to visitors that they were entering the Gould kingdom.

Hiram knocked on the door, gave the maid his card, and seated himself uncomfortably on the too-small chairs in the hallway—Gould didn't even have an anteroom for guests. Hiram felt like a schoolboy sent to the headmaster's office.

Half an hour after the scheduled appointment time, the maid returned and escorted him into Gould's office.

"We meet again, Johannsen. Have a seat, though I don't think we'll be long," said Gould.

"You said you had a proposal to discuss."

"Yes. Thank you for being direct. No need to waste time with niceties. I'll do the same. The AT&SF isn't going to survive on its own long term. The UP is going to swamp it. Maybe not this year or next, but it will happen. I think you've lived to regret not joining me at the beginning. The Kansas Pacific would have died in a year if you hadn't sold. Now it is doing quite nicely."

Gould rose and unfurled a route map, pinning it to an easel beside the desk, and continued. "You can see the new proposed routes. And you can see how the Texas and Pacific is going to overtake the Katy."

"Not necessarily, but continue."

"Oh, it will happen, have no doubt. Dodge, my manager, is working out the details now. The Katy has been a thorn in his side. Here's my deal: I understand you've bought into a meat-packing business, using the Katy and the AT&SF to undercut Chicago competition on transportation costs using refrigerated cars. I admire that—initiative and smart business. I had the opportunity and should have taken it. However, I'm offering to leave that business alone, maybe even help it along. I'll also give you a ten-percent reduction in tariff rates for freight on the AT&SF and the Katy that connects to the Union Pacific or the Texas and Pacific." Gould pointed out the routes, let his hands drop with a smile, and resumed his seat, feet up on the desk.

"In return, you agree to stop expansion of the Katy, stop fighting the UP with the AT&SF, and sell a ten percent interest in the Katy to the UP."

"Ten percent now, and then you'll work to take over entirely, as you have with the other railroads, right?" Hiram's face reddened, and he felt like upending the desk into Gould's lap.

"Business is what it is. However, I can guarantee that you'll come out ahead."

"And if I refuse?"

"I'll destroy you, just as I would have destroyed the Kansas Pacific. And I'll get the AT&SF and the Katy anyway."

Hiram stood, hands clenched at his sides. His mind worked quickly, and he prayed silently. Julia would tell him to accept after their reverses over the past two years. But her comments from years past echoed in his mind: one is a snake, the other a wolf. The wolf was seated in front of him, licking his chops. Think, Hiram!

"I'd like to make a counter offer. We'll give a three-year moratorium on further expansion of the Katy and sell you a five-percent interest at today's closing price in New York so that you have no time to manipulate the stock. You give us a five-percent tariff reduction on freight to the east on any of your railroads and ten percent on meat in refrigerated cars. We pay you directly, not your companies, three percent of the annual profit of the meat-packing business. And no deal on the west and the AT&SF."

Gould leaned back and laughed, but there was no mirth in it. "You've got brass, I'll give you that. You're a fighter. I watched your steamboat line disappear into the Mississippi mud, just as we predicted, but you bounced back. You fought well with the Kansas Pacific. If it hadn't been for the war in Prussia and the Panic, you might have made it. The bridge over the Missouri River was genius. But you'll have to pay cash for everything. Credit in New York and overseas has dried up. I don't think you have the resources."

"I guess we'll find out," said Hiram.

"All right, tell you what—I'll accept your counteroffer and add that I won't buy more of the Katy for one year. It'll be worth it for the breathing room. I'll take a three-percent stake in your meat-packing business in lieu of the three percent in profits. Fair enough?"

Hiram didn't like it but saw no alternative. He didn't want to give Gould any ownership in the meat-packing business. It implied a loss of control and a much larger stake in the business than Hiram had offered. When he shook on the deal, he felt as though he was putting his hand in the wolf's mouth.

Chapter 11

Dallas, 1877

Mary could hardly believe it as her mother helped her to dress. It was here—her wedding day. She and Will were going to marry. Her wonderful, awkward, fun-loving Will, a master of practical jokes. It couldn't be seven years since he'd walked into the bank, could it? Most couples moved faster than they had. Will was impetuous in some things, but courting had required a great deal of her patience. He was a smart farmer and businessman, and there was no one else she'd rather have with her in times of trouble. She wouldn't think of potential problems—not today. He'd asked her to marry him on that frozen pond, and they both took it seriously, working out all the potential problems they could imagine in advance—children, money, family, church, and getting to know one another, how he liked to grab an idea and run with it, while she wanted prayer, planning, and consideration. Most couples had short courtships and longer engagements, but they had courted for six years and been engaged for one. They took care because both believed marriage was forever.

Ann buttoned the back of the ivory gown with its layers and drapes like flower petals overlapping each other, a rosette every foot at the hem surrounding the skirt. A white two-inch belt fit above Mary's hips at the waist, accentuating her breasts and the billowing floor-length skirt. The sleeves were short, ending above the elbow, with layers outlined in seed pearls. A floral pattern went up around the neck and split to go over each breast, with an opaque panel between the floral strips.

"What do you think? Am I ready?"

"As far as your dress goes, yes. You'll have to answer for your heart. But I know you love him."

"I do. I'm nervous, though. I want everything to be perfect, I want to be perfect for him, and yet I feel like I don't know anything about being married except what I've seen with you and Father."

"We may not be the best example, but we've had a lot

of good years. Trust God, talk to Him every day, and you'll do fine."

"Right now, aside from not tripping as I go down the aisle and remembering my vows, what worries me is tonight," she said, blushing. "I want to please him, but I don't know how. We've shared kisses, but no more than that over the last years."

"Listen to your heart. He's your husband. No need to worry or hold back."

Ann adjusted the veil and looked deep into her daughter's eyes. "I will always love you. You're a woman grown now, and it's time for you to take your place as a wife and a mother."

There was a knock at the door.

"Mrs. King, they're ready."

Mary took her bouquet from her bridesmaid outside the door—thank the Lord for early spring flowers—and walked to the rear of the sanctuary on her father's arm. She was surprised to see a tear escape his eye. David signaled the musicians at the front, violins, and cellos, and they began the walk to the altar with Pachelbel's Canon in D playing, just like her music box from Will. Mary looked ahead at Will, standing tall at the altar in a brown suit, vest, tie, and stickpin, a new chain for his pocket watch—but what she noticed most was his smile.

Mary was relieved she didn't trip walking down the aisle. Reverend Rogers, the new minister, smoothly went through the vows and prayers. Her niece and one of Albinia's sons were ring bearers and managed not to lose or drop them. As the minister came to the final vows, she struggled to keep from crying happy tears. This was it, this was the moment, this was the man she would wake up with for the rest of her life. She turned and faced him, hands clasped.

"Do you take this woman to be your wife?"

"I, Will Crump, take you, Mary King, to be my wife, and I do promise and covenant, before God and these witnesses, to be your loving and faithful husband in plenty and in want, in joy and in sorrow, in sickness and in health, as long as we both shall live."

Will's eyes spoke love and promise, and joy surged in her. He'd proven faithful all these years, and she couldn't imagine life without him. He slid the ring onto her finger.

"And do you take this man to be your lawfully wedded husband?"

"In the presence of God and these our friends, I take thee to be my husband, promising with divine assistance to be unto thee a loving and faithful wife so long as we both shall live." She slid a ring onto his hand.

"Then by the authority vested in me by the state of Texas, and God our Father, I pronounce you man and wife. Introducing Mr. and Mrs. William Crump!"

Will lifted Mary's veil and took her face in his strong hands, kissing her softly, once and then again. His eyes filled with longing, and she blushed, turning to face the congregation. She took Will's offered arm, and together they began walking to the rear of the church, smiling at friends as they went.

The pianist and strings started with Bach's first Brandenburg Concerto in F and then halfway down the aisle switched to a lively version of "Laughing Eyes of Blue." Mary almost laughed—it had to have been Will's doing. Life would never be dull with this practical jokester.

Will helped her into their buggy and drove to the hotel where the reception was planned. Her father had spared no expense. With one hundred guests and thirteen tables, a three-tiered cake adorned with white roses, miniature caladiums, asparagus fern, and lovers knots of silver cord, the reception included a menu with filets de boeuf à Napolitaine, green beans, lobster salad, and assorted pastries.

The musicians from the church found their way in, got set up again, and soon quiet chamber music filled the hall.

Will and Mary stood in the reception line, welcoming

guests with the Kings and Robert. Julia stood in for Will's mother as the eldest sister.

After the guests were seated and the waiters circulated serving food, Mary had an attack of the jitters and could barely swallow. She again thought of the night ahead, with a bit of nervous warmth.

The reception lasted two hours, with David and Robert giving humorous speeches. By the end, Mary was more than ready to get away and be alone with Will.

"Let's let them party on," Mary whispered in Will's ear. "I need some fresh air."

Will nodded, and they began their circuit of the tables, Will accepting congratulations as they said their goodbyes.

Will exchanged a handshake and heartfelt congratulations with Charlie Goodnight. Charlie had married. His wife, Molly, came from Kentucky. They had traveled to the wedding by train from Colorado. Charlie talked excitedly about possibly moving to northwest Texas or California.

"There's opportunity out there, Will. Come and see us sometime. I'll be back through here to wrap things up at the ranch, but we're moving west," said Charlie.

Molly exchanged greetings with Mary.

"How do you like Texas, Mrs. Goodnight?"

"Texas is all right for men and dogs, but it's hell on

women and horses!"

Mary laughed and promised to keep in touch.

They stopped at Albinia and Peter's table and exchanged hugs. When she reached Robert, she first curtsied to pay him respect but then responded to his bear hug. Mary hugged Julia and Lydia both at once. Then she watched Will go up the hotel stairs ahead of her, turning as she stopped to throw her bouquet to the waiting girls below. Lydia captured the flowers and looked very pleased. Mary waved and smiled, then turned up the stairs to where Will was waiting.

They entered the hotel room, and Mary saw that Ann had already laid out clothes for her. Even though they were married, it felt slightly scandalous to be alone with Will in a hotel room.

"Can you help me?" Mary asked, smiling. He fumbled with the buttons, ribbons, and other attachments of female clothing, helping her shed them down to her chemise. His whiskers tickled as he planted kisses on every inch of newly exposed flesh until she was laughing uncontrollably.

"Stop, you silly. We'll never get changed at this rate."

"I don't care if you don't," he said. "I want to enjoy you."

"But I do. I want that buggy ride you promised."

She folded the clothes and packed the wedding dress in

a garment bag while Will changed into his usual jeans and work shirt, hanging the finery in the wardrobe. She put on a light brown calico dress with pink floral decorations.

Mary noticed Will strapping on his Navy Colt pistol.

"Do we need that? It's our honeymoon."

Will hesitated, then left it behind.

Soon they were sneaking down a back staircase to avoid people from the wedding. Mary saw the buggy waiting outside and figured Will must have arranged to move it to the rear door.

The afternoon was bright and sunny with a hint of a spring breeze. The land was beginning to turn green after a long brown sleep. Will took the reins, and soon they were speeding across the prairie, laughing at nothing and everything.

Will began singing *"Molly Malone,"* substituting her name for Molly. She joined him on the choruses of *"Alive, Alive O."* It felt good to be alive, to be loved, to begin a new adventure.

They stopped along the Trinity, spreading a blanket over the prairie grass next to a tall cottonwood tree. Mary unpacked the picnic basket Albinia had left for them in the buggy. They lounged comfortably on a bed of moss, leaning against the tree, arms entwined as if they'd been doing it for years. She guessed in one sense they had, but never alone, unrestrained by convention.

Will looked over at her with a twinkle in his eye and stole a kiss about every five minutes.

After they finished eating and put the basket back in the buggy, Will said to her, "I want to do something, something I learned from an Indian friend. Will you trust me?"

Curious, she said, "Of course, what is it?"

He pulled a ringlet of hair free from her bun and cut it. "Now you do the same to me."

Unsure, she grabbed a lock of his hair and cut it, handing it to him.

"I'm going to mix our hair together, and we'll bury it. It's the Indian way of marriage. In the future, if one of us ever wants to break the marriage bond, we have to come back and find the hair and separate it. The Shoshone would have a third person bury it, but you'll have to trust me. Turn around so you won't see."

She turned around, but with one eye cracked open she could still see him as he dug in the dirt at the base of the tree and buried their hair.

"All right, turn around," said Will.

Mary thought it odd, but it touched her that he would think of such a thing to preserve their love.

"You needn't worry. I'll never leave you," said Mary.

She turned to him, wanting to give him everything, and Will embraced her, hugging her tight and drawing her into a long open-mouthed kiss that lit fires in her.

They broke apart for air and looked at each other with lights of love and longing. He took her hand, and they walked along the river as the sun set, golds, oranges, and reds blending in a prairie fireworks display of the wonders of God.

When they returned to where the horses stood with the buggy, the stars were beginning to show in the sky as twilight set in.

Mary looked over and said, "I guess we'd better be getting back to the hotel."

"And miss the light show God put in the sky for us? Why? Look around—there's no one for miles," said Will with an impish grin.

Will spread more blankets on the ground and invited her down beside him.

Mary couldn't imagine what he was thinking—surely not here, in the open! She felt both excited and uncomfortable at the same time but wanted to please her new husband. She tucked her skirts underneath, lying next to him. He fluffed up a coat as a pillow for her head. They lay quiet, watching the stars appear one by one as the sky turned from twilight blue to inky black, the large moon poking above the horizon.

Will rolled onto his side, kissing down the length of her neck, stroking her face and her breasts and drawing her to him. After a few minutes, they stood, shedding more clothing until they were naked in the moonlight, and lay down again.

Mary laughed self-consciously, breaking the tension.

"I don't know what to do," she admitted. "But I want you. I love you, Will."

"We'll figure it out together."

They did—hands everywhere, lips meeting and parting until she drew him into her, and their lovemaking increased in intensity, leaving them passionate and breathless. When it was over, he tenderly covered her, and they rested together in each other's arms beneath the starlit sky.

***

April 1876

Will stretched and rubbed the sleep from his eyes. After a few weeks, they had settled into a new rhythm of living, adjusting to each other, Mary getting used to life on the ranch instead of in town. Robert and Lydia had moved back into the apartment over the store to give them privacy.

The cattle needed tending, regardless of how wonderful it might be to stay in bed with his bride. Mary had been talking about changes she would like to make in the cabin, and he supposed it was only natural. He wasn't sure how to tell her what he had in mind. He'd been on the ranch for almost seven years, but the last two had been lean ones.

The cattle markets in the east weren't buying for high prices. The grasshopper plague two years ago hadn't run itself out yet, meaning that the cattle didn't eat well. In some months, he'd been forced to buy grain and haul hay from the south. He wasn't ready to sell the ranch, but he wanted to lease it and strike out on his own with a store. He was restless. Charlie's talk of opportunity in the west had stirred him.

There was a town northwest of them called Henrietta. Hiram had told him that the railroad was likely to go through there soon. More people were moving to Henrietta all the time, including a group of Quakers intent on starting a fellowship there.

Will got up and went to the creek for water, then added coal to the wood fire in the stove to start the coffee. Mary stretched but turned over to go back to sleep. After only a few weeks of marriage, she was still getting used to not having servants to cook and clean. She never complained, and she worked hard, but in the morning, he'd learned, she was a sleepyhead.

Coffee started, he grabbed his Bible and thought more about his moving plan. He read in Genesis 12 about Abram, *"Now the Lord had said unto Abram, Get thee out of thy country, and from thy kindred, and from thy father's house, unto a land that I will show thee."*

Maybe God was calling them west. Wouldn't Mary appreciate being in a Quaker meeting? He thought he could make a better living with a store for the people moving to Henrietta than he was doing with the cattle right now. If he leased the farm, when cattle prices went back up, he could make a choice. The economy couldn't stay bad forever.

Meanwhile, he could keep the land and still have a financial base.

Will went out and fed the horses and loaded hay in the wagon. When he returned to the cabin, Mary rose and put on her dressing gown, padding in bare feet to the kitchen after making the bed.

"Good morning!" She gave him a kiss and a hug. "Thank you for starting the coffee. I'll get breakfast shortly. Flapjacks all right?"

"That'll do fine, Mary." Will smiled. He'd learned that her cooking repertoire was limited. At the Kings', Miranda made food appear on command effortlessly.

She poured coffee for both of them and set out strawberries from their garden.

He read a psalm, and after the coffee was down to a quarter cup, Will asked, "Are you awake enough to talk?"

"Sounds like I'd better be. What's on your mind?" she asked, rattling pans to start the flapjacks.

Will considered and decided to plunge ahead. "Sweetheart, you know I have loved this ranch and looked forward to living here with you."

Mary turned to him, eyebrows raised. "Yes . . . What are you saying, Will?"

"You've seen the cattle, how thin they are. Cattle prices have dropped a lot. George and Lydia are thinking of relocating to St. Louis after they marry. Pa may close the store and go with them."

"You can't be thinking of us moving—you've worked hard for this ranch, and we're just getting started together here."

"To the northwest, there's a town where they are starting a Quaker fellowship. People are moving there, and Hiram says the railroad will go there."

Mary set the hot flapjacks on a plate in front of him and poured more coffee. Will laid out the other arguments in favor of the move that he had rehearsed, ending with, "And they have a school. When we have children, it would be miles for them to go to school here."

"And the ranch?"

"If we rent it out, we could come back if things improve with cattle."

"But you said there's no railroad. How would I ever see my family? Or yours? Why not buy out your father's interest in the store in Dallas? We could rent this and get a place in town. There are schools there, and while it's not Quaker, there is the church I grew up with, where we got married."

"In Henrietta, we'd have a chance to be part of something new. The town is just forming again. They were burnt out by Indians a few years back, and there was a tornado . . ."

"Sounds lovely," Mary said sarcastically.

"I want us to be part of something that we create together. At least promise me you'll pray about it, think it over."

Will saw her mouth set in a thin line.

"All right. You're my husband. We'll pray together."

***

May 1876

Mary hung the wash out to dry. She was tired most of the time now—married life was harder than she had imagined. The tension with Will over a possible move wasn't helping matters, and cattle prices continued to plunge.

Will was going into town today. She decided she would go along and visit her mother. It was time for some maternal advice.

When Will dropped her off at the Kings' house, it felt odd to enter the place she'd grown up as one who didn't live there. Her mother greeted her as Will went off to do his errands and visit Robert.

Ann and Mary embraced, and part of Mary wanted to cling to her mother as she had done as a child.

"What's wrong, Mary? I'm delighted to see you, but I can tell something isn't right," Ann asked with quiet concern.

Mary debated a moment and then it spilled out.

"Oh, Mother, I don't know what to do. I want to be a good wife, but . . . Will is thinking of moving, leasing out the ranch, and going west. He wants to go to Henrietta. All I know is that there are Indians and no railroad. It is over a hundred miles away. It would take days to get here. When would we ever see each other?"

Ann sent Miranda for tea. "Let's sit together. When your father wanted to move, first from Tennessee to Pennsylvania and then here to Texas, I wasn't thrilled. I did my best not to show it, but after losing two babies, moving far from family wasn't my idea of how to live. You'll remember your baby brother John had just died when we went through Indiana. I wasn't myself. To be honest, I was fighting the move to Texas. If we were going to move, I wanted to go home to Tennessee. But your father was convinced that there would be an opportunity in a frontier town for a bank. He was right, of course, but I couldn't see it then."

"How did you decide?"

"I cried, all alone where no one could see. I prayed. In the end, it was faith—faith in God, faith in your father. I'd given my word and joined my lot with him. You know your father and I love each other. What could a woman with children do besides follow her husband? I'm sure you never knew of my anguish. I tried to give you a happy time here, though you were already an adult in many ways."

"So that's what you think I should do? Pray and follow?"

"Just weeks ago, you said you loved him and bound yourself to him forever. You know he loves you. He's a good man, or your father and I wouldn't have allowed the courtship to continue all these years. What would you do? Throw it away or create war in your home?"

Mary sat, lost in thought. "You're right, of course. We don't know what blessings God may have in store down the road. I suppose it's best to look for them rather than dread the problems. Will you write to me? Often?"

"Of course, I will. And come to see you when I can."

When Will returned for Mary after his business in town, Mary said, "I've talked it over with Mother and God. If you think Henrietta is best, then we'll go."

***

Henrietta, Texas, June 1876

Will rented a freight wagon, and Mary helped him load it with all their goods. Then they set off on the drive to Henrietta. As soon as they arrived, Will rented a building for a store.

The new store was close to the proposed rail line, and the area was growing. He thought it a good place to raise a family. He and Mary would live above the store until he could build a house nearby. He didn't want a cabin, but a real house from sawn lumber. He wouldn't have David think his daughter had married down in the world.

He knew Mary had misgivings about the move—far from the railroad, far from family. But once she'd made up her mind, she had a cheerful attitude and worked alongside him. Quakers had moved to the area and built up the town. Mary was happy to have a Quaker meeting to attend and like-minded neighbors.

Will had written to Luther to tell him of his marriage and the move to Henrietta and received an answer written by Ruth. They were planning to leave Topeka and start the colored town Luther had dreamed of in western Kansas. Will said a prayer for them, hoping for the best.

Will worked tirelessly, making shelves for the store,

display cases, a new bedstead, wardrobes for Mary's dresses, and signs to advertise the store. He hoped the railroad would come soon so he could get regular restocking and fresh meat from the Fort Worth packing plant. Mary displayed a flair for doing the books, and he let her handle it, never having liked the drudgery of ledgers. Her background with the bank stood her in good stead. She consulted him occasionally with vendors reluctant to deal with a woman, but Will scolded them into submission.

"Will, what do you think of getting some chickens? We could set up a coop and sell eggs through the store."

"I think it's fine, Mary if you can handle it. I'm willing to build the coop, but I want to concentrate on building the house you deserve."

"I can do most of it. I was thinking of hiring a girl to help with the counter in the store and starting to display some custom needlework from Lydia. She has such a fine hand. I think the women here will snap up her creations."

"Whatever you think. You're doing a great job. And I love you and your management skills."

Will noticed the smiling response. He wondered ahead about children, but Mary had given no sign as yet of being pregnant, and he didn't ask.

He noticed that Mary ordered a few extras—flower

vases, knickknacks, a braided rug—to make the apartment over the store home. With the move and the adjustments, they hadn't had much of a honeymoon. When he locked up and came upstairs from the store, he smelled a roast cooking; she must have gotten some recipes from Ann. Her hair was swept up like she was going to a ball, and she wore one of her best gowns with an apron, along with the necklace he'd given her.

"What's the occasion?" He smiled.

"Do I need a reason to dress up for my husband?"

"I suppose not. Though you might give me ideas."

"I hoped so. The roast won't be done for an hour."

Will grinned and led her toward the bedroom.

***

April 1877

Will and Mary had been in the little community of Henrietta for almost a year, building and growing. The Dallas farm had been sold. Lydia had married her beau and moved to St. Louis, with Robert following her. Lightning was getting old, and had gone with Robert. Mary missed being close to her family, especially with no railroad connection nearby. She accepted it as part of being a dutiful wife, following her husband.

In late April, she missed her monthly and began feeling sick in the mornings.

She waited until they had finished work for the day and Will was sitting in his favorite chair. He'd been working at the house all day, and it was nearly ready for them.

"Will, I wanted to talk to you. I think we need another clerk at the store. The girl we hired is doing well, but I might not be able to do as much in the next few months."

"Are you feeling sick? Is something wrong?"

"No, nothing's wrong. It's just . . . I think I'm pregnant."

Will gave a whoop and embraced her.

"That's fantastic! When? I mean . . . I don't know what I mean! Let's celebrate!" He picked her up and whirled around. "Oh, sorry, I guess I shouldn't do that. Here, sit down. I can finish getting supper."

She laughed. "I hoped you'd be pleased. I'll have to get more rest, but I won't break. You might be on your own for breakfast for a few weeks—I was sick this morning."

"Whatever you need, Mary. We should telegraph your parents and my pa."

"Not yet," said Mary. "I debated about telling you, let alone everyone else. If I lose the child, having everyone know would be embarrassing. Let's wait a few months. When we're more sure, or I begin to show, then we'll spread the news."

"You're right, of course. I'm excited, that's all. A son!"

"And what if it's a daughter?"

"Then we'll love her just as much."

"Yes, we will."

***

The store prospered as the little community grew. One day a freight wagon came with supplies, and Will began talking with the muleskinner.

"How was the trip from Dallas?" Will asked.

"Blamed hot, as usual. First two days, I didn't see a soul. Then on the ridges from the trail, I began to see lines of Kiowa, like they was just letting me know they were there."

"Did they approach?"

"No, but I don't know why. I didn't have a soldier escort, and I had all these trade goods. Lucky, I guess. Even with my Winchester, I couldn't have fought off that many."

"Maybe you'd better spend the night here in town. They might be waiting for you west of here. It's a long way to Fort Concho."

"Maybe you're right. Got a place with enough room for my mules?"

"Talbot barn, just up the road. I hear his wife makes a mean stew."

"Much obliged."

Will mulled over what the man had said. He had heard of the Kiowa chief and his hatred for whites. Later in the day, as he was about to close, a wagon and a lone horseman rode into town, tying up in front of the store.

The horseman dismounted and helped a lady down from the wagon.

As they entered the store, Will recognized Charlie Goodnight.

"Charlie! Where did you blow in from?"

"Colorado and Dallas. Finally sold the last of everything in Dallas. I'm headed to the Llano Estacado. I heard you were in Henrietta, thought I'd stop by on the way. So this is your store?"

"Yes, sir. Been here about a year with my wife, Mary."

"Marriage looks like it suits you. It's the best thing in the world for a man. You remember Molly?"

"Mrs. Goodnight, it's a pleasure."

"We're just passing through. I have a new ranch up near Palo Duro Canyon. Best cattle country I've seen. Just a few Indian problems, though. Speaking of which, I saw signs of a large party of Kiowa not five miles from town."

"I was just talking to a muleskinner about it. He must have been a few hours ahead of you."

"Then they aren't trying to hide their presence. I wouldn't go far out of town, and I'd keep my rifle handy if I were you."

Will made a face. "This community is mostly Society of Friends, Quakers. They don't believe in violence. They think if you treat the Indians right, they'll mostly leave you alone."

Charlie snorted. "The day I see a Kiowa I can sit and talk with is the day I'll know the Second Coming has happened already."

"I know. But they are determined and say they'll welcome the Indians with meals and open arms. It's plain crazy," said Will. "It would be like someone stealing your cattle and then you invite them to dinner."

"Their hair will be hanging in a tipi," said Charlie.

"I was just closing up. Is there anything I can get you? And would you like to stay for supper?"

"Matter of fact, there is. Molly, you have the list?"

Molly handed him a pencil-scrawled list. "We'd be much obliged to stay to supper, right, Charlie?"

"Of course."

Over supper, the ladies chattered and Will heard about Goodnight's exploits. "Mind if I smoke?" said Charlie, drawing out a pipe.

"Not at all, Mr. Goodnight," said Mary. "It sounds like you've had a long day."

Charlie lit up, took a drag, and said, "Not nearly as long

as tomorrow might be if those Kiowa get itchy."

Will finished with the livestock and was thinking about breakfast. He figured Charlie and Molly might like a bite to eat before they hit the trail. He went into the house and saw a half-finished cup of coffee on the table, but no sign of Mary.

"Mary? Mary, where are you?"

There was no answer. He looked upstairs, but no one was there. Then he went out back. The clothes were flapping in the wind on the line, and a laundry basket was on its side on the ground, rolling side to side in the breeze. Mary wasn't there. He turned and was about to go back inside when he noticed the tracks of horses, heard a gunshot, and smelled smoke. A glance in the direction of the shot showed flames leaping up from a neighbor's house.

Kiowa! Will ran to get his guns and saw Goodnight hunkered behind his wagon.

"Charlie! They got Mary!"

Charlie signaled that he understood and then aimed a rifle at a brave that was bearing down on him. Will had to stop to load his rifle because Mary didn't like keeping loaded guns around. Goodnight felled that Indian, but there were three more coming. Will got the last of the seven cartridges into the Spencer and began looking for targets. He tried to fire, but the Spencer jammed. Two Kiowa rode whooping around the next-door neighbor's house and shot a little boy racing out the door toward their barn. The mother came out trying to save her son, rifle in hand, and she too was shot, falling in a rag-doll heap. Will got the Spencer working again but couldn't fire fast enough to save them. He took aim, and the two Kiowa dropped in the dust.

Will half heard Goodnight firing off to the side and saw others run out to join the fight, taking cover behind water troughs and barrels. He ran to the house next door to see if anyone was alive there, but the half-eaten breakfast on the table was the only sign of life. He found the husband on the back porch, sprawled on his stomach in a pool of blood, skull caved in from a war club. Seeing nothing to be done, he cautiously moved around the side of the house, looking for more people. He saw another Kiowa, drew the Colt, and fired.

The Indians began to retreat. Will aimed and shot two more as they left, wounded or killed, he couldn't tell. But where was Mary? Half a dozen houses were ablaze.

He moved from one hiding place to another until he was on the outskirts of town. Seeing the retreating band of Indians, his heart sank. What if all this made her lose the baby? He refused to give up, though, while there was a chance. He ran back toward his barn. Charlie stood, comforting Molly.

"They've gone. But I still haven't found Mary. Do you think they've taken her?"

"Most likely. I wish I could be encouraging, but . . ."

"She won't fight back. They may have taken others. I have to go after her."

"Feeling suicidal? There's probably more of 'em wherever their camp is. You're gonna ride into a hornet's nest."

"I don't care. I have to go. What if it was Molly? Will you come with me?"

Goodnight hesitated, then said, "I'm probably loco, but we can't leave her. It would take too long to get soldiers. Let's get Molly to a house with protection. Send one of the other men to the Texas Ranger station to ask men to come—we may need help. Rangers move faster than soldiers. Grab any extra guns and cartridges you have and bring her horse. Let's ride!"

Within fifteen minutes, they left Molly in the schoolhouse with two men standing guard. Five others rode with them, chasing the Kiowa.

The sky was growing darker as a storm threatened the riders, and a hard rain would wipe out tracks. If they lost the trail, there were hundreds of miles of prairie that the Kiowa knew better than they did. Will rode Dusty with Printer on a lead behind him. He was impatient—his horses could outrun his helpers, but arriving alone would be no help.

The dust cloud ahead of them and the tracks were all they had to go on. They pushed the horses hard, trying to keep the pursuit hot. Sometimes the dust cloud vanished for a minute behind a hill but reappeared as soon as they topped the rise.

A lightning bolt cracked, splitting the sky from top to bottom, and large raindrops began to fall. It was darker and harder to see. Goodnight took the front as the most experienced tracker. With the rain, there was no more dust cloud to follow. What must Mary be thinking? Would she think he would give up or follow? When he found her, he certainly wasn't planning a peaceful palaver with the Kiowa.

Another thunderclap and flare of lightning. Surely the Kiowa would stop soon and not try to continue in this weather.

Ahead, Goodnight raised a hand, signaling a top. When Will and the others caught up and gathered around, Charlie said, "I know this country, maybe not as well as the Kiowa, but I do know it. Up ahead about a quarter of a mile is an arroyo. In this rain, it'll be a flash flood. Just behind it is a little rise with a cave. I'm betting they'll hole up in there until the storm passes. If I'm wrong, we'll lose them. But if I'm right, we can surround it and be ready when the weather lifts. Remember, they have at least one woman, and we don't want to get her shot. Make sure you know where your round is going."

One of the men said, "I think it's crazy to keep going in this weather. We should turn back and pick up the trail tomorrow."

Will protested. "That's my wife out there. Maybe your family is safe back in town, but I'm not leaving her. I'll go on alone if I have to."

Another said, "My Wilma disappeared too. Seems like they killed the women that tried to fight, took the others."

"Will's right. We can't stop now. If she slows them down, they'll scalp her and leave her. If you want to go back, go ahead. But remember, it might be your wife next time," said Charlie.

The men looked at each other in the dimming light. A lightning flash lit their faces.

Charlie pointed. "You, you, and you, come with me. The rest follow Will. Watch my signals as long as you can. We'll split up, with my group going around to the north and

Will's group to the south. The storm will cover us some, but be quiet as you can. Our best bet is to catch one outside the cave and kill him, leaving the body near the entrance. Kiowa believe evil spirits come from the dead and won't hang around a dead body. If it's at the entrance, as soon as they discover it, they'll all come out."

Goodnight turned his horse north, and the others followed. Will stayed south of him but within sight, a good trick in the rough terrain. Within a few minutes, they came to the arroyo, which looked like a raging river.

The horses snorted and didn't want to cross, but Will urged Dusty through, and Printer followed. In the failing light, with help from lightning, they saw the cave, with a crowd of Indian ponies outside it. Will took up position behind an outcrop and motioned the others to dismount. He tied Dusty to sagebrush. He knew Dusty wouldn't spook, but he was less sure about Printer.

Waiting in the soaking rain wasn't pleasant, especially when Will's mind conjured up images of what might be happening to Mary. He looked at his pocket watch. Three hours since the attack, an hour here at the cave. At least the horses were resting. If the Kiowa had set a guard for their horses, he wasn't showing himself.

After another ten minutes, it was approaching full

dark. There wouldn't be a moon tonight with all these clouds. Visibility for shooting would be poor. His nerves were stretched like a banjo string. Part of him wanted to jump up and storm the cave entrance, but his head told him to wait it out.

There! A quick flash from Goodnight's side. Will strained to see. A man was coming out of the cave, checking on the horses. Will started to move but stopped when he saw someone from Goodnight's side slithering on the ground, darting forward when the guard's back was turned, then going still, then moving again until he was only two feet from the guard. A clap of thunder and the figure was on his feet, arm around the guard's neck, knife slashing. The guard dropped without making a sound. The next flash revealed that the figure was Goodnight. He pushed back against the hill around the cave, making himself invisible to those inside. When it was dark again, Will saw the horses move—whatever had been tethering them was no longer there. Goodnight motioned and fired a shot. The horses took off in different directions. The body of the guard had fallen forward, across the cave door. Shouting echoed above the thunder, and the Kiowa poured out of the cave, jumping over the dead man. Finding they had no mounts, they took cover as the bullets from the waiting white men swarmed them. They fired back but didn't know except by muzzle flashes where their assailants were. At last, there were only two left, and they took to their heels in pursuit of the vanishing horses. Goodnight signaled to let them go.

Will rushed to the cave entrance, Colt drawn, peering around the side. There could be Kiowa still inside, and he hadn't located Mary. What if she wasn't there at all? What if the one that kidnapped her wasn't part of the group they'd chased? He signaled Charlie, and they both jumped into the cave. No one attacked. After their eyes adjusted to the dark, Will saw three women tied to poles and seated on logs, all with gags. They thrashed trying to get free. He rushed forward, heedless of anything except the look in Mary's eyes and the bruise on her face. He drew a knife and cut her free. Charlie freed the other women.

As soon as she was loose, Mary collapsed into Will's arms, sobbing and holding on as if she'd never let go.

Relief flooded Will. "I thought I'd lost you. But you're safe now, you're safe." He stroked her hair and rocked back and forth with her in his arms.

Chapter 12

Ellis, Kansas, September 1877

The train screeched and groaned to a stop at Ellis, and everyone in the party with Roundtree and Luther looked around at the empty prairie north of the town. The land sloped gently downward.

The chaos of getting all the people off the train, along with the horses, dogs, and a few cages of chickens reminded him of getting troops moving in the army during the war, except then they had more horses and wagons to carry both people and supplies. There wasn't a single wagon in the group, and if Luther had bought one, it would have been mobbed with people seeking passage. The tiny town of Ellis, population six hundred, was no metropolis, and the town had never seen so many black people of all shapes, ages, and sizes.

Except for the handcarts and supplies they bought, Luther suspected the town would be glad to see the back of them.

When they had organized into family groups and filled canteens, they started out, walking north.

Luther, Ruth, Ned, Katy, and Olivia were all together. They'd sent word to Mark, but so far he had declined to come.

The whole group looked like the Israelites walking to the Promised Land. At first, they sang, and even the little ones joined in. Roundtree stayed at the front, leading and encouraging. They were walking to freedom. Talk buzzed about what it would be like, what they would grow, and most of all, how each man would be his own boss. Emotions ran high.

"Ruth, how many rooms do you want?"

"Three for us, and we should help Ned and Katy with their place."

After a few miles, they fell mostly silent, realizing they needed to save their strength for the walk. The sun beat down, and it must have been more than eighty degrees. The toddlers began crying to be carried and were scooped up. They made about five miles that first day, stopping only for drinks and to relieve themselves, trudging on through the barren landscape. Luther had always traveled by horse or train in this country.

"Let's make camp here by this stream tonight," called Roundtree. "We still got a long way to go."

Luther pulled up beside him. "What all these people gonna eat? You expecting manna?"

Roundtree grinned. "No, sir. I think most gonna eat hardtack and jerky that they brung along."

"And three days from now?"

"We'll see what the Lord provides."

Makeshift tents from canvas tarps sprang up along the river, and campfires winked in the night. A harmonica played a tune, and a few voices rang out in song. After the sun was well down, quiet lay like a blanket over the camp. Luther unrolled a blanket under a tree and was asleep within minutes.

Chapter 13

Fort Worth, 1877

With the time limit expired on his deal with Gould, Hiram was free to expand the Katy Railroad. The pause had given Gould the advantage on key routes in the west but also allowed Hiram time to concentrate on the meat-packing business and pay off his debts. While he was no longer rich, he wasn't drowning in creditors either. Having already lost the advantage in the west, he decided to proceed more slowly, building only what they had the capital to do. The meat business had grossed a million in its first two years, but he knew how quickly that could disappear when building miles of rails and buying locomotives and rolling stock, and the profits were split with George Sceafors, Swift, and other investors. Their railroads inched rather than leaped their way west, but they remained solvent and thus out of Gould's grasp.

Hiram closed the ledger with a heavy thud and rose, rubbing his eyes. Too many late nights with too little food lately. He wondered if Julia would be home from the meatpacking plant yet. They seemed to be running parallel lives again, like rails on a track, close but not touching. Maybe it was his fault. Being poor had thrown them together more, but as their fortunes improved, the distance widened as well, each keeping their portion of their businesses running.

It was time for a night off. He grabbed his hat and drove as though chasing the sun down to the meat plant. As he suspected, Julia hadn't left and was going over accounts.

"C'mon," he said. "Leave that till morning. I want an evening with my wife."

Julia looked up, amused. "Not that I mind, but why the sudden urge?"

"Does a fellow need a reason to spend an evening with his wife?" Hiram grinned at her. "We're doing better in the bank, but not with us. I want to go to dinner, spoil you, and forget about work for a few hours. Is that so wrong?"

"Not at all, but you could at least give a girl some warning so that I could dress."

"Never mind that, I'd take you in a flour sack."

"And I won't! Let's go home and change. You shave and wash off that I-have-been-at-the-office-all-night look, and I'll find something appropriate to wear. Where are we going?"

"I thought maybe the Lone Star on Main, down by the river."

"All right. Let's go!"

Within an hour, they had changed and were entering the Lone Star for dinner. Hiram ordered fish, quail, and oysters. The orchestra played, and he got Julia to dance with him. They laughed about the dance at her uncles' those years ago when they met and Julia had sprawled on the dance floor, tripping another couple. They switched to a polka and smiled as they stepped forward and began circling. After three minutes, they collapsed at a table, out of breath and dizzy.

They drove home and made slow, passionate love to each other, falling asleep just before sunrise.

When Hiram groggily arose and made coffee, he decided to let Julia sleep. Maybe he could surprise her with breakfast: Swedish pancakes, hot and ready. He proceeded to make them and grabbed the newspaper from the porch before gently awakening her.

"Mmm, smells good. What have you done, my Swedish giant?"

"Pancakes and coffee. Nothing special."

She pulled him down for a kiss, then sighed. "I suppose we have work today."

"We do, and we're late. But I don't care. The office will still be there in another hour."

Julia stood and threw on a dressing gown, following the smell of the coffee. When she was seated with a cup, she saw the newspaper under Hiram's arm.

"So what's the news of the world today?"

Hiram opened the paper, exclaiming in a low voice, *"Gode gud!"*

"If you're speaking Swedish, it can't be good. What's wrong?"

He silently turned the paper so she could see the headlines.

Railroads Strike - Miners Strike - Thousands Out of Work

With coffee only beginning to stir her brain, Julia pushed aside the memory of the previous night to concentrate on what Hiram showed her. She decided to ask her more awake husband.

"What effect does it have on us? At least it's not our railroad."

"No," Hiram said slowly, "but it could be soon. These unions tend to expand their reach to unrelated areas for leverage. The miners in Pennsylvania and the B&O Railroad aren't directly related to us, but we should keep track of it and make sure it doesn't expand to our interests. As it is, the traffic backup between Chicago and the East may cause us headaches—meat in ice cars only keeps for so long sitting on a siding waiting for passage."

"Let's think like Gould," Julia said. "Instead of moaning about the disaster, let's look for ways to exploit it. How can we get meat to New York City and avoid B&O routes entirely?

"Beat Gould at his own game, eh? I like it. There's the Grand Trunk Railroad and the Providence Railroad. If we sent some of our refrigerated cars north to Canada or even Vermont, we could move meat south from there. We can pass the tariff on in higher prices because they'll still be lower than what suppliers going over the B&O can charge if they can even get through."

"While Gould is fuming about the strike and tied up with union lawyers, we can expand south and west—as long as we can get the rails."

"What about that company in Illinois we worked with before?"

"We can contact Latimer. I can send a note to Mrs. Latimer, and you follow up with him. Maybe they can help with the unions too. Is the steelworkers' union connected to the railroad unions?"

Hiram said, "I don't know, but it's worth looking into. There are so many connections these days."

"Let me work on it. I'll get one of the managers to take care of the meat for a week," said Julia.

"All right. I'll work on the Canada angle and see if that's something we can put over on Gould. I should be getting to the office. See you tonight?"

Julia put on her sweetest smile and kissed him. "You can count on it."

***

August 1877

Julia paced at the door of the apartment, waiting for answers to her telegrams.

When she thought she would scream from the waiting, she heard a knock and made the door fly open so quickly the messenger boy jumped.

"Mrs. Johannsen?"

"Yes, that's me."

"Sign here, please."

Julia scribbled her signature, accepted the envelope, and tore it open.

```
Mrs. Julia Johannsen
AT&SF Railroad
Fort Worth, TX

    The rails and crossties you re-
quested would be available in one month
from the date of order. The quantity
you asked for would be $10,000 if paid
at once or in installments of $2000
over six months.
    Please advise.
    Mr. Hugh Latimer
```

"Boy? Can you wait? I have another message."

She wrote to the foreman in Colorado, telling him to proceed with the grading. She wanted to have all in readiness for the line south through Raton toward Santa Fe. Then she wrote another message to Latimer to order the rails and crossties and have them shipped to the end of the track in Colorado. The expansion into New Mexico was going to work!

***

Through a stroke of luck, the AT&SF managed to gain the right-of-way through Raton Pass ahead of Gould and the Durango Rio Grande. Julia celebrated the news with a special dinner for Hiram. It was mixed, however, because Gould had taken control of the Katy, buying up the bonds and forcing the board to name him president. The AT&SF countered with the acquisition of the Gulf, Colorado, and Santa Fe Railway and their lines to south Texas. Gould was like a spider with multiple entrances and exits from his lair, unpredictable and deadly.

The extra rails Julia acquired allowed the line built through Raton, a coup for them, but the construction was extra costly due to the terrain and all the switchbacks.

Railroads were coming and going, rising and falling, and the AT&SF struggled to keep up, buying an interest in this one, selling an interest in that one, always trying to stay one step ahead of Gould and find a way across the Texas plains, west and south. As new towns sprang up, entrepreneurs would come to them offering incentives to route the new line through their town. They would promise cash or land, and some would simply plead.

Julia and Hiram wanted to help them all, but business

dictated that they gauge profitability and let that guide them. Decisions that were life and death for towns had to rely on population, amount of goods shipped, and whether Gould could undercut them on rates and tariffs. Sometimes a spur was built from the main line to connect a grateful city, but more often smaller towns were passed by.

Gould frustrated their attempt to build an east-west line across Texas. With the new revenue through Raton and the western line, AT&SF built south to Galveston, and then from Temple began building north and west, going around Gould's Katy and Texas and Pacific. It was an expensive detour and a gamble. It had the potential to open west Texas to them, but it kept them awake at night as to whether it would pay off.

"What we need is a killer product that Gould can't match, that only we can ship because of our routes," said Hiram. "Wheat and cotton are great, but not enough to beat Gould."

"I don't know what it could be. There's some oil, but it isn't worth that much."

"For now, we'll have to keep shipping wheat, cotton, and beef, with Gould getting a cut of our profits."

"Maybe eventually we can link back to the Kansas line from West Texas, ship cattle from Dodge or that area east."

"What about passenger rail? Could we interest people in going to the Texas coast for vacations?"

"Possibly. It would be seasonal. Nobody would pay to go to Galveston in January."

***

Galveston, Julia

Passenger rail was more successful than expected. Julia and Hiram were exultant about having a profitable route that Gould did not control. The extra revenue allowed them to build west to Coleman and San Angelo.

Today Hiram would meet with investors—one of whom was Henry Ford—about the possibility of extending the AT&SF north through Brownwood toward Abilene. Unbelievably Gould had offered the town a deal, albeit an unfavorable one, and they'd had the brass to turn him down. Today they would find out the town's conditions for this prime route along the Colorado River. If successful, it could carry them north in Texas all the way to hook up with their line through Raton Pass in New Mexico.

"Gentlemen, I am pleased to meet with you today. Mr. Ford, I understand you work with steam engines and that has given you some capital to invest. May I present Mr. Weakley, a local investor, and Mr. Brooke Smith, a local banker with railroad interests?"

Everyone shook hands and took a seat.

Hiram resumed, "I can't tell you how crucial it is that the AT&SF and GC&SF gain access to north Texas. We know

314

that you had an offer from Jay Gould and that his company refused to help with your recent losses due to a fire in the town. We stand ready to help, to the extent we are able, and ask your requirements to be able to build through your town."

"It's quite simple. We need help to rebuild. Part of that will come from railroad revenues and expansion, but we need cash upfront and assurance that the railroad will be built. We've read of Gould playing a shell game elsewhere. We can't afford to be a victim," said Weakley. "The stage link has proved unreliable, being robbed five times in the last month, and it takes nearly two days to get to Fort Worth. We require $31,000 in cash and a railroad yard and depot."

Hiram felt his throat tighten. When other communities were paying them to come through, paying a town thirty-one thousand for the right of way was legal robbery.

"I see. Suppose you talk to your local businesses. I'm sure they will see the benefit of the railroad. You could sell subscription bonds and reduce the amount of cash required."

Ford said, "I'm prepared to risk five thousand, at an appropriate interest rate, over five years."

Weakley smiled. "Kind of a lot of money for a farm

boy with a steam engine. Are you sure?"

Ford smiled in return, but there was no warmth. "I don't play games, sir. Transportation is the lifeblood of the country."

"Very well. Then we can reduce the cash amount to twenty-six thousand."

Hiram said, "Twenty-six thousand is impractical, sir. We have no assurance this line will succeed, even with your town's recent foray into oil. I offer five thousand cash to build the yard and the terminal. In return, you supply twenty-one thousand in subscriptions and the right-of-way. I offer an additional two thousand toward rebuilding the burned buildings. Shall we meet back here for lunch tomorrow? You can tell me what your local investors think then."

"Very fair," said Smith. "These gentlemen are making you an honest deal, Weakley. You should grab it."

The following day, the deal was signed, and the AT&SF entered into a plan to build lines from Lampasas to Brownwood, Fort Worth to Brownwood, and north through Abilene across the Brazos.

North Texas was within their grasp.

Chapter 14

Nicodemus, 1877

The sleepy little colony began to sit up and stretch. More dugouts sprouted, and Luther resumed his role from Colorado days of driving a wagon to the railhead for supplies—only now there were no paying passengers to finance the trips. He used savings to buy more land, looking to spring, but for now, all the money was going out, and none was coming in.

The colony was three times the size it had been. Because they had arrived in September, there was no time to grow crops before the onset of winter, and by late October the wind took on a bitter chill. Roundtree was a cheerful source of encouragement, but Hill seemed to have deserted them, concentrating on the founding of a white town north of them named Hill City.

Luther began to worry about the winter—how would all these people eat and stay warm? There were no trees to burn for fuel. Bison numbers dwindled, which meant less meat and fewer buffalo chips for fires. And when the road to Ellis became impassable for wagons due to winter snow drifts, then what?

The camaraderie among the people was a joy. They had many hands working together. The first two buildings erected were the blacksmith shop and the church. The church was the center of the community, both for services and for socializing. On one trip to Ellis, Luther hauled back a potbellied stove and a load of coal. At least one space in the town would be warm. The coal also fired up the blacksmith shop, where he and Ned began shaping raw iron into tools and other necessities for the community. The sense of working together for a common goal—not someone else's goal, but theirs—was invigorating.

Luther was at his forge, making plows and hoes for springtime when Roundtree came to visit.

"Howdy, Reverend. What can I do for you this morning?"

"If we could multiply the loaves and fishes like Jesus, that would be a help. Are you and Ned able to make guns?"

Luther scratched his head and considered.

"We could probably figure it out. Never made one before. They're complicated, not like making a plow blade. Why?"

"Lot of the people don't have money to buy one. They don't have money to pay you either. But somehow we got to eat this winter, and I figure a few more guns would help us do that. Not saying anything against plows and hoes—you and Ned doing good work. But guns for this winter, and horses or mules to pull those plows in the spring, we gotta have those too."

"But horses got to be fed over the winter. Best wait until closer to planting time to get more. You think we'll be able to get through to the railroad all winter?"

"No," Roundtree admitted. "But each family has their garden plot and a few vegetables they've grown to last the winter."

"At least the Indians have left us alone, thank the Lord."

"That's right. They's always blessings."

"I'll think on the gun making and talk to Ned. We'll let you know what we can do."

***

When the first snow came, Luther tried to be cheerful. He built a snowman with the children. He pretended to be a horse and gave the children rides, rearing and pawing at the snow. When the children were off laughing and playing with friends, he took Ruth aside to talk.

"I have to be honest. I don't know how we're going to make it this winter. If the railroad came through here, then maybe, but we have nothin' to sell, and the Colorado money is beginning to run out. I checked my traps today, and they were empty. I'll have to move farther out. With all these people, what bison are left are staying far away. A man hunting out on the plains in the winter could get lost and freeze or starve."

Ruth's brow furrowed, and her hands went to her hips. "So what we going to do? Is freedom just the freedom to starve to death?"

"I don't know right now. But we best salt some meat and cut back on rations. Better to be a little hungry now than starving later."

Luther kept an eye on their dwindling stores. Roundtree prayed in services. All the families were in the same predicament. Those who had been there longer were sharing what they had, to their detriment.

He went out setting more traps and snares, looking for anything edible. He always took his Colt revolver in case of trouble, animal or human. Just before Christmas, as he checked the traps he saw horsemen approaching—twenty or thirty of them. They didn't ride in lines like soldiers. It was hard to tell who they might be in the snow that fell in white feathers from the sky. As the riders drew closer, he could see details . . .

Indians!

Luther gathered his belongings and broke into a run. He had to warn the town. Slipping, falling, and gaining his feet again, he arrived minutes ahead of the Indians and raised the alarm. People began running everywhere—children to their dugouts, mothers looking for their children, men grabbing whatever weapons they had, with much shouting. The dugouts were holes in the ground, sometimes in mounds, some like rabbit holes. Luther felt terror and despair like a suffocating blanket. Would they lose everything now? They hadn't the men or the guns to survive an Indian onslaught.

Ruth gathered the children and huddled at the back of their dugout, moving the makeshift table and chairs in front of the entrance to bar access.

Luther organized the men, Roundtree and ten others on one side of the town, Luther and the rest opposite, to have a crossfire as the Indians rode into the town.

Luther couldn't see how they could fight off so many with the few guns they had. Not enough men, guns, or bullets. And what about the women and children?

Luther hunkered down at the entrance to the dugout, behind the table, preparing to fire as the lead Indian rode into the town. Why was he riding at a walk? Why not swoop down on them?

The Indians stopped about thirty feet from a dugout, looking around. They seemed to be looking for people, mystified that they didn't see any.

Luther aimed, making sure he would take down the leader. It was then he noticed that many of the horses had travois behind them. That wasn't typical for a war party. None of the men had war clubs or bows at the ready. As the Indians gazed around, Roundtree slowly came out from his hiding place in a dugout. The Indians were startled, and one started to raise a bow, but the leader prevented him. He rode over to Roundtree, and Luther watched them pantomime and sign back and forth for a few minutes. The longer they "talked," the more the tension lapsed. After about five minutes, the leader slid off his horse and pulled back the covers over his travois, revealing fresh buffalo meat.

"It's all right," Roundtree called out. "Put down your guns. Everyone come out and welcome our new neighbors. These are Pottawatomie, and they've come to feed us!"

As Luther and Ruth sat around their fire that night, they realized it was Christmas Eve, and the Lord had brought them presents.

Chapter 15

Henrietta, Texas, 1877

After the Indian attack, Will telegraphed Fort Concho and Mary's parents in Dallas to let them know what had happened. Fort Concho responded that they were spread thin, but would send a troop north as soon as feasible. David and Ann immediately telegraphed back that they should come back to Dallas—they were welcome any time.

Charlie did a few patrols out from Henrietta without saying much. He reported to Will that the band of Kiowa seemed to have moved north and further trouble was unlikely at present.

"There's strength in numbers, though," said Charlie. "And experience counts. Why not join me at the JA Ranch in Palo Duro? At least come see the country. It makes the range here look pitiful."

"I might just do that. Mary's itching to go back to Dallas. I'd like to stay here a while, then maybe move farther west."

"I've been all over the Llano Estacado. There's no finer land for cattle and cotton." Goodnight helped Molly up to the high wagon seat and mounted the driver's box.

"Thanks for your help," said Will. "If ever I can do you a good turn, ask and I'll be there."

Mary was shaken and took it easy. She hadn't miscarried, but she cried and had nightmares. Will felt helpless and guilty. He'd come to Henrietta thinking that town life would be good for them and the Quaker community a blessing for Mary. For the first year, it had been. Now the community was frozen in fear. Mary wouldn't leave the building without him. She didn't want to be alone, even upstairs while he was tending the store.

"Can you tell me what happened?" he asked for the dozenth time.

"I don't want to talk about it. I don't want to remember. They hit me when I wouldn't do as they wanted. I was terrified—for the baby, for my life—so after that, I cooperated, and they didn't hurt me more. At least they didn't rape me. It's not so much what they did as what I was afraid they might do—and the thought of never seeing you again. I knew you would come, and I was afraid for that too, that they might kill you. At that moment, it felt like God had abandoned me, though I know that isn't true. I just want to go home!"

"This is our home. You know there are families here that are our friends. The Meeting surrounds us, and God watches over us. You're safe."

"But I don't know if I will feel safe ever again. I'll try. But if something like that can happen here in town, when I'm hanging out the laundry, how can I ever be safe? Will, what is it that you're looking for?"

"I wish I knew, Mary. Peace. A place for our family. Community. To feel part of something bigger than myself."

"I want to love and follow you, to honor all those things I said, but is it worth risking our lives, our future together, this thing that you're seeking? Please think about it."

A few days later, a troop of sixty cavalry with a small field piece came through. Will never thought he'd be glad to see the blue uniforms, but he was, and Mary almost emptied the store to fix them a good meal. They sent word back a few days later that the Kiowa had been chased to Fort Sill in Indian Territory, and Chief White Horse, the leader of the band, had been killed.

With Indian troubles apparently behind them, Mary settled more. Will was still concerned for her and stayed close.
He began wearing his gun belt whenever he went out, and
she did not object.

Will worried about the baby. "Have you talked to the
midwife?" he asked.

"Yes, now that things are quiet, I spoke to Clara to
make sure the jouncing on the horse, the blows to my face,
and my terror didn't harm the baby. They didn't know I
was pregnant. She said I need rest, and that as far as she
can tell the baby will be all right. The birth will most likely
be after Christmas."

"I know the Indians have moved on, but we don't
know when they might return. Won't you practice some
with the Winchester? With a baby coming, we can't be too
careful. And I have to be gone sometimes to haul supplies
for the store."

"No, I don't want to shoot guns. I'm glad you and
Charlie saved me. I don't know what would have happened. But it pains me to think about our neighbors who
were killed and the Indians as well. I don't think violence
has any place in our lives. God protected me, and He will
continue to do so. Violence just breeds more violence."

Will pursed his lips, was about to say something, and

then kept silent. There was no point arguing this with Mary, but he knew there were times when force was the only answer.

***

January 1878

The pains were coming closer together now and intensifying. Mary groaned, sweating even with the cold of the winter morning. It had been an uncomfortable night, with neither Will nor Mary getting much sleep. At about 3:00 a.m., Will woke Ann, who had come for the baby's delivery, and took the buggy to fetch the midwife. Now he waited nervously downstairs, sipping coffee and tending the stove, while the women took care of Mary. He wanted to stay, but they shooed him out, saying it was no place for a man. They'd call him when Mary wanted him. With first labor, it could be hours—or minutes. Will tried to read the Bible and pray for her, but it was tough to concentrate. There was nothing worse for a man than having his wife in pain and no way to help or relieve it.

When the sun peeked over the horizon, weak, as though it didn't want to get out of bed, he went out to feed the horses and chop the ice from their water trough. It needed doing, and it was something to do besides wearing a hole in the floor and listening to Mary's cries. Both Ann and Mary had refused chloroform for her, worried about the effect on the baby. Will wondered if she regretted it now. Back in the house, it was quieter at the moment, maybe resting between contractions.

"Will!" called Ann. "Have you any ice from clean water?"

"Yes, Mary planned ahead."

"Can you bring some ice chips?"

"Yes! Anything to help," said Will, thinking he might also catch a glimpse of Mary. But when he ascended the stairs with the ice in a pan, Ann barred the door.

"Thank you," she said, shutting the door with finality, and leaving Will in the hall at the top of the stairs. Will couldn't remember when Lydia was born since his parents had shipped him off to the neighbors. Was it always this long?

He'd hung a sign on the door of the store saying they were closed for stork delivery. He knew the instant there was an announcement, Mary would be mobbed with lady friends from Meeting, wanting to see the baby and congratulate her. No one talked about the common worry, that either Mary or the baby might not survive. Mary at least wasn't too old. She was still young and strong.

Will warmed yesterday's soup—a fella had to eat, no matter what. When he finished, he pumped water into the sink and rinsed the dishes. He was wondering what to do next when he heard Mary calling him.

He went up the stairs two at a time, heart pumping, ready to do whatever was needed, The door opened and he saw the most beautiful sight a man was privileged to see— his wife holding a baby wrapped in a clean blanket.

"Say hello to your son," said Mary. "Though at the moment, I think he's more interested in food."

"What will you name him?" asked the midwife.

"We agreed on David, after my father, for a boy," Mary said. "Would you like to hold him?" she asked Will.

Will took his new son and felt his chest might burst with love and pride. This delicate little human was now his responsibility. Whom would he become? Will wondered if he was ready to guide and be an example for another human being. It gave him a new appreciation for his pa, and he wondered what he was doing and when he would be able to introduce this little one to his grandpa. He looked over at Mary and saw pride, love, and fatigue. The baby began to cry and Will handed him back.

"He's so small. I bet he's hungry. Better let him eat so he can grow."

"Easy for you to say," said Mary. "But we can try." She bared a breast and let little David try to figure it out.

Will watched the miracle—a baby thrust into a foreign environment, moving and exploring until he attached and found food. Life as a family of three had begun.

Will decided that, with the new baby, the apartment over the store simply wasn't enough. He hired some help and completed the white frame house he had started, with four bedrooms, a kitchen, a dining room, and a parlor. They made one bedroom into a nursery and Will let Mary order whatever she wanted to decorate it. They moved in, using the old apartment for store storage.

They had a real home at last.

Chapter 16

Nicodemus, March 1878

Luther heard the call between blows at the forge. Roundtree was calling a meeting in the church. Almost everyone came, crowding around to hear the news. A new group of settlers from Kentucky was coming. They were walking right now from the Ellis train depot.

"You know what that's like, some of y'all just done it not a year past. The Lord's been good to us. He got us through the winter. It's time to plant, to prepare. We ain't got much, but we got brothers and sisters coming. God calls us to share, like the widow and Elijah. She didn't have enough to eat, but God called her to share it, and she did."

"You're right, Reverend."

"We need to make a couple of houses or dugouts, a

place for these new folks. Some of them are sick, I hear. What does Jesus say about when we see the sick?"

"Tend 'em. Heal 'em. But, Reverend, what they sick with?"

"Measles—those red bumps you get with the fever."

A gasp went through the crowd. Measles was very serious. People died from measles.

"Why should we let them bring that here?"

"Because they got nowhere else to be free. Just like you. That's why we're gonna make some dugouts for the sick ones, a little way over from the rest of us. Maybe then we don't get it."

There was murmuring in the crowd. Not everyone was positive about this new development.

"And I need a favor. Someone with a wagon and a team make the drive to Ellis so the little ones with fever don't have to walk here."

Luther looked around. No one was stepping forward, and several were looking at him. Should he volunteer? What about his family—wouldn't he be putting them at risk? He looked at Ruth, then Katy. They each nodded. He thought about the risk Albinia had taken, the time in jail she'd served for helping others like them escape.

"Reverend Roundtree, I'll go."

"No, you won't," said Ned. "I'll go. Whoever goes gonna have to stay away from everyone for a time. The community can't spare you at the forge. I'm old and getting slow. I don't have any little ones anymore."

"But, Ned . . ."

"No buts. Listen to me. You take care of that family of yours."

"All right," said Roundtree. "I guess that settles it. Don't argue with a man with a hammer! Ned, we got some food and water you can take in the wagon and a few shoes in case they don't have any. My daughter will ride along to tend them while you drive."

"Let's go."

***

Four days later, Ned returned. He'd driven slowly, sticking with the walkers so the children in the wagon wouldn't be far from their parents. Simon's daughter had been tireless, wiping foreheads with cool cloths, praying for the sick, lifting heads to spoon in broth. She showed no signs of sickness, but it was too early to tell. Ned asked a doctor in Ellis, who said it could be two weeks before any sign would show up and to keep people away for two weeks after the bumps stopped coming. Ned hoped for help with the spring planting, though he knew Katy and Ruth would help. He answered endless questions from the new-comers. He shook his head—he didn't think they believed him about the dugouts. But as they walked, they got round-eyed about the lack of trees.

About ten didn't have shoes and were grateful for those sent from the community. Roundtree's daughter had a good voice and kept their spirits up by singing songs and reciting Scripture.

As they walked into Nicodemus, one of the women in the wagon raised her head at the excitement from the more than one hundred walkers.

"There's Nicodemus!" one of them yelled.

Looking confused, the woman said, "Where's Nicodemus? I don't see it."

Her husband pointed at the smoke coming from the ground, a hundred or more dugouts, and the blacksmith shop and church. The dugouts were little more than holes in the ground.

"There's Nicodemus."

Ned felt sorry for her. She was so sick, and to arrive and find no buildings to speak of was heartbreaking. She began crying quietly.

The town soon turned out, but they warned everyone back. Roundtree led the way over to a group of freshly made dugouts. The sick were placed carefully in them. Ned carried the few that couldn't walk. The cool earth felt good to hot limbs. The healthy ones set up tents they had carried. They had a dugout for Ned, but he said he would sleep outside until he could rejoin his family. Everyone came out, stood at a distance, and prayed. Simon agreed with his daughter that he would leave a pot of soup on a stump near the "sick town," as they called it, every day.

As with the first group, twenty or so looked at the conditions and said they would leave and try their luck in Ellis. Roundtree didn't try to stop them. If the sight of the dugouts was enough to discourage them, a Kansas winter like they had been through would have them in full revolt. Nicodemus wasn't for everyone.

***

Nicodemus, November 1880

The new families had settled in. The measles abated, and fortunately, no one died. Roundtree's daughter had a mild case but was healthy within a month. Ned never caught them. He told Luther he was too ornery for some white man's disease to get him down. Crops were planted, and the harvest was good. This winter, they wouldn't starve. The Pottawatomie came to the village at times to say hello. Some of the Indians had learned English at the mission school near Kansas City.

Nicodemus was now composed of thirty-five structures, including three hotels, two churches, two dry-goods stores, and a lumber yard. White people had also moved to Nicodemus, which meant there were both black and white students in the school. One of the dry-goods stores was run by a white man. Wagons went back and forth regularly to the railhead.

Luther could hardly believe the transformation of the town. When Thanksgiving came, there was plenty to shout for joy about. The November winds blew, and there was a little snow, but the people had warmth, food, and most importantly, freedom. Freedom to come or go, to work or be idle, to worship however they pleased. No one needed to look down when a white person came—it was the white person's choice to be among them.

Luther reflected on the blessings, then chuckled. It wasn't perfect harmony. You couldn't get five hundred people together and have absolute peace. There were quarrels and not a few romances; some worked, and some didn't. Most of the time when someone was in need, the community pitched in to help, but some preferred to mind their own affairs.

As the year came to a close, he was happy that his children had school. Olivia had rejoined them and taught at the school. They had food, and work in the blacksmith shop was now a paying proposition and not charity to neighbors. Other people had wagons and teams.

There were spirited community meetings where Roundtree presided, though he was no longer the only minister. Everyone got their say—and some more than their say. Prayer and the vote decided.

When spring came, the cattle drives from New Mexico and points south resumed to Dodge City and other towns along the railroad.

One morning as Luther, Ruth, and the children sat at the breakfast table, they heard a rumbling. Looking out the entrance of the dugout at a clear blue sky, they knew it wasn't thunder. It grew louder, and the earth above their heads in the dugout began to shake.

"Is it an earthquake?" Ruth asked.

Before Luther could answer, the ceiling of the dugout cracked, and a huge longhorn steer fell through into the middle of their table.

The table, miraculously, didn't crack. The animal snorted, twisted, and turned, shook his horns, causing everyone to duck, and let out an enormous bellow that echoed off the dirt walls. There wasn't room for the steer to jump down, and he wouldn't have fit through the door.

"Luther! What are we going to do? The children!"

Luther yelled over the noise of the steer, "I don't know! Everyone stay put, as still as you can be. Let's see if he quiets down."

The hole in their roof was about a four-foot diameter circle. Luther might have made jokes about it under other circumstances, but an angry thousand-pound steer was no laughing matter. If he could get to his gun, he might kill it, but what if he missed or made it angrier without killing it? The steer pawed and thrashed, reared up on its hind legs, trying to reach the roof, and slammed down again. Outside, the ground continued to shake as more cattle ran over the top of the dugout, so far avoiding the hole. After two or three minutes, the herd passed, and the lowing of the other steers could be heard fading away.

The steer on their table seemed frightened as well as angry. Luther crawled toward the back wall where his .36 caliber Navy revolver holster hung on a peg. He saw no alternative but to kill the beast—at least with the revolver he could fire five fast shots. One cylinder was always empty for safety. He got to his knees and was about to push up, grab, and fire when the beast gathered itself like a spring, gave a mighty roar, and jumped back through the roof. Its front legs made it outside, and it hung, struggling until a back leg managed to get on the earth, and pushed itself out of the hole, chest heaving, breaking into a run to catch the rest of the herd.

***

Henrietta, Texas, 1882

The town buzzed with excitement. After years of waiting, today the first train would arrive in Henrietta. The
town had grown, now having over three thousand people.
Will and Mary had done their part, as they were now the
parents of three very active children. Dave was four and
followed his father everywhere. Bob, their second son, had
made his appearance three years ago, and the noisy laughter
of the boys, along with their penchant for mischief, kept
Mary running. Mamie, their daughter, was beginning to
walk, clinging to first one table, then a chair, and giggling
with glee when she fell and regained her feet. Will and
Mary hoped her parents would visit often to see their growing brood of grandchildren. As they entered their sixties,
Ann and David were thinking of retiring. Will knew Mary
hoped they might move closer since he hadn't been willing
to go back to Dallas.

Will helped get the children dressed. There was to be
a band, sausages, and a clown to celebrate the railroad. He
and Mary went together, making it a family outing. The
town would benefit much from the train, and Will knew
Mary was looking forward to it. He wasn't going to mind

not making the long wagon hauls to supply the store and hoped to be home more with the children. At least as much as he could—there was a burgeoning business in buffalo hides and bones. Will had resumed hunting as he used to, in support of his growing family.

Mary carried Mamie, with Bob hanging on her skirts, as they walked downtown.

The band began to play, and Will looked around to see where Dave and Bob had gotten to—if the train was coming in, he didn't want them in the way. Looking over the crowd, he spied Dave with some friends, not too near the tracks, and Bob followed his big brother, trying to imitate the older boys as they pretended to be locomotives, blowing their whistles. Then Will heard the train whistle.

"Will! Look!" Mary panicked as Bob moved closer to the tracks. She was about to pick up her skirts and run over when Will beat her to it, lifting Bob up onto his shoulders.

Mary sighed in relief. "I swear, keeping track of these three could make a woman old."

"Nah, they keep us young and close to God. He knows we couldn't do it without Him," Will shouted over the noise of the train wheels screeching to a stop. "Hey! Look who's here!"

Mary looked in the direction he pointed and saw both

of her parents, Hiram, and Julia descending the train stairs.

David and Ann waved on seeing them, and the boys ran to their grandparents.

"What an unexpected surprise!" Mary said, hugging them all.

Will shook Hiram's hand.

"The man of the hour. We have you to thank for this magnificent train."

Julia hugged Will. "Hiram and I can't stay long—we have to take the next train back. But we couldn't resist seeing you. It's been a long road, but it's time to celebrate! Now that the AT&SF and CSU railroads have merged and joined the Katy at Fort Worth, and now that the Katy has reached Henrietta, we'll be able to see more of one another."

Will said, "We will indeed."

Turning to David, Will said, "Good to see you, sir!"

"We couldn't miss the first train!" Ann enthused. "We've been wanting to see you and the children. I hope it's not an imposition."

"Not at all," said Will. "Especially if David would like to come along on a buffalo hunt tomorrow. I hear there's a herd about five miles west. I thought I'd take Dave and Bob along."

"Do you think it's safe?" said Mary.

"I don't see why not," said David. "It would be an experience."

"Safe enough," said Will. "They can stay in the buggy with your father. I'll take the Sharps or the Winchester. They'll be a quarter mile from the herd, at least."

"Please, Ma?" said Dave. "We haven't gone hunting with Pa before. He's told us about buffalo hunts from the old days, but I've never been on one."

Mary looked at Ann helplessly with an expression that said, "Men!" and raised her hands. "All right, but promise to do just what your father says, and stay far away from the buffalo."

"Yay!"

Bob jumped up and down too, though it wasn't clear that he knew what about.

"Let's get back to the house and find some food. I'm starved," said Will. "We can have buffalo steak tomorrow."

***

The men were up early and piled into the buggy. Will was amused as it seemed like David thought he was going on a real western adventure. They bumped along the dirt trail, the boys excitedly pointing at every pheasant, prairie chicken, or ground squirrel they saw. After three hours, they saw the dark specks on the prairie that might be the herd. In the last five years, nearly all the Comanche and Kiowa had been forced into Indian Territory. The great herds of the past were gone. Will felt that if he didn't profit from the great beasts, someone else would until the herds were gone altogether. Cattle were the future. In the dry Texas climate, it took thousands of acres to support the cattle herds and make them profitable. The buffalo would get squeezed out in any case.

"Look, Pa! There they are!" yelled Dave. "Grandpa, see?"

Will smiled. "Good thing we're so far away—with all that noise, you'd stampede the herd."

Chastened, Dave sat down, "Oh. Sorry, I didn't mean . . ."

"No matter," said Will. "They didn't hear you. Wind's blowing from the north, carrying sound away from the herd. But when we get closer, you do need to be quiet."

"Yes, Pa."

"Can I get a buffalo?" asked Bob.

David said, "Why don't you help Grandpa watch? We'll make sure none get past us here."

Will winked at him. "Grandpa's smart. Let's see if we can get a little closer without spooking them."

He lifted the reins and drove quietly over two more rises until he was within about eight hundred yards of the outside buffalo. He didn't need to be quite that close, but he wanted the boys to be able to see.

He stopped the buggy and put on the brake. Dismounting, he went back and grabbed his 1874 Sharps, an upgrade from his old one, and stuck it in the rifle scabbard of the saddle horse he was trailing behind. Dusty was too old for such ventures, and Will had left him at home. He mounted and pointed the horse at the herd. This would be child's play unless they stampeded the wrong way. Maybe he'd better warn David.

"I don't think they will, but if you see the herd run this way, fire three shots in the air with the Winchester and then drive away as fast as you can."

David nodded, gripping the rifle.

Will rode out over the valley until he was within

about five hundred yards of the herd, choosing a point between the herd and the buggy. He hobbled the horse and crouched behind a boulder. As he watched, a large bull moved to the edge of the herd. Sighting over the boulder through his scope, he mentally calculated the wind resistance, adjusted an inch higher, and fired. The bull bellowed once and fell, chaos breaking out in the herd.

Will aimed again and again, two more falling. The herd took flight.

Will acquainted his guests with the hard work of butchering and harvesting the hides. Bob was too little to be of much use beyond sitting on the dead animals and riding them.

Once they had the hides and meat they needed, Will marked the spot for the bone harvesters to come back and collect the rest—buffalo bones were often ground for fertilizer back east.

The boys were tired and fell asleep in the buggy on the way home. Will and David came across a wagon and crew with surveying equipment and stopped to talk to them.

"What you boys doing way out here?" Will wondered.

"Surveying for the railroad. We're finding the best way west, clear to Amarillo. You?"

"Buffalo hunting. Don't expect the herds will last much longer."

"Just as well. They get in the way of trains. My name's Frank Wheelock."

"I'm Will Crump, and this is David King. David runs a bank in Dallas. I'm a storekeeper."

"I have a big ranch, the IOA, out west of here near Palo Duro," said Wheelock.

"Palo Duro, that where Charlie Goodnight is?" asked Will.

"Yes, how did you know?"

"Charlie helped me out of an Indian scrape a few years back. I did a cattle drive with him. Invited me to come out to the Estacado, but I never made it."

"You should. Bring Mr. King here too. There's money to be made in the land out there. Me and a couple of Illinois investors are thinking about a town, maybe get the railroad interested," said Wheelock.

"My brother-in-law does railroads: Hiram Johannsen. He's with the Atchison Topeka and used to own the Kansas Pacific."

"Come out and see, then. Bring your family. With a new town, a railroad makes all the difference."

David seemed skeptical but said, "New town, eh?

Well, I suppose that's natural now that the Indians are out of the way. But what makes you think there's money in it?"

"There's going to be a lot of new towns, a lot of competition. Buy up land now while it's cheap and resell it to farmers and families. There's a guy from Michigan, C.W. Post, that's starting a town. He thinks the farms will generate cheap grain for his cereal factories up north. There's talk of oil and, of course, cattle and cotton. In ten years, the Estacado will be civilized. Now is the time to get in on it. I'm working with Lofton and Harrison of Fort Worth."

"I know them," said David. "Let's make an appointment. Where are your offices?"

"Fort Worth," said Wheelock.

"Thanks for the tip. Charlie's been after me to do it for years. Maybe now is the time."

"How about two weeks from today, lunch, in Fort Worth? That'll give me time to finish this survey and get the papers in to the railroad."

"Two weeks it is. I'll look forward to it," said David.

The men arrived back home with bison and excitement. Will and David told their wives of the chance meeting on the plains with Frank Wheelock and the new events on the Llano Estacado, full of dreams and plans. The women were considerably less enthused.

"What do you know of this man? How do you know it isn't all for show, just speculation?" asked Ann.

"How can you even think of being involved in this, Will?" asked Mary. "We're established here in Henrietta. The store is doing well, and the railroad means growth. Why would we want to leave this for a gamble farther west?"

"Simmer down, ladies," said Will. "We're going to meet with the man, that's all. Mary, you and the kids can come along—you've been wanting to visit Dallas. You could stay with your mother while David and I hash out business in Fort Worth. I'll get someone to watch the store."

"It sounds awfully risky to me," said Mary. "But if Father's on board, I suppose we should consider it."

"Don't worry," said David. "I will check it out thoroughly."

"And I'll talk to Charlie Goodnight," said Will. "We won't make a move without letting you know."

Mary and Ann looked at each other, each mirroring the other's worries.

After the evening meal, Mary said to Will, "Let's take a walk. My parents can watch the children."

They strolled down Graham Street in the moonlight. Will wondered at her stiff posture and clipped words.

Mary said, "I can't help it. I have to speak my mind— you knew that about me when we married. We've been here six years, and it's only in the last few that I've relaxed enough to feel safe walking down the street. You wanted us to come and raise a family. You wanted to give me a fel- lowship of Quakers. We've done that, and I'm grateful. But now, just when the railroad comes, you want to move again to the middle of nowhere. At least here, there was already a town. Dave and Bob have gotten to go to school."

She wrung her hands and moved a step away from him.

"Mary, I know this is hard for you, but look at the oppor- tunity!"

"Opportunity for what, Will Crump? We had a perfectly good ranch in Dallas. Times were hard for a bit, but you can see how it has recovered. The hard times are over. We left the ranch, and while the last few years have been good, and I love our children, I went through hell the first years we were here. Molly Goodnight was right that Texas is good for men and dogs but hell for women and horses—especially women. We have a good business here, friends, all the things you said you wanted for us, and you want to move again? I can finally see my parents on a regular basis. We can see your family too. I don't understand you. You've even got my father thinking about it."

"I know it may seem crazy, but Charlie has been urging me to come and look for years. That's all I'm doing—looking," said Will.

"But what's the point if you aren't seriously going to consider it? I'm telling you now—I don't want to go."

"Mary, please pray. Give it a chance."

"I will pray, but God is going to have to send me a special light to change my mind."

She turned and walked back to the house, leaving Will standing in the street.

***

Will walked out on the prairie. What was it that drove his restless spirit, looking for the next challenge, the next obstacle to overcome? In some sense, Mary was right; he had everything he had dreamed of—a wife, children, a community. Mary had moved with him, even when it was unexpected. She'd been kidnapped. Through all of it, she hadn't complained, she had worked alongside him. Maybe she had a right to complain about another move. The thought weighed on his spirit.

He put his hands in his pockets and looked at the stars. The whole country was growing and changing at a frenetic pace. Men were starting new businesses and new towns. Dallas had something new, David said, telephones that let you talk to people far away. Fortunes were being made and lost.

Men had left good farms in the east to follow the Oregon Trail or race to the gold fields in California. Was he so different from them? Would he race to the stars if that were possible? Maybe it was that when things became too settled, he became bored. Was that selfishness? Why were some men admired for their spirit of adventure—Daniel Boone and Davy Crockett—and other men lived ordinary, farming or running a business, quietly raising a family?

A coyote howled out on the prairie, and Will realized the moon had come out full, enough that he could see his shadow.

Who did God want Will Crump to be? He had tried to be faithful to God, loyal and honorable, keeping his word. He always trusted and always moved forward, no matter the odds. Even in Camp Douglas, the prison the Federals had put him in for keeping his word to Morgan, he never gave up. He tried to treat everyone by the Golden Rule, white, black, or Indian, to reach across the things that divided men from each other.

There was always another challenge, another mountain to climb or river to cross. He thought of Davy Crockett's maxim, "Be sure you're right, then go ahead." Was he right? Was this challenge of a new town dividing him from Mary? It seemed as though it was. He reflected on the fact that God had three possible answers to any question: yes, no, and wait. The answer now seemed to be "no" or "wait."

Will sighed and turned his steps back to the house. Everyone had gone to bed. It was quiet and dark. He tried to be silent taking his boots off. Mary was asleep. He would have to apologize or at least talk things through in the morning.

***

Will stretched when he heard the clatter of pans in the kitchen. Mary and Ann must be getting breakfast together. He'd overslept. He washed up and threw clothes on, hurrying to check on the children. Mamie was still sleeping, but the boys were playing on the back porch. Ann and Mary were talking, though he couldn't hear what they said, which was probably just as well, he thought. He went to the animal shed and fed the horses, giving Dusty a pat. He wondered if Dusty would last through another winter.

When he finished, he made an appearance in the kitchen.

"Morning, Will," Ann said, smiling. Mary glanced at him but said nothing. It was not a good sign.

"Where's David?"

"He grabbed some coffee and went to the telegraph office—bank business, I suppose."

After breakfast, Will debated taking Mary somewhere to talk. They would have to open the store soon. He decided against it. Ann needed to hear this as well.

"Mary, if you'd rather talk privately, we can go upstairs. But I think your mother needs to hear this too."

Mary frowned. "If you mean to try and convince us more of this scheme of yours, you're wasting your breath."

Ann said, "I don't mind listening, but I can't see much point if you want to push moving."

Will said, "I want to start by apologizing. I should have realized how attached you've grown to this place. We do have an appointment with Wheelock, and we'll keep it. But I won't consider moving right now. I think in the end, west Texas may be the best place, but I won't even go look at it until we can agree. In the meantime, I hope you'll continue to pray, as I will. Whatever we do, we'll do it together."

Mary started to cry. "You have no idea how happy that makes me," she said. "I know you will keep your word, and I'm going to hold you to it. Go talk to Wheelock. I know it's important to do what you've promised. But tell him we're not moving now and maybe not ever. God will guide."

Ann said, "I'm proud of you, Will, for taking your wife into account first. I will let David know of your decision. Money has never been your first concern, and I'm happy to see that you aren't letting it rule you."

Will stood, and Mary opened her arms, enveloping him in a hug.

Chapter 17

Henrietta, Texas, 1887

Five years had passed since Will and David met with
Wheelock. The children and the town grew. More stores
opened in Henrietta. The train made supplies easier to get
but also increased competition, the same worry Will had in
Colorado. One edge that kept him going was negotiating a
discount on freight and meat with Hiram, something the
other stores couldn't match. Albinia had resumed being a
seamstress as well as teaching, now that her children were
older, and Lydia contributed her needle skills as well. Lydia's and Albinia's dresses, brought by train, sold well. Each
was original, not from a pattern, again something the other
stores couldn't equal. Will still worried about what would
happen when another store that was better funded came in.

Telephone service came to Henrietta, and Will was one of the first to install one, charging customers for its use. He could order goods from Dallas and Houston without using a telegram or mailing printed forms. Mary chattered happily to her parents and traveled to Dallas with the children periodically.

Will usually had to stay with the store on these occasions. But it made Mary so happy that he could hardly deny her the pleasure. They had acquired a calico cat to keep mice out of the storage area above the store. Mamie heard the Bible story about the Queen of Sheba and liked the sound of the name so much that she went around saying, "She-ba! She-ba!" so that's what they named the cat. Sheba liked to wrap herself around Will's feet when he did ledgers in Mary's absence, much to his annoyance.

It was when Mary was gone on one of these trips that disaster struck. Will had been working late, doing inventory and preparing orders to be ready for the Christmas season. Exhausted, he went home to bed rather than sleeping on a cot upstairs, as he often did when Mary was gone.

Later that night, his tired brain heard a crackling noise. Thinking it was mice, he thought he might go get Sheba from the store and go back to sleep. He pulled on his boots and looked out the window. Flames shot up from the store roof and danced in the windows.

He raced toward the store and saw Sheba leap from a second-story window. He must have left the lamp lit—that window was right next to the upstairs desk. Perhaps the cat had knocked it over. He tried to carry goods out of the store, piling them in the road. The fire was too big to put out, and unlike Dallas, there was no fire department to call. Back and forth, back and forth he went, carrying what he could. A few neighbors woke up and saw the blaze, coming to help. Within an hour, the flames were too hot, and the store was an inferno.

When the morning light came, there was nothing left but the charred boards and ashes, along with the little that Will had saved.

He sat on the porch of the house, holding his head in his hands. He had to tell Mary. He should send a telegram. But what would they do?

Will prayed and remembered the verses from Job, that the Lord gives and the Lord takes away. Maybe instead of a telegram, the best option was to catch the train to Dallas and talk to Mary in person. He could get a neighbor to feed the horses for a few days.

He caught the noon train and was at the Kings' house by nine in the evening.

***

Will knocked, and Miranda answered in her dressing gown.

"Mr. Crump! We weren't expecting you. Mrs. Crump and the children are in bed, as are Mr. and Mrs. King. What's wrong?"

"Please, Miranda, get Mary. And some hot tea if you can spare it."

"Yes, sir. Please come into the parlor. I'll light a lamp."

Within minutes, Mary bustled in, and Miranda returned with a tea tray.

"Will! What is it? Why are you here?"

"I'm sorry, Mary. I'm so sorry. There was a fire at the store. I'm afraid we lost almost everything. No one is hurt, and no other buildings were affected. I think it might have been my fault—I was so tired. I probably left the lamp lit, and the cat knocked it over, I'm guessing."

"Oh, Will!"

She was on her feet, hugging him.

"Thank God you're safe. But whatever will we do?"

"I don't know. We have some savings, but I don't know how much will be left after paying what we owe for orders.

We don't have a store to sell from, and the other places in town will take our customers by the time we rebuild. With no money coming in, it will be difficult."

Will finished his tea. He felt like an utter failure.

"Morning will bring ideas, if not a solution," Mary said. "Come and get some sleep. Tomorrow we'll pray and decide what to do."

***

The next morning at breakfast, David and Ann heard the story.

"What will you do now?"

"I'm not sure, sir. We have to start over. We have the house, our savings, and some merchandise. We will also owe for everything already ordered. I can send telegrams to cancel for what I can remember, but most of the records were in the store."

"If you need a loan . . ."

"Thank you, sir. I hate to be beholden, but we may have to do that. I need to contact Hiram and cancel meat orders as well."

"Sir?" Miranda interrupted. "There's a telegram for you. It's from a Mr. Wheelock. Shall I bring it in?"

"Yes, please do."

David scanned the telegram and frowned.

"What do you think of this? It's Frank Wheelock. I haven't heard from him since that meeting a few years back. He says the town got delayed, but he and his Illinois investors are ready to start. It's now or never, he says. He's inviting me to join the investment and wonders if Will still has any interest in being part of a new town. He says they plan to send a plat for the town to the Land Commissioner in Austin next month. Anyone who invests will get land for less than a dollar an acre."

Will looked up. "It sounds great, but we don't have the money. And Mary wouldn't want to go."

Mary said, "Haven't you learned after all these years to let me speak for myself? It's a little different now than it was five years ago. Losing the store changes things. We have to start over anyway. The children are older. The land price is attractive and would give us a boost. Maybe we should at least look."

Will grinned. "So much for predicting Mary!"

David said, "If you think it's worth pursuing, let's call Wheelock and get more information. If you still like it, Ann and I could keep the children for the time it would take you two to go and look. Does that sound acceptable?"

"Yes, yes, it does," said Will.

Mary put her hand on his. "Together?"

"Together. God will show us if it's right."

Bob pushed back from the table. "I know I'm supposed to be seen and not heard, Grandpa, but I'm eight, and if Ma and Pa are going to look at a new place, I want to go too."

Mamie spoke, "I'd rather stay with Grandma. Riding in a

wagon sounds boring."

Dave said, "I'll second that. I'd rather stay and help Grandpa at the bank, if there's a choice."

Will and Mary looked at each other, and Mary gave a slight nod.

"All right, Bob. You're old enough to help drive the team," said Mary. She turned again to Will. "You did say our horses and barn are all right?"

"Yes, they are. We could drive the draft horses and the wagon from Henrietta. But let's see what Wheelock has to say first. And, Mary . . . are you sure? It would mean selling the house and uprooting, starting with nothing. When we got married, I had land and money from Colorado."

"Will, I know it's been your dream. You've never let go of it, even these last five years. Let's look at this dreamland of yours."

Will, Mary, and Bob rattled along in their wagon, mile after mile. They followed the fork of the Red River toward Palo Duro and the Goodnight ranch. The red dirt and yucca gave way to scrub juniper as they climbed through the canyon. They startled mule deer and earned a scolding from a pair of blue-headed painted buntings. Will enjoyed showing them the new sights. It would be a welcome relief to stay with Charlie and Molly after a week of sleeping in a tent or the wagon bed. They would travel south across the plains to the Llano Estacado, perhaps stopping at the town of Estacado, ten days south, a Quaker community.

As they neared the ranch house, cattle roamed freely around the rough stone walls. Will was amazed. It looked like a house transported from back east—two stories with a gabled roof, steps to a large porch, two chimneys, in the middle of well-kept grounds, surrounded by a rail fence. It would have been at home in a Kentucky city.

He pulled up before the barn and corral, put the brake on the buggy, and helped Mary and Bob down.

Will took Bob's hand, walked over to the house, and knocked. A housekeeper opened the door.

"Yes, sir?"

"I'd like to see Mr. Goodnight, please."

"Come in and have a seat. You are?"

"Will Crump."

"I'll check whether he'll see you."

After a few minutes, Charlie came out. "Will! You finally made it out here! Welcome. Good to see you again, Mrs. Crump."

"Good to see you, Charlie," said Will. "I'm hoping for a bunk for the night and information—what you can tell me or show me about the country. I'm talking with Wheelock over at the IOA about starting a town. It's just an idea at this point, but some investors are interested."

"My competition, eh? No matter, a friend is always welcome. I'm sorry, Mrs. Crump, Molly's off visiting, or she'd welcome you too. Wilma?" Charlie turned to the housekeeper. "Will you set extra places for dinner and make up the guest room?" They stared around the huge elegant house with high ceilings and chandeliers.

When Will and Bob were seated in the morning room around a small table, Will began asking questions.

"This is quite a place, Charlie. I had no idea. How long have you had it?"

"Oh, something's been here since before the war, but we built this house in '79, adding on to the original cabin. Kept adding things until Molly said stop," he chuckled.

"Had trouble with the Indians at first, then Quanah and I became friends, reached an understanding. I give them a few beeves now and then, and they leave the rest alone. Comanche are mostly friendly now, but it doesn't pay to get them riled."

"How much land do you have?"

"Around twenty-five hundred acres and the grassland south of here. The river provides water, but it's pretty dry to the south."

"I see what you mean about it being great land for cattle. We're looking farther south, down around Yellow House."

"Fine country, just dry, as I say. You might have to dig some deep wells, more than fifty feet, I'd judge. 'Course there is Buffalo Springs to the southeast. You'd have it to yourself for sure."

Will and Charlie continued talking over dinner, some beer, and into the wee hours of the morning. Mary eventually left them and went to bed. When the sun rose, Will and Mary set out for Yellow House Canyon.

***

"Pa, if we move here, can I have my own horse?" asked Bob.

"Well, I don't see why not—except you got to pay for it. You might find a horse for seventy dollars. A grown man makes maybe two dollars a day. But then you got to feed and take care of it. A horse is a mighty fine thing. You can travel far with him, and he'll be your friend—no railroad will do that. Are you willing to work for one?"

"Sure, Pa. I'll do whatever you say." Bob thought for a minute, staring at the wide cloudless sky.

"Do I have to let Mamie ride him?"

Will chuckled. "If he's your horse, then you decide who rides him."

"Good! Then I won't let any girls ride him."

"' Course, you might think on that. When Mamie's old enough to bake pies with Mama, she might not let you have any."

"I never thought of that. Well, maybe she could ride him sometimes. Like Fourth of July or Christmas."

Will's eyes crinkled in the corners. "Yeah, maybe then."

They drove on for mile after mile, the land rising to the Caprock. When they crested the top, it was like they'd climbed onto a table that stretched endless to the horizon. At sunset, clouds blew in, like wispy sailing ships on a sea that changed color from blue to deep orange and fiery red. They were quiet, taking it in. There was no sound but the wind and the occasional chirp of birds. They were utterly alone.

After several days' drive, following Goodnight's directions and the sparse landmarks, keeping the sun on their left in the morning and on the right toward evening, they saw smoke rising from the prairie and knew Estacado must be ahead. Will didn't know what he'd expected, but he could hardly call it a town.

"Is this it? Is this all there is?" asked Mary. They saw rows of tents, a general store, a post office and church, two or three frame houses, and a lot of soddies. The sign on the store proclaimed *George Singer Emporium, Goods of all Kinds*. He looked around. There didn't seem to be a hotel. Maybe he could get Bob some penny candy and pick up some information at the store.

"Howdy! What can I do for you? I'm George Singer."

"Will and Mary Crump. We need some jerky and penny candy for the little guy here. And information."

George bustled about getting the jerky and candy and asked, "What kind of information?"

"Where to get water for the horses, a bed for the night, if there is one, and what lies to the south here."

"There's a pump over behind the church and a trough for the horses. Bed? 'Fraid not. Half the people live in tents. I built this store last year and had to haul the lumber from the railhead south of here at Colorado City. That's one long, dry hundred miles. But it's the closest railroad, so I make the trip every few months." George handed Will a bag with his order. "That'll be three bits."

"Food comes high here, does it?"

"I guess you might say that. I'm the only store in fifty miles, and I have to haul everything in by wagon. The buffalo are gone, and the deer get scarcer, so I have to buy salted beef."

Will tipped his hat. "Much obliged."

They camped under the broad canopy of stars again that night and attended a Quaker Sunday meeting the next morning, waiting quietly on God. A few verses were read, but the time passed mostly in silence. Bob fidgeted, even though he was used to it from Henrietta. Will felt a sense of communion and knew Mary would like this place if she gave it a chance.

When he woke just before dawn, he saw a great light across the sky, moving south. It had a bright head and tail that stretched over half the sky. Will supposed it must be a comet. He'd heard of them but had never seen one.

"Mary, look!" Will whispered, poking her.

She stirred sleepily, looking up. "That's quite a light show," she said.

"I think God is saying to us, 'Come, follow me. I will show you a place.'"

Mary kept watching. "Maybe so," she whispered.

She took Will's hand, and they followed the progress of the comet across the sky. Bob never stirred.

With supplies from the Singer store loaded, they continued south, reaching Buffalo Springs, and then farther west they turned back north. The horses quickened their pace, and Will wondered if they sensed water. Charlie had told him how to find Yellow House Canyon, which had water running through it. It wasn't a lot, but there was water, green grasses, and good land. Something clicked in his spirit—this was the place. The half-mile-wide canyon stretched across the prairie as far as he could see.

As they explored the canyon, they came to a shallow lake. The horses drank their fill.

"What do you think, Mary? Could we make a home

here? It's where Wheelock and the others talked about coming."

"Is this it?" said Bob. "I see nothing."

"It's a pretty place, but how would we live? There's no one here, and it's a long haul to any store."

"Let's talk to Hiram. Towns spring up out of nowhere when the railroad comes. What if it came here?"

"Maybe. But with no people, why would it come?"

"I don't know," Will admitted. "Wheelock and the others seem to think that the land is good enough to draw people."

"I'm still skeptical, but let's keep praying and talking."

***

After their excursion to Yellow House Canyon, Will
and Mary collected their other children from the Kings in
Dallas and went home. They cleaned up the remains of the
store and tried to re-open it, but it was a struggle. Will and
Mary agreed the place didn't feel like home anymore. They
couldn't explain it, but the canyon called to them.

Wheelock and others began plans to build. There were
no trees except scrub pine near the water in the canyon, so
lumber would have to be hauled from the railhead. Hiram
advised them that the railroad would pass near the Goodnight ranch within a month.

"Mary, I have an idea. What if we sell the house and the
business here? You could move in with your parents until I
have a place in the canyon. I got word from Wheelock—
next month, George Singer is going to move his store to the
canyon from Estacado. Twenty families are moving with
him. They'll need supplies and lumber. I could use our
wagon and team to haul it south from Amarillo. I could buy
land with what we get from the sale of the house. Wheelock
says we could get several hundred acres, and cattle are
cheap right now. We could restart our herd buying from
Charlie for about two hundred. If we wait, it will cost much

more. Hiram thinks there's a good chance of a spur from the railroad south."

"All right, Will. The store here certainly isn't prospering. There is something I need to tell you, though. I think I'm pregnant."

Will hugged her. "That's wonderful! It's been so long . . . I mean, Mamie is almost seven. I didn't think we'd have any more children. Does that change your mind? I know one of the reasons you said we could move was that the children were older now."

"I have to admit that it isn't convenient. But perhaps spending time with my parents would be good at a time like this. I'd miss you, but I don't want to be alone in the canyon while you're away hauling things from the railhead. I can come when things are more established."

"What if I kept the boys with me and then came back for the birth? We could come on the railroad after it gets to Charlie's. Wouldn't that make it easier?"

"You'd come and visit? And be there for the birth?"

"Yes. I'd certainly do my best. You could telegraph Charlie when the time gets close."

"All right, then. The boys can go with you and help. They'll miss some school, but I doubt Bob at least will mind. We can make it up later."

They put the house and store up for sale. Mary and Mamie went to the Kings' house in Dallas. Will and the boys loaded the wagon and set out on the long drive to Yellow House Canyon.

Chapter 18

Nicodemus, March 1887

There was a stir in the town. After Luther played in the baseball game today against the visiting white team, Roundtree wanted to hold a meeting. The Kansas Pacific Railroad had been taken over by Jay Gould's Union Pacific and was on the move again, building more lines and extensions. Gould had sent an engineer out to look things over, Virgil Bogue.

"Afternoon, Mr. Bogue. Are you enjoying our fine town?" asked Luther as he selected a bat.

"Very interesting. I thought I'd sample the local culture. It's not often you see an all-black town—and a successful one at that."

Luther smiled. "Glad you can see it. We're very

proud of what we've accomplished. From the old-timers like Simon there," he said, motioning toward Roundtree, "to the relative newcomers," Luther pointed to some more families, "everyone pitches in to do their part. We have over five hundred people here now, our newspaper, literary society, and a baseball team."

"I believe baseball is becoming very fashionable. In Seattle, where I come from, there's a black team, the Seattle Steelheads," said Bogue.

"Yes, sir. We have just about everything—except a railroad."

"That's why I'm here, to choose the best route for the railroad. I don't want a repeat of the Northern Pacific's Stampede Pass fiasco. Wasted money, building over a pass too high and drilling an extra tunnel. What we're looking for is something along the Solomon River. If we don't have to cross and build a bridge, so much the better. The more cuts and bridges we have to do, the more it costs. I'm sure even you can understand that."

Luther caught the insult but let it ride. "Yes, sir."

Bogue continued, "Of course, town participation and support matters too. The railroad has to go where it will get the most freight business. Passengers are nice, but freight pays the bills."

"Yes, sir. We want to ship wheat and cattle. We're having a meeting this afternoon after the game, raising money for a depot and support for the railroad. We'd be pleased for you to attend."

"Fine, fine. I'll look forward to it."

"If you'll excuse me, I believe the band is starting, and my team is taking the field."

Luther found it hard to concentrate on the game, worried about Bogue. There was something very slimy, very white about the man. Luther had grown used to the day-to-day relations in Nicodemus, where none of that deference and eyes-down foolishness was needed. He looked the white storekeeper in the eye and called him by his first name, just like everyone else. But it wasn't like that everywhere—he knew that well from Topeka. He'd heard that the governor was discouraging black people from coming to the state now, even though Ed McCabe, a Nicodemus resident, had become state auditor.

The bat cracked loud, and the fly ball soared at Luther in left field. He scuttled back, trying to get under it, and almost lost it in the sun. He corrected, caught it, and threw the man out at second. Two out, one to go.

Luther focused on the game and got a double when he came up to bat. The score was three to two at the end, and the Nicodemus team was triumphant. After water, back-slapping, and some good-natured teasing, everyone gathered around to hear Simon Roundtree.

"Praise God for good weather, good harvest, and fun times! I bless every day I spend in Nicodemus. But you can't get complacent. You can't sit on your hands. You got to keep working, keep listening to the Lord.

"What we're here today to talk about is the railroad. You know how hard we've worked. But unless we get the railroad through here, it might all be for nothin'. We can't let freedom slip away. We got to hold on to it, tie it down. We have a gentleman here today from Union Pacific. He's looking at the ground, the hills, and the rivers, but he's also looking at you! The UP wants to know, how bad do you want a railroad?"

"We want it!" said the people.

"But they ain't gonna do it all for you. They want to know, are you behind it? Will you support it? Will you send your crops to market on it? Today they're asking for a pledge. We're going to vote on a bond in support of the railroad. What will you give? How much does it mean to this town? We're not rich, but we want our children to grow up free. We need the railroad, and the railroad needs us. Now we got some sausages down here for everyone.

Y'all come to the front, get your sausage, and write your pledge. We'll total it up for Mr. Bogue."

Luther helped serve the sausages, then gathered the pledges for Roundtree. Simon counted, "One thousand, five hundred, another one thousand . . ." When it was all totaled, the community had pledged sixteen thousand dollars for railroad bonds.

Simon presented it to Bogue with a flourish. "Here you are, sir. This is our people, giving all they can. They don't know what's coming—maybe hail, maybe plenty— but they want to support your railroad, giving even more than they got."

"Thank you, Reverend . . . Roundtree, was it? I will take this back to the directors at the UP. When we finish our land surveys, we will let you know."

***

Nicodemus, July 1888

Luther and Ruth decided they'd had enough work for a Friday. Lindy could watch the other children while they took a leisurely ride along the Solomon. They had two fine saddle horses, and Ruth had become an accomplished horsewoman.

They rode west, up the gentle slopes, and then down again to the banks of the South Solomon, crossing at a low point. Luther thought about challenging her to a race, but right now he liked this lazy feeling of a peaceful ride, no purpose in mind, no pressure or cares. He pointed his mare farther west once they crossed the river. The wildflowers were competing to see which could shout the glory of the Lord the loudest, and the birds played a symphony just for them.

"It's pretty near heaven, isn't it, Ruth?"

"Pretty near. We got to start thinking about the children, though—what will they do when they grow up? They don't know much outside of Nicodemus."

"Maybe they won't have to find out," said Luther with a grin. "I bet Lindy could run a hotel, the way she cooks and cleans. One of the boys takes over the blacksmith

384

shop."

"We can dream. Say, what's that up there?"

Luther looked in the direction she pointed and saw stakes driven in the ground, connected by strings.

"Let's get a closer look."

When they got up close, Luther saw digging had been happening between two rows of stakes. The stakes made a track about five feet apart—just wide enough for a railroad.

Luther swore, and his tone caused Ruth to draw back. "Let's follow these stakes and see how far they go."

They trotted beside the rows of stakes, yellow flags fluttering in the breeze, the peace of the ride shattered. After about two miles, they saw a board sign:

**Welcome to Bogue, where your dreams come true.
Home of the Union Pacific Railroad.**

"That no good scoundrel Bogue! He's already decided on the railroad and the town. They never meant to give us a chance," said Luther.

Ruth frowned and said, "C'mon! We got to get back and tell Simon."

Omaha, 1888

Roundtree, McCabe, and Luther cooled their heels in an outer office, waiting for someone to see them. They'd telegraphed ahead but received no assurances nor any notice.

"I'm afraid Mr. Bogue is very busy today," said the assistant. "Can I help you?"

"You got the power to decide where the railroad goes?" demanded Luther.

"No, sir, of course not."

"Then we'll wait for Mr. Bogue," said Roundtree.

After another two hours, the assistant reappeared. "I'm sorry, he's just too busy to see you today. If you'd care to make an appointment in two weeks, I'll see if I can find a spot on his calendar."

McCabe spoke up. "That is unacceptable. Either find a way for us to meet with him or Jay Gould or I will telegraph the governor."

"It just won't work today, gentlemen. I'll show you out."

"We'll see about that," said Luther, pushing past the assistant and opening the frosted glass door. McCabe tried to restrain him, but Luther shook him off. McCabe and Roundtree followed as Luther read the doors until he found one that said "Bogue" in gold lettering. The assistant spluttered and said something about calling security.

Luther threw open the door to find Bogue behind his desk, sipping claret and going over maps. Bogue looked up. "What is the meaning of this? I clearly told my assistant I have no time to see you."

"And when were you planning to tell us about the new town across the river and the railroad route?"

Bogue sighed. He took off his glasses and stroked his forehead, as though soothing a headache and hoping they would disappear. "I saw no need to concern you. We looked at your town. The directors do not believe a black town can generate enough commerce to be competitive. It's as simple as that. The banks should return your bond money. Now if you'll excuse me . . ."

Roundtree said, "There ain't no excuse for hatred."

Luther rounded the desk and picked up one of the maps.

"Hey, you can't do that! That's company property!"

"Uh-huh. And this shows a new town with a UP line and depot, all platted out, named after you, with you as the owner of the lots. I see the stamp from Topeka, and it's dated before you came to that baseball game. You never intended to give us a chance, did you?"

McCabe protested, "That's unfair, sir. What's more, I've looked at your route—does the UP and the legislature know that your route involves two bridges and three cuts to reach Hill City and Bogue? When on the north side of the river none are required at all?"

Behind them, three security guards entered, tapping billy clubs on their hands.

Bogue stood and said, "This interview is over. You will leave now, or these gentlemen will throw you out."

Luther looked at the guards and saw that resistance was pointless. Fighting the guards would hurt their cause and get him arrested, hurting Ruth and their children. He clenched his fists, and his stomach rolled with fury. Once outside, they could talk.

"Not fair doesn't cover half of it," said Luther. "Cheats and swindlers. They plan to get rich, lining their own pockets, from the railroad."

"It sure looks that way," said Roundtree. "But what can we do?"

McCabe shook his head. "Not very much, I'm afraid. They are not using state money. I can petition the governor. But once they start laying rails, it is unlikely that we can overrule them. The best we can hope for is a spur, a bridge over the river to Nicodemus someday."

"It's always some other day, isn't it?" said Luther.

***

Luther returned to the house he'd built with Ruth, next to their old dugout and the blacksmith shop. His face gave away the discouragement he felt. She knew without words and came to hug him. There would be no railroad. He sat at their table and pounded a fist on it in frustration. How could he tell her?

"They won't budge. They cheated us. Not even an attempt to pretend. It's all because we're black. We'll try to get the bond money back. McCabe will talk to the governor and the legislature. As state auditor, his voice may carry some weight."

"Oh, Luther. After all our work. What can we do?"

"Pray. Keep working. We still have the land. Maybe, if we work hard . . . someday."

Luther began to sing, almost a whisper, using the melody of the old song, "Wake Nicodemus!" changing the words:

"Nicodemus, the town, home of black and brave
They worked the land, they earned the gold
Their freedom they tried to save
Their story not told, the Good Comin' sleeps

Don't wake Nicodemus today
Their spirit lives yet, in the Kansas plains
A few souls brave enduring the pain
No longer in dirt caves lined with tears
It echoes still, down through the years
Lord, will we ever be free?"

***

Nicodemus, December 1889

Luther stretched and shrugged into his clothes. He had projects at the forge waiting. This cold winter morning, he felt every one of his forty-five years. The hammer was heavier; the iron materials took longer to shape. There were other blacksmiths in town, at least for now. He couldn't crawl back into bed. The ground might be frozen, but the stock still needed tending. He massaged his right shoulder, which ached from the cold. He walked out to the shop and stoked up the fire for the forge. He'd let it warm up while he fed the horses. It was Saturday, only four days until Christmas.

When he opened the shop door, he saw someone coming toward him.

"Luther? Is that you? It's Mark, Ned's son."

"Mark? Ned said you might be coming. Somethin' about losing the store in Georgetown, after all these years."

"I'm afraid that's true. I let myself get involved in the silver boom, and I was doing well. I had a little too much to drink one night and got involved in a poker game. Ever seen a woman play poker before? I figured she'd be easy to beat. Her name was Alice—I discovered that they call her Poker Alice. It wasn't two hours and I had lost the store, my claim, and my ready cash. I wrote to Pa, and here I am. Can you show me to him?"

"No need for that, here I am," said Ned. He grinned and walked over to hug his son. "I'm happy to see you."

"Are you sure? I guess I'm a little like the prodigal."

"We can talk about that. But for now, let's go see if your ma can find you some breakfast. It's good to have you home. We've missed you. There's always room in our house for one more."

Chapter 19

Dallas, August 1889

During the past year and a half, Will and the boys had used the train to visit Mary and the girls in Dallas whenever there was a pause working on the town.

Due to the lack of everything, especially timber, their first jobs had been to get shelter and a steady supply line. Frank Wheelock, George Singer, and William Rayner, with the families who moved from Estacada, worked tirelessly at the new townsite, clearing rocks and planting to make the town self-sufficient—when there was a town. Due to the lack of trees, Will hauled logs from the railroad to Estacada, and they put Singer's store on them, rolling the structure with oxen more than twenty miles to the new townsite. Wheelock bought lumber for a hotel, the Nicolett, and built it in North Town. A few months later, information came in from Hiram about where the rails would run, and it caused sharp disagreement among the town planners about where to put the buildings and how to plat the town. William Rayner wanted to put everything on the north rim of the canyon, even though all indications were that the railroad would run along the south rim. Rayner insisted he was right and started a rival town that he called Monterey, though everyone else called it North Town. When the information about the railroad came in, Wheelock used tremendous engineering skills. He put his three-story hotel on logs, and moved it to South Town, near Singer's store.

As Will finished helping with that feat, a messenger galloped into the settlement. Will wondered what the excitement was about. He discovered it was a telegram for him from Mary. She said that the midwife thought the baby might come within a few days, and urged him to come.

He packed and got the boys ready to go. George Singer agreed to drive with him to the depot. George could pick up supplies to bring back.

When he got on the train, he wished that he could make the train go faster, like pressing his heels into the sides of a horse. He was impatient with each turn of the wheels. Babies were unpredictable—what if he was too late?

When the train pulled in, David King met him at the station, and they drove to the King's house as if bluecoats were chasing them. Miranda motioned him upstairs, and there was Mary. She wasn't too far into labor yet.

"Will. You made it."

"Thank heavens for trains." She stood, and he gave her a hug, interrupted by a contraction. The midwife came out of the corner.

"All right, you've seen her. Now shoo. There's women's work to be done. Go wear out the floor in the parlor."

Katy Bell Crump arrived in the middle of the night, before dawn on August 22, 1889. When Will saw Mary again, she was exhausted. She was holding their new daughter, and that was enough for any woman to do. She wanted to rest in the moment, to glory in this new creation.

When they got Katy settled in a bassinet, they had a short time of quiet and cuddling before sleep claimed Will and Mary had to nurse. Will got to introduce the boys to their new sister, and they stayed for two days before taking the train back to the new town.

The Founding

Caprock, Llano Estacado

Wheelock and the other men were discussing how to proceed.

"We need lumber. We all know the scrub trees here are no good for buildings. And we've watched what happens to towns that rely on soddies or dugouts—eventually they get real buildings or they die," said Wheelock.

"Hauling lumber is expensive," objected George Singer. Turning, he saw Will. "How's the new baby?"

"Beautiful daughter, and loud," said Will. "Let's get this town done!"

Wheelock filled them in on the doings at the state legislature and the investors. "We've floated some bonds. There are those in Illinois that have faith in us. To succeed, we'll need to make this place the county seat. Austin thinks the county should be named Lubbock, after Francis Lubbock, the state treasurer, and former governor. We could come up with a different idea, but since we want Austin on our side, I say we go with it. To make things simple, we can name the town Lubbock as well and curry some favor for it as the county seat."

Will shrugged. "Sounds sensible. Remember - the town that gets the railroad takes off and prospers. The town that is passed by withers."

"I can attest to that," said Singer. "Estacado is dying now for lack of a railroad connection and a store. I moved it here in hopes of the railroad."

Wheelock stared at the sky a moment. "We need to move quickly. Rayner will try to pull population to North Town and influence both the railroad and the legislature any way he can."

Will looked over at Dave and Bob. They had stacked boots, pans, and boxes, trying to build a fort. Will smiled at them, and Bob said, "We're making the fort for the town so there won't be Indians."

"If Rayner persuades the legislature and the railroad, we could lose the county seat. The sooner we have some-thing that *looks* like a town here, the better."

Will considered. "What do you think of Rayner's chances?"

"Hard to say. Information from your brother-in-law gives us a slight advantage. On the other hand, he's done another town southeast of here called Rayner. The state government knows he can do it."

"Can we talk? Maybe re-join forces?" asked Will

Wheelock shook his head. "He's a stubborn cuss. He thinks the railroad will more likely go to the north side of the canyon. There's a chance it could get ugly. Other counties in this situation have had gun battles over which town gets to be the county seat. The faster we build and bring in people, the less likely violence will happen. And the sooner that lovely wife of yours can join you."

"All right. Then let's get busy."

***

South Town, or Lubbock, as they began to call it, had a store, the Nicolett hotel, a trading post, and a post office. The town was beginning to take shape. A preacher came and held services in the store. Will got used to the trip up to Amarillo, hauling lumber and other goods. Sometimes he picked up extra supplies for farms along the route and delivered them. They would leave money in a box on the road to pay. Will used the fees from this to buy more lumber and worked hard in whatever spare time he could manage to build a little frame house. Dave was becoming a good carpenter. The house was close enough to the Yellow House Draw, the water that flowed through the canyon, that they could fill buckets for household water. Will telegraphed Mary on his next trip to Charlie's and the little town of Amarillo that was growing up around the railroad there, asking her to come. Three days later, she and the girls came on the train. Mary brought news that Will didn't want to hear – his father Robert died.

"Lydia thought it best not to tell you in a letter or a telegram, since I was coming. The doctor said it was old age, no other reason. I'm sorry, Will."

"Thanks for bringing the message – you're right, a telegram isn't the same."

Mary and Will fell into each other's arms. They were a family again.

***

South Town, 1890

As they worked, more people came in, and Will spent most of his time as a freight driver between Amarillo and Lubbock. Lubbock now sported a saloon.

Mary spoke about it to Will at dinner one night.

"Why on earth does the town need a saloon? It will make trouble if the railroad comes. Remember what Julia told us about Abilene? Why couldn't they build a proper church?"

Will shrugged. "The men work hard. Some of them aren't churchgoers. They need a place to blow off steam."

"Get drunk, you mean. And probably whore, though no one talks about it."

"You may be right, but if they don't do it here, they'll go to North Town to do it. No sense giving Rayner an advantage."

"George doesn't carry liquor in his store. I think it's commendable."

Will decided retreat was the best course of action. Why fight about something he wasn't in favor of either? The reality was that some of the men were going to drink, regardless of what the women thought.

Will worked together with the other men to move more buildings, to build up the town faster and cheaper than building from new lumber. They moved houses and shops from Estacado and surrounding towns. One day he discovered that someone had dug a gully across their usual path to move the buildings. Wheelock looked at it with him and started cursing.

"Damned North Towners! So that's how it is, is it? Not enough to throw lawyers and bribes at us in state government, now they resort to sabotage. They must have done this at night."

"It was done on purpose, that's for sure. Do we need to set guards on the road to Estacado?" asked Will.

"We could, but they might just come at it from another way. We've got more buildings than they do," said Wheelock.

"And more people, but they could sure slow us down with devilment."

"We can't afford that. We need to settle this by Christmas. Governor Ross is favorable to us, but who knows who the new governor will be in January?" Wheelock fretted.

"Well, let's get some men on it. The gully won't fill

itself. And I smell rain coming from the north," said Will.

The next day, they found the supports for one of the houses removed and the porch roof caved in. As they were examining, Rayner rode up. His long-limbed gray horse appeared to labor under his six-foot-four frame. Black hair spilled out from under his slouch hat, and his black eyes carried a look of disdain.

"Now ain't that too bad," Rayner sneered. "Looks like one of your buildings fell apart. Guess you weren't gentle enough moving it down. You really should be more careful."

Wheelock said, "I think we are careful, but we have to watch out more for snakes like you, Rayner."

Will was hot, tired, and angry. "If you think you're going to stop us by tearing things up, you might want to think hard before things get ugly."

"Oh, threats, is it? Well, come ahead. I have a few boys of my own. Some of them right handy with that Remington 1880 revolver."

"Will, let it go," Wheelock said. "We don't want anyone hurt."

"That's right," said Rayner. "Y'all could come over and join me—or go back to Fort Worth. Either way is good for me. But this little pit in the road," he motioned at South

Town, "is never going to succeed. When I convince the AT&SF to build the spur to Monterey, everyone here will leave, just like Marble Falls and Estacado."

"Since my sister and brother-in-law control the AT&SF, that seems unlikely," said Will.

"And what if 'accidents' start happening in North Town?" said Will, carefully avoiding calling it Monterey, as Rayner preferred.

"Now that would be real unfortunate. We have armed guards at night, and some during the day. Coyotes, you know. We want people to feel safe in our town," said Rayner. "'Course the Comanche could come out again. Now that the government opened the Indian Territory. The Sioux up north are getting troublesome. Could be some Comanche bucks will get tired of the porridge at Fort Sill. If they was to shoot up or burn your little trash pit here, that would be a pure shame."

Will glared at Rayner. "We'll see, Rayner. We'll see."

"Will! When you have a nest of vipers, don't go sticking your hand in it," said Wheelock.

***

Lubbock, August 1890

Will joined for lunch, but Mary was nursing Katy, so he made sandwiches for everyone. Katy was crying fitfully and not latching on, her face red from the heat. At one year old, the hot Texas plains were hard on her.

"It's the heat, Will. She has a hard time with it. I'm thankful that we agreed for me and the girls to stay in Dallas until there was a house here. I can't imagine giving birth under these conditions."

"I'm sorry the house is so small and lets the heat in so much. We'll fix it or make a better one. It's the best I could do for now. I missed you and Mamie so much I wanted to hurry and finish to give you a place to live."

"I don't like to complain, but the house is situated so that the sun beats down on it in the morning and heats it like a baking oven. No trees, so no shade."

Will watched her wipe the sweat away from her and Katy.

"I feel like a roast goose," said Mary.
She tried moving Katy back and forth, a gentle rocking motion.

"At least the boys have endless room to run," said

Will. "All that flat land stretching to the other side of the canyon. That much is a blessing."

"I wish there were more families. I suppose I should be grateful for twenty, but I rarely see the women, mostly just the men, intent on working to build the town. I'm starved for adult female conversation. All I hear is the next thing needed for the town."

"I wish I could do something about the weather. But I am glad to have you here. Maybe Dave can watch the other kids for a bit this evening after it cools off. We could walk down by the draw. With the weather hotter than usual for north Texas in August, it's a wonder we haven't been fighting. That's thanks to your patience, Mary."

"Do you think we'll soon get well? And I miss my garden in Henrietta—we have no vegetables stored for winter."

"Maybe we can plant a few things, but it's late. Do you think Bob or Mamie could water them?"

"Yes, but it's hard for me to supervise with Katy. Still, it's worth a try, if George has seeds this late in the season."

"I'll ask," said Will. "Well, I should get back to work."

He left, walking over to the Singer store, thinking as he went.

Occasionally petty disputes broke out, but there was no recognized authority to settle them, he mused.

Everything pointed ahead to someday. Someday they would have a regular church and minister, maybe a Quaker meeting. Someday there would be a school, though whether there would be any learning before the snow fell, no one knew. Someday they would have a farm, a business, and a normal life. Someday there would be a sheriff, courts, and laws. Here on the prairie, hell seemed closer than someday. He'd never imagined starting a town would be this hard.

Will came back at the end of the day's work. He'd been moving more houses, building, hammering, sawing, and hauling. Sweat poured off him, even dripping from his beard. He wanted a clean shirt, a drink, and dinner. Mary looked drawn and haggard. He didn't want to ask her. He thought if he did, she might scream. There was no escaping the heat—unless they stripped naked and jumped in the draw! That made him chuckle.

"What's funny? I could use a laugh," Mary said.

"Oh, I was just feeling sorry for myself, nothing you want to hear. This heat makes us both cranky, so I had this vision of throwing off our clothes and jumping in the draw."

Mary grinned despite herself. "That would entertain

the town for sure! We might have to try it."

"Mary! I was joking. I appreciate all that you put up with. You are up for sainthood, in case you hadn't noticed," said Will.

"I hadn't, but I'll take it."

Will frowned and said, "Rayner finally came over. He wanted to gloat and tell us it's as likely as snow in August that Lubbock will succeed. He even as much as admitted that he was sabotaging houses and roads. He threatened violence, pretending to be Comanches."

"That scum."

"Why dear wife, I'm surprised at you!" Will grinned without humor. "But you're right. He is scum. None of this would have happened if he hadn't insisted on his way. Well, we'll be ready for him. He's not the only one that knows how to be violent."

"Will, no! You can't. I won't have you teaching the children killing."

"Mary, I don't want to kill anyone. I want him to leave us alone."

"And so he will. God will tend to him. We're to love our enemies."

"If he tries to burn a house over here, I'll love him to death," said Will, loading a cartridge into his revolver.

"You'll do no such thing. We'll pray and trust God. Violence and guns are not the answer."

"I won't let them hurt you."

"They won't. You'll see."

"I'm going to follow up on the idea of jumping in the draw. Then I'll take Katy so you can have a break."

As Will left, she murmured to his back, "None of this would have happened if you hadn't insisted on *your* way."

***

September brought rain—sheets of it. Will's frustration grew as he saw the plains turn into a muddy mess. In surrounding areas, crops were left in the field unharvested due to the rain and not being able to get equipment into the fields without getting stuck. Dan and Rod, their draft horses, developed sore tendons from the effort of pulling their huge hooves out of the muck. Worse still, it left the children little place to play, and Mamie looked like she'd become a mud pie.

Mary came to Will, holding her skirts above the mud.

"Where am I supposed to do laundry? I'm sorry, Will, but these conditions are beginning to get on my nerves. First the heat, now the rain. There's no room to hang laundry to dry, and if the children play outside, they come back looking like filthy groundhogs. We need more space. Winter will come, and then what? And I'm not the only one. I talked to a few of the women at the store. I had to go buy food, and if I didn't get out for a short time, I'd go crazy. We're all in the same fix."

"I know, Mary, I do. I wish I could command the weather. The women aren't the only ones frustrated. A month of rain? Charlie said our main problem here would be how *dry* it was. I don't think there's a dry spot in the county. I'll speak to Frank and the other men and see what we can do."

Will found Frank Wheelock at Singer's store.

"Frank, we've got to do something, or the women will revolt. I know you're as frustrated as they are, but they have to have somewhere to do laundry and get the children out to play. Any ideas?"

"Pray for dry weather, but I know everyone has been doing that. As soon as the weather breaks, we need to haul lumber and build a courthouse—it can do double duty and serve as a community center and church, and let George and Rachel have their store back."

Frank paused, scratching his head. "I guess I could let the women use some rooms at the hotel to hang laundry. I've got no customers anyway. No one wants to come to a town that doesn't exist, and no one can get through the muck."

"I'll tell Mary. Would it be all right to let the women have one of the two large common areas for the children to play in until the sun comes back?"

"I guess so. We'll have to clean up and not let them go crazy. I hope to have a business next spring."

Moving buildings or freighting anything became impossible. The town construction slowed to a crawl in both North Town and Lubbock, as if God had sent two recalcitrant children to their corners to cool off.

The one bonus was that since Will couldn't drive the team to Amarillo, and couldn't build or haul, he was home more. True, the space got cramped for six of them, but he always had a joke, a story, a song, or a game to keep the children happy and engaged. Mary gave him high marks as a father.

The sun did return, but the canyon floor took several days to dry. Temperatures hit the seventies, quite bearable after the summer heat.

Will and Mary looked over their brood.

"I don't care what anyone says," said Will. "I'm taking time to build two extra rooms onto this place. My next trip to the railhead is going to get lumber for us and coal for the stove."

"You'll have time? I know it's important to get the courthouse built."

"Look at these kids. It's so cramped in here that if they wiggle, someone gets an elbow in the eye. The cabin I grew up in was bigger than this. Only two rooms, but bigger."

"It would be a help," said Mary. "But if you got the courthouse built, wouldn't it be a lot bigger? Could we just live there for the time being? There's bound to be new people in the spring, looking for land—this could be temporary quarters for them. If some of the men dedicated their time to it, working together, couldn't it be up before Christmas?"

Will considered. "You've got a point. We plan to go all out advertising, getting people to come. The problem is where to build the courthouse. This foolishness with Rayner has made everything uncertain, and cost weeks of extra work."

"Then maybe it's time for some of that peace on earth," said Mary.

***

With the return of the sun, the minor acts of sabotage resumed. Will only hoped it would die out of its own accord.

A thought nagged at him—what if it didn't? What if as things dried out, it got worse? Will hadn't heard of any peace overtures. Mary and Will prayed nightly for resolution and harmony, but when the men talked at the store, the resentment still boiled.

The ground dried enough for horses and wagons to get through, and Will resumed hauling goods, taking Dave and Bob with him this trip to give Mary relief. He posted letters to his sisters and Robert and one to Luther as well. Will wondered how he was doing. Hiram sent word that the UP had bypassed Nicodemus, and Will wondered what they would do now. He invited Luther and any of his family that was willing to join them in Lubbock.

"Papa, what happens if the railroad doesn't come to Lubbock?" asked Bob.

"I don't know," Will admitted. "We'll keep working and trying to convince them. Your uncle Hiram thinks the railroad will come, but he has investors, men that have put out money for the railroad. He doesn't make all the decisions anymore. Julia is my sister, but decisions have to be made on a business basis, whether they think they will get enough freight to make a profit from building the line. That's why it's important to get more people to come."

"When are we going to get a real house again?"

"I don't know, Bob. I just don't know. This trouble with Rayner is holding everything back."

Dave frowned. "In another month, it's going to be Thanksgiving, Papa. Are we going to visit Grandpa?"

"I don't think so. There's too much work to do on the town."

Will's heart ached, looking at his sons. Was it too much to ask of them, this dream?

They arrived at the depot and loaded lumber, nails, coal, and the items on George's list for the store. Looking at it, he knew this wasn't sustainable. They couldn't supply a whole town this way forever, even with an army of wagons. They simply had to get the railroad. The town would come together so much faster if Rayner worked with them instead of against them.

While they were loading, Bob asked, "Papa, why do we have to fight with Mr. Raynor? Why not work together?"

"It's complicated. We have to build where the railroad will come. Not everyone agrees about that—even your uncle Hiram doesn't know for sure. We have a good guess from his engineers, and that's what we're working from.

Do you remember I talked about my friend Luther? Despite all his work and the town's effort, the railroad bypassed them. The railroad men disagreed with them, saying the town couldn't produce enough to make the railroad work. When men disagree, it's hard to get them to change their minds. Let me tell you a story from when I fought in the war—a nice story about a time when at Christmas, in the middle of the war in Virginia, the blue and the gray called a truce. They stopped fighting and shooting at each other and exchanged what poor gifts they had, in the name of the Savior. For one day, they set aside their differences and declared peace on earth. They went back to fighting, but for that day they joined together as just men. And eventually, there was peace."

Dave said, "Why couldn't we do that with North Town? Not the fighting, the peace part. What if we got Uncle Hiram to come to talk to Rayner about the railroad and make peace? We could invite them all to a Thanksgiving dinner."

Will wondered, could it work? Was it that simple? If Hiram could give them some better assurance of the railroad route . . . Will had an idea he'd been holding back because it meant extra work. But what if . . . ?

He told the boys to keep loading and went to the telegraph office. Amarillo had gained the telegraph ahead of Lubbock because of the railroad. He sent a message to Hiram.

Of course, it might not work. Hiram's board might be opposed, or Hiram himself. And what if Rayner wasn't convinced and refused to participate? What if it degenerated into fighting? He knew about Rayner's size, strength, and nastiness. But the sabotage hadn't gotten better, and anger was rising among the men—probably on both sides. What if there was a battle and Will killed Rayner, or worse, Rayner killed him? He could shoot well, but he knew from the war that no man was invincible. And then there was Mary. If violence could be avoided . . .

He would try to wait long enough in town for Hiram to answer. If Hiram thought the idea was worth a try, he'd float it to Frank and Mary.

***

Will was elated. He got a positive response from Hiram. He said he'd have to come with some engineers to be sure and talk to the board, but he thought Will's idea had merit. Will was hoping Hiram would come in the next few days. They hadn't yet talked to Rayner, wanting to be sure first.

It was midmorning when Will's neighbor came, calling everyone who could come to a meeting at the Nicolett Hotel.

"Please come if you can. Wheelock's got an announcement, and we need everyone there."

Will looked at the weather, threatening rain again, then at Mary holding a crying Katy and said, "I'll go. Can't be anything that requires both of us. You take care of Katy, and I'll tell you all about it."

"Promise? I don't want the edited lady version—after all, I was invited."

"Promise. I'll tell you everything I hear."

Will left, grousing to himself about going out. Maybe he needed to build an ark instead of a house, the way it rained here. He returned an hour later. He hung up his wet coat and took off muddy boots, putting them in the box provided for the purpose at the door. He didn't say anything. Katy was sleeping again, and he saw that Mary had set the boys and Mamie to doing sums, to keep them busy and quiet. He poured a cup of coffee and sat, looking grim.

"What has happened?" she asked.

"It appears that someone tried to poison the water in the draw. That would end the town for sure, at this stage. If we have more rain and flooding, who knows what else it might affect? It would kill livestock. It might kill people. They saw a person dumping some barrels into the draw: cow manure. The person ran away and didn't get caught. But it wasn't accidental, and it doesn't take much to figure out who's responsible."

"How horrible!"

"Right. Wheelock wants to get some men together and go to North Town. I don't think there's much prospect for peace now. If we find any barrels of cow manure there, we arrest Rayner and hold a trial. If they resist, we fight."

"But, Will, someone will get killed!"

"I hope not. But they've gone too far. We can't ignore it."

"When are the men going?"

"Tomorrow, before noon."

"What about Hiram?"

"He won't get here before late afternoon. There's no

way to warn him that the visit might be for nothing."

"We can't let this happen, Will. We have to give Hiram and the engineers time. You and Hiram should go talk to Rayner—tonight. At least try. Peace for a day? Isn't that the story you told the boys?"

Will thought a minute. "All right. If Hiram is game, we'll give it a try. No need to involve anyone else yet."

***

Hiram arrived as the sun was setting. It was almost seven in the evening. Will greeted him and had Dave tend his rented horse. Hiram had dropped the engineers at the Nicolett Hotel, as agreed by telegram.

"How was the trip, Hiram?"

"Exhausting. We had trouble with a switch, and I didn't get to Amarillo until two hours late. Then we had trouble finding a buggy. I had to pay extra and get someone to cancel their reservation."

"Why don't we get you some food? I'm sorry to tell you, but things have changed. We need to act tonight."

Will told him about the poisoning and Mary's plan to stave off a fight.

"We need to talk to Rayner tonight."

Hiram groaned. "All right. I'll eat and drop my things at the hotel. I don't think you have enough room for me here."

Will gave a wry smile. "You barely fit in the door, so no, I don't think so. Thanks for coming on short notice, though."

After they ate and Hiram returned from the hotel, Will outlined more of his idea using Hiram's maps.

"It does look workable, but can you sell this Rayner on moving his buildings? And your people on the extra work of moving what they've built?"

"If it gets the town built faster and the railroad to come, I think so. Everyone knows how important the railroad is."

Will took his gun belt off a hook by the door. Mary gave a disapproving glare.

"Will, don't take your guns. You're trying for peace, remember? I will pray for you. Trust God and not how well you can shoot."

He hesitated, then hung the gun belt back on the hook and walked out the door to the buggy.

They drove across the canyon to North Town. It was dark. As they entered the main street, a guard appeared and looked them over.

"We've come to see Rayner," said Will. "I'm Will Crump, and this is my brother-in-law, chairman of the AT&SF railroad. Tell Rayner it's urgent."

"What's so all-fired urgent? It better be good—it's late, and I'm not looking to get skinned alive."

"We have a business proposition. By tomorrow, it may be too late."

"Rayner usually does that kind of business long before this hour."

Will bristled and then thought, Lord, forgive me. It's violence we're here to prevent.

With all the patience he could muster, sounding like the firm father of four children he was, he held a lantern his little higher to show the man's face. "We don't want to have dinner or dance with him at this hour. We have information and a proposal for the town. If he'll listen, it may save him a lot of money—and potential bloodshed."

The guard sighed and shrugged, slinging the rifle back on his shoulder. "All right. You'd have a better chance if you were a pretty lady at this hour. Remember that I warned you."

Hiram's presence helped propel Will up the stairs to Rayner's room. He hoped they weren't interrupting a nighttime tryst—Rayner would be angry, and they'd be embarrassed. Doubts assailed him. Whatever gave him the idea this could succeed? Another two steps. What if it came to shooting? He cursed himself for listening to Mary about the guns. They were at the door. He raised his hand to a tentative knock, but Hiram beat him to it, thumping on the door, demanding entry.

"Mr. Rayner? Please open the door," said Hiram.

The knob turned, the door cracked open at first, then opened the rest of the way. Rayner walked toward the desk with his back to them. There were two Mariinsky damask couches in forest green with gilt frames around the edges, a matching footstool, and a large oak desk with a chair, where Rayner sat. A thick golden carpet and matching wallpaper completed the decor. A door off the right was discreetly closed, probably the bedroom for the suite.

"State your business, gentlemen. This is hardly visiting hour. I don't want your small talk. Just tell me what brought you here so I can get back to sleep. And be quick.

You're big, but I can call more guards and have you thrown out." He pulled out a pocket watch and laid it on the desk. "You have two minutes, and then Jake and the boys will throw you in the horse trough."

"I'm sorry to interrupt your sleep—"

"One minute and forty-five seconds," interrupted Rayner.

"All right!" snapped Will. "Rude it is. I have come, Mr. Rayner, because my brother-in-law here, Hiram Johannsen, is head of the AT&SF, building north through Texas. I don't like to fight, and I don't like wasted money. I believe if you'll listen, I can show you a plan to avoid both, to the benefit of everyone in the towns."

"All right, Crump. You bought yourself five more minutes."

"May we show you our idea on a map?"

Hiram spread his rolled-up map on a table.

"What exactly is your proposal?" asked Rayner.

"Hiram has brought railroad engineers with him to check this out. In the past, they have surveyed this area as far as Amarillo. See here, the two ridges of Yellow House Canyon. There are several geological impediments to connecting the railroad to North Town called out in Hiram's notes. South Town might be slightly better, but neither location is ideal," said Will.

"That's right," said Hiram. "But Will has proposed an alternative. We just need time to evaluate it."

"And time is scarce right now. Your last stunt, polluting the water, has all of South Town hopping mad. Don't bother to deny it. Either we resolve this tonight or there will likely be bloodshed tomorrow," said Will. "I don't want it to come to that."

Rayner smiled with malice.

Will ignored him and continued, "George Singer moved his store from Estacado to South Town partly because the railroad passed them by. You don't want that to happen here."

Hiram pointed at the map, turning up a nearby oil lamp for better visibility. "Here," he pointed, "according to my men, south of the canyon just a short distance would be a much better place for the railroad—and the town. Closer to water, which is always important for the locomotives, I'm sure you know." Will couldn't resist smirking at Rayner.

Hiram continued, "And coming from the southeast, this area is more level—easier for buildings and roads and fewer bridges or cuts for the railroad."

Rayner looked at them as if seeing them for the first

time. "Does Wheelock know about this?"

Will spread his hands and answered, "Not yet. They've been too busy building and countering your she-nanigans. As you can see on the dates of these messages, Hiram and I only got all the information this past week. I intended to show them over the next few days, but your at-tempt to poison the draw has everyone reaching for their guns."

Hiram said, "Will might not tell you, but he was a sharpshooter in the war. I've seen him drop a bison at a thousand yards. Can't we stop this pointless squabble and save lives—and the town?"

"Your threats don't impress me. But your business case might," allowed Rayner.

Hiram rolled up his papers, replaced them in the oil-skin, and walked back to the door side of the desk.

Rayner appeared to be considering, sitting again at the desk chair. "You say the AT&SF has looked at this?"

"We need time to check thoroughly, but yes. We need to buy time, though, to calm down Wheelock and the others in Lubbock. Will says an armed posse from Lubbock is planning to come and visit you in the morning. I shouldn't tell you that, but I trust God that you will be a reasonable man. If you all work together and move the town to the site

Will and I arc proposing, I believe we can get on with making this a good place to live. I watched it happen with Dallas; it can happen here."

"Very well," said Rayner. "What you've said has merit. If you can convince the South Town people, and your delegation comes unarmed, we'll talk. It may be that as you say, we've been too stubborn in not considering the options."

"Then Will and I will depart, and messengers will come in the morning. Good night to you, sir."

Will and Hiram turned to leave.

***

Hiram yawned his way into the hotel, declaring that he was going to catch a few hours' sleep.

Despite Will's fatigue, he was too full of fizz from his visit to Rayner to try and sleep. He brought life to the coals in the stove and made coffee. It must be after seven, as he could see rays of light clawing their way over the horizon. In this land, you could see forever, so unlike the green rolling hills of east Texas.

Once he had his coffee, he pulled out his Bible and spent time reading and praying. It would take God to resolve this town mess. He'd done his little part. No one hurt so far. He hoped Mary would be pleased. The rest was up to God.

By the time the sun was fully over the horizon, he had breakfast cooking. He heard Katy stir. Mary picked her up, cooing at her, and changed her, then gave her medicine for croup.

"Good morning, sleepyhead." He smiled at her. "There's coffee and breakfast. Would you like me to hold Katy?"

"She's been coughing a lot. You were out late . . . and up early. The children missed you."

A wake of early morning chatter followed the boys

into the kitchen.

"Only the children?" He raised an eyebrow.

"Me too, of course," she said, setting Katy's medicine bottle on the table. "How did the meeting go?"

"I think Rayner's going to go for it. That guy isn't going to make it onto my Christmas list, though. I still have to talk to Frank Wheelock."

When they had eaten and Katy was fed, Mary got the boys to put on their worst clothes and told them they could go and play as long as they wouldn't exclude Mamie too much. The boys decided on working on their fort and letting Mamie help.

Before Will could get out the door, Frank Wheelock walked over to them, with ten other men from the town, all wearing guns.

"Ready, Will?" Wheelock asked. "Bring your rifle."

"No need, Frank. Hiram and I visited Rayner last night. I think he's willing to listen."

"But the water," one of the men said.

"I believe he might see to cleaning it up," said Will. "If we divert the draw and run the water through screens, sand, and gravel for a time, with all the rain we're having, it should be safe within a few weeks, as long as no more contamination happens. We can boil the water we use for drinking until then."

"There's no need for violence," said Mary. "There are times when men behave like pigheaded bulls, horns locked and pushing each other nowhere. Frank, I want you and the other men to listen to Will. Can we walk over to the store? There's more room there, and he has something to show you. Then if you want to go shoot up the town, we won't try and stop you."

Will looked at Frank. "She's right. If you'll listen, I think we can solve this."

Frank seemed impatient at the delay but said, "All right, Crump. Let's go over to the store. I hope this won't take long."

"Bob, can you go over to the hotel and get Uncle Hiram? Tell him I promise Swedish coffee later. Dave, can you take Katy? That will speed it up."

When they were all assembled in the front room of the store, which doubled as school and church, Will stood in front of the men. Mary said a silent prayer.

"All right, I'll try not to take long. I didn't call you here for coffee and cakes, though Rachel makes wonderful cakes, I've discovered."

Rachel circulated among the crowd, passing out cups of coffee and currant muffins.

"Last night, my brother-in-law Hiram and I went to see Rayner. Some of you may know about my brother-in-law Hiram Johannsen, who runs the Atchison, Topeka, and Santa Fe railroad along with the one down south in Galveston. I had an idea from doing my freight runs and deliveries and ran it by Hiram. It turns out that the AT&SF has already run surveys of this area, though they weren't ready to use them. The surveys show that neither North Town nor South Town is in quite the right place for the railroad."

He looked around to make sure he still had their attention. Some were wolfing down Rachel's delicious muffins, others rubbing their eyes, a couple scratching various parts, but Wheelock seemed to be paying rapt attention.

"I can show you the maps that Hiram provided. I've already shown Rayner. The railroad believes that about two miles south is the proper place for the town to get railroad support. I've shown Rayner Hiram's notes, and he's convinced enough to talk. You can look for yourselves. If you agree, there's no need for guns or bloodshed. Rayner will work with us instead of against us.

"George, can you clear some table or counter space? I need somewhere to spread out these maps."

Everyone gathered around the counter where George had made space.

Hiram came in with Bob. He and Will went through the same presentation they'd made to Rayner the night before, drawing more and more favorable comments when they explained the problems with the two current locations.

"If we send a messenger to Rayner this morning, and you men go over *without guns*, he's willing to talk and consider the proposal. We need a truce, a day of peace, to check everything out."

Chapter 20

The railroad engineers did a thorough survey on the site Will and Hiram identified, with favorable results. After much negotiation, on December 19, Rayner, Wheelock, and the other men shook on the idea of moving to the new location. Rayner set a crew to fixing the Yellow House Draw.

Wheelock came to Will. "I swear, locating this town is worse than arranging the furniture for a new bride. I hope we got it right this time."

"It's a pretty good Christmas present. I hope so too. It's been a trial. Moving buildings with draft horses and oxen is not fun."

"At least we haven't got the courthouse yet. We can build it in the right place."

A lot of hard work followed, including moving Wheelock's three-story Nicolett Hotel and George's store on logs, as they had done with both earlier. They agreed on a layout for the town. Will made a petition and got all the men to sign, asking the state legislature to make Lubbock the county seat. Wheelock, Will, and Rayner all traveled to Austin to finalize it.

Today they were meeting in the relocated Nicolett to have a recompilation ceremony for Lubbock, Texas.

Will, Wheelock, and Rayner addressed the crowd.

"Gentlemen, at long last, we can say we have a town!" said Wheelock. "As a result of our trip to Austin, the town is incorporated and accepted as the county seat."

Cheers went up, followed by foot stomping. Mary and Rachel Singer hugged each other.

Will said, "We've all worked hard, and there's still more to do. But from today forward, we can all agree to work together in peace and harmony."

Will extended a hand to Rayner, and they shook in front of everyone, then Wheelock and Rayner shook as well. There was loud applause and another cheer.

Raynor said, "We've agreed on a location for the courthouse, and Mr. Farris over there has agreed to sell two lots back to Mr. Wheelock and the county. Will Crump will commence hauling lumber and stone for it. We'll hope to havc it rcady by the end of 1891. In the meantime, I am leasing one of my buildings to the county to use for commissioners' meetings and court proceedings."

In the following months, Will and the other men dug a well and put in a windmill. For a time, Will worked hauling lumber and freight for the new town from Amarillo and Colorado City. It took four days each way.

When Will returned from one of these trips in April, he called a meeting with Wheelock, Rayner, and the county commissioners.

"Gentlemen, we have a problem. Everything has been going well, and the railroad spur from the north was about to begin construction. Hiram informs me that the state has formed a new railroad commission, and we must now wait while they review the proposal to build the spur."

Wheelock groaned. "Government interference. Is there anything we can do?"

"Not much, I'm afraid. The delay has us dealing with a new governor, Hogg. We'll have to wait and see. Once the courthouse is built, I might take another trip south to see him," said Will.

Once enough lumber was hauled, Will worked with the other men and built the courthouse, which doubled as a community center. With permission from the county commissioners, Will moved into the courthouse with Mary and the children while he worked on building their house on the farmland they now owned, near the site of the old South Town house.

Will used his investment with Wheelock to form the Ripley Township Company, holding over two thousand acres of land. He borrowed using the land for collateral and began ranching purebred Herefords again, and then he started another store.

When the house was finished, the family moved again.

"Will Crump, this is the last time. I don't ever want to move again," said Mary.

Will answered with a twinkle in his eye, "Can't promise that, Mary. But I'm sure we'll be here a long time. If we can just get the railroad to come."

Soon after they moved in, Ned, Katy, and Mark came to Lubbock. Will's letters north had kept them in touch, and he'd offered them a place in the new town. Mark was going to help out in the store, as he used to in the Colorado days. Ned would help with the cattle.

"We're glad to see you, Ned! Sometimes old friends are the best friends. I'm sorry things didn't work for you in Nicodemus. Is Luther still doing well?"

"They're getting by. It's either been a flood or a

drought. After the railroad passed by, people and businesses began to move out. There's a core of people that are determined to make a black town work, and they may make
it. I think we'll try our luck here, even though you don't
have a railroad yet. The people in Nicodemus haven't given
up, but I don't think it will ever happen. The Union Pacific
just doesn't care about black folks."

***

Will arrived home from his trip to Austin and spun Mary around, lifting her off her feet.

"What in the world, Will? What's come over you? I'm glad to see you, but put me down!"

Will laughed and sang a few bars of "*Laughing Eyes of Blue*." "It's done, Mary. They've approved it. The railroad is coming!"

Mary's eyes lit up, and she clapped. Mamie and Katy heard and began making a pretend train through the kitchen, imitating a train whistle as loud as they could.

"When, Will?"

"Now that the railroad commission is done fooling around, it will be here in a few months, Hiram says. His board is still willing. Our population is small, but they have faith that it will grow. Before next Christmas for sure. And that's not all."

"What could be more wonderful than that?"

"Remember I mentioned taking soil samples with me?"

"Yes . . ."

"Oil, Mary. Oil. They think our land has a lot of it. They'll come and drill at the test hole. If it works, we'll be rich. Sun Oil Company wants to try. I can give you the life

I always wanted to, right here."

"Oh, Will, all I want is you and the children. God has already blessed us. We have a house, thanks to your hard work. The Quaker meeting here is growing. Rachel Singer has gotten to be a good friend. We should count our blessings. When the railroad comes, you can give up hauling. Mark is doing a great job with the store. We're at peace," said Mary, hugging him tight.

When she let go, Will picked up each of the girls, who squealed as he swung them around, singing songs about the railroad.

"You should invite my parents and your family to come on the first train. Luther too. I don't know if he will, but we can ask."

"I will do that. I'll invite Charlie and Molly too. We'll have a regular party."

***

The great day came. Mary dressed in her finest and insisted the children dress up as well, much to Bob's complaint.

A band played on the bandstand near the courthouse, and it could be heard a block away at Chestnut and First as the locomotive steamed into the new Lubbock depot.

Will and Mary craned their necks with Ned and his

family to see people get off the train—and there they all were. They saw Hiram and Julia first, as Hiram towered over the crowd. Then Albinia and Peter with their children, then Lydia and George and Charlie and Molly. Will was hugging everyone when he looked over at Ned's and Mark's disappointed faces. Maybe Luther hadn't come. When he could break free, he went to speak to the conductor.

As he reached the train, from the last car Luther, Ruth, and their children spilled down the steps into the train yard. Ned limped over to them, and Will followed. After Ned and Katy greeted Luther and Ruth, he and Albinia welcomed Luther. He stuck out a hand, but Luther responded with a hug. After all these years, they were able to reach across the great divide.

Author's Notes

Introduction

The entire *Across the Great Divide* series is a work of biographical fiction. Various changes have been made to suit the story, and many discoveries were made in the process of research. The Crumps, despite founding two towns, Lubbock and Shallowater, are not overall famous people, which has made research more difficult. Even in Lubbock today, as I experienced in March of 2022, you can ask any one of the 264,315 people there about Will Crump and get a blank stare. Even Mary Lou Crump, his granddaughter, said to me in correspondence, "We don't know much about him. We'll look forward to your books."

Mary Lou has since published her own short nonfiction account of her family titled, *We Could See Nothing*, echoing her father, Bob, and grandmother Mary's comment when they arrived at the Caprock.

Notes

- I uncovered evidence about Robert Crump's Colorado prospecting after *The Search* was written from several new sources and Will's involvement in Colorado. Robert did invest in the Tiger Mine, which failed. Robert's alcoholism is my invention, though it seemed plausible as a result of grief over Sarah's death, PTSD from the war, and losing everything while in Colorado.

- Will worked on several ranches, including the Colorado Goodnight ranch, was a jack of all trades, and operated a store in Georgetown.

- Due to the long time span this novel covers, it would have been unrealistic to have the dog, Lightning, and the horses Dusty and Printer survive through the entire book. To spare my animal-loving readers, I simply let them fade away, not mentioning their demise. This was intentional.

Georgetown, Colorado, Silver Works, 1867

(Courtesy Western Mining History, Public Domain)

Georgetown, Colorado, 1867

(Courtesy Western Mining History, Public Domain)

Freight Wagons Ute Pass, near Georgetown, similar to
Luther's *(Courtesy Western Mining History,*
Public Domain)

- For *The Founding*, I relied heavily on family notes
  and stories in the voluminous paper archives at the
  Southwest Collection at Texas Tech University in
  Lubbock, Texas. I spent days reading through boxes
  of dusty papers. I also used the excellent nonfiction
  accounts in *The Legend of Jay Gould* by Maury
  Klein and *The History of the Atchison, Topeka, and
  Santa Fe Railway* by Keith L. Bryant Jr.

•   The evolution of the railroad through the late nine-teenth century in Kansas, Nebraska, Colorado, and Texas is a complex story with many players, over which the shadow of Jay Gould towers. The AT&SF had many more managers, presidents, and workers than are depicted in the book. Hiram Johannsen is a fictional character of my own invention. I tried to follow the actual history of the AT&SF, neglecting the various management changes. His wife, Julia, is a fictionalized person drawn from Will's sister Sarah Moseby Crump and the Civil War spy Pauline Cushman. Much of Julia's story is from my imagination. Hiram's meetings with Gould are necessarily fictional but in line with Gould's character.

A locomotive from the AT&SF that was used in Will's lifetime, still operating on the Abilene and Smokey Valley Railroad. (*Copyright © 2022, HistoricalNovelSRUS*)

AT&SF Locomotive, Michael Ross photographer, *(Copyright © 2022 HistoricalNovelsRUs)*

- Samuel Pomeroy was a real US Senator, and while he had some questionable dealings, particularly with the Pottawatomie tribe, he was a driving force for getting the AT&SF through Congress. Other notable AT&SF players were the Civil War Confederate General Braxton Bragg, one of the worst managers in AT&SF history, and W. B. Strong, one of the best. I patterned the character of Hiram on

Strong for most of the book. Bragg appears in *The Clouds of War* as Julia's judge.

Senator Samuel Pomeroy of Kansas *(Library of Congress)*

- The impact of the railroad on the indigenous tribes cannot be overstated. It was devastating. The tribes lost their main source of food and the lands that sustained wildlife. *The Founding* barely touches these topics since they were dealt with extensively in the previous book, *The Search.*

- The Kiowa attack on Henrietta, Texas, did happen

several times. The Kiowa raided Henrietta, trying to stamp it out, in 1860. By 1862, it was abandoned. A settlement was again attempted in 1865, but the inhabitants were massacred and the town burned to the ground. In 1870, a few years earlier than depicted here, Goodleck Koozer and his Quaker family attempted to resettle the ruins, and again the Kiowa attacked, killing Koozer and kidnapping his wife and daughters. Koozer's son escaped. Since the Quakers did not believe in violence, Koozer had no weapons. His wife and daughters were later released. In a similar attack, Charles Goodnight rescued a family. *Source: Texas Handbook Online, Texas Historical Society*

- Charles Goodnight is a legendary but real figure in the American west. The Pulitzer Prize-winning novel *Lonesome Dove* is based on his story and his friendship with Oliver Loving. Goodnight had land around Dallas but lost everything, relocating to Colorado and then Palo Duro Canyon, Texas, near Lubbock, with a palatial house near Amarillo. Goodnight encountered Will Crump in real life in Colorado, much as shown in the book, became friends, and invited Will to Texas. Without that chance encounter, Lubbock might never have happened. I discovered it in the archives of the Southwest Collection at Texas Tech, as well as their later encounters.

- George and Rachel Singer were real people. George moved from the east to Estacado, Texas, with Paris Cox, a Quaker visionary. Their attempt at founding Estacado spluttered when the Quakers found the blue northers of the Staked Plains and the lack of trees to use for lumber too much. The settlers began to desert, to go back to their eastern homes. Rachel had a reputation for a mouthwatering kitchen, and she had her own "fast food" joint at the back of the store, feeding any travelers who passed, often without pay. When George joined forces with the Lubbock settlers, she willingly followed and supported him. The Singer store served as the first school, church, and all-around meeting place in Lubbock. You can read more about the Singers at Singer Store.

- Mary King married Will Crump on March 1, 1877, in Dallas at the First Baptist Church, which still stands. The real Mary was born in Lisbon, Texas, in 1853, now engulfed by Dallas, about ten miles from downtown. Her parents were Ann and David King. David was a physician rather than a banker, one of the first in Dallas. At the time of the writing of *The Clouds of War*, where she first appears, this information was not available. In *The Clouds of War*, she appears as Peter's childhood friend, traveling across the country from Pennsylvania, through Indiana, to Texas. The Kings were in Dallas from 1853 forward, with David King coming from Tennessee. Mary's mother, Ann Smith, was also from Bedford County, Tennessee, and married David there in 1850. The elder Kings tried Morgan, Alabama, but found it not to their liking and moved to nascent Dallas before the year was out.

David King did initially oppose the marriage of Will and Mary, but Will won him over.

Mary didn't want to move from Henrietta in real life. Will moved the family from Henrietta to Benjamin but received an invitation to think about the Staked Plains from Charles Goodnight. The family abandoned Benjamin after only four months. Mary did take the girls and return to Dallas, whether with Will's agreement or not is unknown. She stayed there while Will adventured to the Staked Plains with the boys, as depicted.

- W.E. Rayner was a historical person; his physical description in the book is derived from Will's notes. Since Will was only five foot eight, there was a considerable size difference between them. Much of Rayner's personality in the book is derived from notes about his actions rather than actual descriptions; any error is mine. He was originally part of the Wheelock/Crump group but split off and went his own way, creating the conflict about town location.

The area between North Town and South Town in 1890
(Courtesy of the Crump Family)

On the left at the back of the above picture, you can see the outline of the three-story Nicolett Hotel, later moved on logs to present-day downtown Lubbock.

- Will and Hiram's confrontation with Rayner is fictional, but it could have happened. No one, even the folks at the Southwest Collection, knows why the two groups reconciled without violence, only that a meeting of reconciliation did happen on December 19, 1890.

- Lubbock was incorporated in 1909, the same year that the spur rail line on AT&SF came in. Texas Tech College started in 1923. I have moved this date closer to 1890, the year Lubbock was incorporated, for the purposes of the story.

Will Crump and Family, 1920s, Bob driving, Katy Bell front seat, Mary, Mamie, and Will, standing *(Used by permission Crump Family)*

In real life, neither Dave Crump nor Katy Bell Crump married or had children. I don't know why, and the records do not say. As I was only four or five when I knew Katie Bell, it wasn't a question a child could ask. I was always told to call her Mrs. Crump, a common thing for spinsters in the south.

Grave and headstone of Will Crump (*Copyright (c) 2022 HistoricalNovelsRUS*)

Will Crump with granddaughter Mary Lou Crump Koeh-
ler, 1930s *(Used by permission of the Crump Family)*

- Dusty, Will's horse, was modeled on the famous
  Foundation quarter horse, Steel Dust, who came to
  Texas about the same time as Will. Mary's horse,
  Printer, is meant to be another founder of the quarter horse breed, Printer. They were the fastest horses
  over a quarter mile of their time and set records that
  stood well into the twentieth century.

- The Panic of 1873 was one of several major financial crashes of the nineteenth century, but it was specifically about railroads and was caused in part by wars in Europe and the fact that the railroads were heavily financed by German investors. It was also called the Long Depression and was lengthier than the Great Depression of 1929. Jay Gould's Credit Mobilier scandal wasn't too far back, and the main US investor, Jay Cooke Bank in New York, went bankrupt, as did many railroads. Jay Gould landed on his feet, using the crisis to snap up railroads that were stretched thin financially.

- **Luther and Nicodemus:** Luther is a returning character from *Book 1 The Clouds of War,* the first in the *Across the Great Divide* series. He and his family are fictional. His character and experiences are taken from hundreds of slave diaries and stories. In *The Founding*, Luther is driven out of Indiana because he is an escaped slave. Immediately following the Civil War, border states Illinois and Indiana passed laws, known as the Black Codes, to prevent a wave of formerly enslaved people from entering the states. Slavery was not officially repealed until the 13th Amendment was ratified (12/6/1865), and black people were not citizens of the United States until the 14th Amendment was ratified (7/9/1868). There was a Supreme Court case to cover cases like Luther's where a former slave married a free black who wanted to bring their spouse to Indiana. The court ruled against them since the 13th Amendment had not gone into effect, and the Fugitive Slave Law was still technically in effect, though widely ignored following the war. This left the couple with the choice of being separated or moving to a different state. Mimicking the real-life case, Luther decides to move and begins a new odyssey for his family. Following the Civil War, when the federal government removed troops from the states that had been in rebellion, most of those states passed restrictive laws that brought back the trappings of slavery, known as Jim Crow. They could not reinstitute slavery, but they could and did make black people second-class citizens—nor was this confined to the South. This spurred a movement known as the Exodusters, little taught in high school history, of formerly enslaved black people moving west to the new states and territories, looking to escape Jim Crow and find real freedom. The majority of the

Exodusters that came to Nicodemus were from the Lexington, Kentucky, area, just like the fictional Luther. An excellent reference on this topic is *Exodusters: The Black Migration to Kansas* by Neil Irwin. There were half a dozen towns in Colorado, Nebraska, and Kansas that were founded by these Exodusters, with the idea that an all-black town would not have discrimination. Few of the towns survived. Nicodemus in Kansas was an exception. It thrived until two events took it down—the railroad passed it by, and the Great Depression forced people to leave, as there were no jobs and no market for the crops.

- In the 1920s, the Nicodemus crops raised exceeded the value of the land, but that plenty came to a halt in the 1930s. Nicodemus has produced at least two NFL players, not identified at the families' request. Edward McCabe, mentioned in the fight to get the railroad in Nicodemus, was a real person and the first African-American state auditor in Kansas.

- One of the families that came in the last large migration to Nicodemus was the Bates family. Today a sixth-generation descendant, Angela Bates, runs the Nicodemus Historical Society. Angela is responsible for getting Nicodemus designated as a National Historic Site, placing the town under the National Park Service, which provides funding for preserving the buildings and continuing the story. Angela Bates has my heartfelt thanks for her help in writing the Nicodemus story. She went above and beyond, answering all my questions, inviting me to her home (lunch included!), and taking an interest in Luther's story. Luther could not have existed in *The Founding* without her. If you're interested in scenes from a Nicodemus Founder's Day celebration, where descendants tell the Nicodemus story, check out my YouTube channel, Nicodemus, and The Nicodemus Historical Society website, Nicodemus Historical Society. A few descendants still live in Nicodemus today.

• The railroad was a driving force in the last half of the 19th century and the beginning of the 20th. Towns rose or fell on whether the railroad chose them. In some cases, such as my own town, Newton, Kansas, the railroad created the town. The continuing version of the AT&SF, Burlington Northern and Santa Fe, now part of Union Pacific, is still the largest employer in Newton.

- Whatever town was at the "end of the line" in the 19th century became a wide-open saloon town, a destination for cattle drives glamorized by Hollywood in such fantasies as the John Wayne movie *Chisum* and the long-running TV series *Gunsmoke*. These film adaptations carried little actual history. The western era of cattle drives, Pony Express, and Indian battles were relatively short-lived, and Hollywood stories were often told through a biased lens. Newton had its brief period as "the end of the line" and sported several saloons and a now-famous gunfight. You can read about it at Gunfight at Hide Park. Abilene, Wichita, Dodge City, and other Kansas and later Texas towns took their turn as "the end of the line" until the railroad extended and moved to the next town. An excellent nonfiction resource on this period is *Wicked Wichita* by Joe Stumpe. Wichita has the Old Cowtown Museum, a living history with several of the original buildings from cattle-drive days, including the saloon with dance hall girls (no alcoholic beverages).

- Thanks to Harper Collins for their help with the first book. Covid struck in the middle of the second, and layoffs forced the series into independent publication. I hope you've enjoyed following Will Crump and his family as much as I have enjoyed writing about them. I became interested in the Crumps because Katy Bell Crump, Will's daughter, was a friend of my grandmother's, and I used to listen to Katy tell stories when I was a child. As an adult, I became fascinated with Will's story and thought it should be told. As I pored over the archives at the Southwest Collection, I experienced a thrill as I found documents jointly signed by Will Crump, Bob Crump, Mary, and my father and grandfather.

- Robert Crump does not appear at the final gathering because he died in 1899 before the train arrived in Lubbock.

- There are conflicting dates for the death of Will's mother, Sarah Dorsey Crump. I have chosen the earlier date to fit the narrative and the best facts available.

- Kind readers, if you read this book or the entire series, please leave reviews.

Please subscribe to my monthly newsletter at http://www.historicalnovelsrus.com/contact for news on upcoming books.

My website, http://www.historicalnovelsrus.com/blog, has a blog that offers historical profiles of interesting but little-known people, usually weekly, and http://www.historicalnovelsrus.com/store offers a way to buy books directly from me, signed or Kindle, at a discount.

The line drawing locomotive at each chapter heading is licensed from Michael Schisler, Drawn There, Temecula, Ca. His shop can be found on Etsy.

Thanks to my wonderful and patient editor, Jennifer "JennyQ" Quinlan, at HistoricalEditorial.com. Her advice has been invaluable through out the Across the Great Divide series.

Cover Design: Jennifer Quinlan, HistoricalFictionBookCovers.com

As always, in whatever you do, please reach Across the Great Divide.

www.ingramcontent.com/pod-product-compliance
Lightning Source LLC
Chambersburg PA
CBHW070306040726
47501CB00018B/200